Escape to
JUSTICE
and
LOVE

Escape to
JUSTICE
and
LOVE

Not Water Over the Dam,
A REVISIT

LARRY LEE JORGENSON

Outskirts Press, Inc.
http://www.outskirtspress.com

ISBN: 978-1-9772-4541-0

Library of Congress Control Number: 2021917066

Cover Photo © 2022 www.gettyimages.com. All rights reserved - used with permission.

Outskirts Press and the "OP" logo are trademarks belonging to Outskirts Press, Inc.

PRINTED IN THE UNITED STATES OF AMERICA

FOR DAD

PROLOGUE

EARTH'S SADNESS

In 1970, on a chilly, clear night in October, not long after the muddy waters of the Missouri River wiped out the island on which she had lived, Charlie Red Tail's grandmother, Yellow Bird, walked above the reservoir created by the dam and stopped on a hill overlooking what had been her former residence.

A full moon shone overhead and the guiding stars were bright. She could see where the island had been, as it had been straight down from the draw full of fruits and nuts like she had gathered in many an autumn, and where she now stood in sadness. Her thoughts were filled with grief and vengeance. She cried out, "How can they take the land long belonging to our people? The land in and along the river was blessed with the 'three sisters'-squash, corn and beans—and with herbs, fruits, other sources of food, and materials for medicine. The brush and trees were home to many birds.

It was an important winter stop for the birds. We hunted game for food. The island in the river was where I first lay in the tall grass with the young brave I loved. He became the powerful voice of my people during many years of peaceful existence. It was an island that provided joys and challenges with the gifts of the wind, soil and the water. It was where my daughter died in childbirth while delivering a son on the soft leaves of the island fallen under the tall cottonwood tree as she lay on the colorful blanket I weaved over time. It is where my grandson wandered free and upright as one with Mother Earth and with our people."

Grandmother Yellow Bird lifted her hands to Wakan Tanka, the Great Spirit: "I am old and will no longer live the life the Great Spirit has provided me and my people, but what of the little children and my grandson. Will my grandson be strong, and will he lead our people in revenging this terrible war of water? Will he lead us in war against the white man for this crime?"

Then, as she sat on the hill above the gulch under the cold, clear moonlit sky, it was as if the heavens opened up and the moon moved aside. She gazed in awe as a large, dark cloud suddenly appeared out of nowhere and moved from the north to the east, passing above her and then disappearing in the eastern horizon. Wakan Tanka caused a grizzly bear to roar. Black and red clouds rose above her as she sat on the hill above the former island. After a few minutes of wonder, Grandmother put her hands to her eyes, not knowing what was to happen, but all the while knowing Wakan Tanka was talking to her.

Then—something did happen. A Bald Eagle suddenly appeared in the sky, changing colors as it circled low above her. Yellow Bird was not afraid. She knew the eagle is the strongest and bravest of all birds. It symbolizes what is highest, bravest, strongest, and holiest. She stood up with her arms outstretched to the sky and silently understood she was to seek revenge for the wrong that had been done to her people when they took her tribe's lands on which to build a dam on the Missouri River. Grandmother Yellow Bird knew to whom she must give the honor and duty of seeking revenge. Her "vision" was clear.

As she trudged home on this night, Yellow Bird vowed she would tell Grandson Charlie, when the time was right, of the vision given to her by Wakan Tanka. Grandmother knew her grandson was the right one (the chosen one) to bring justice to her people, now the hope-seekers of the barren hills above and beyond the waters, people denied a better opportunity to provide their own sustenance and continue their empowering culture, long developed as they lived along the river bottom, and for her, on an island in the river.

Historically, the Lakota were considered warriors—strong, brave, and feared. Charlie was a Lakota, an enrolled member of the Ogla'la tribe; his paternal great-great grandfather, Many Fast Horses, led his people during times of harsh living with foresight and bravery, raiding other tribes when they invaded the Ogla'la's lands, moving into other tribes' territories when they had greater numbers of Buffalo roaming the land and his people were in need of food. Many Fast

Horses was a beloved leader.

Charlie's paternal grandfather, Brave Elk, followed in his father's footsteps and became chief of the tribe when the reservations were imposed on the Lakota, for the great plains had been stolen by the white man's government and the reservation system stole the Indian way of life and their freedoms. Yellow Bird told Charlie of Chief Brave Elk becoming saddened as the numbers of his people rapidly declined; disease and addiction were crushing the spirit; hope for a better life became contingent on white man's edicts and the white man's handouts of food and clothing. His life ended by his own hand, not in the glory of a fallen warrior on the battlefield.

Grandmother Yellow Bird was Charlie's closest family. She gave him his sense of being, for Charlie never knew his father, killed with Charlie's mother in a car wreck when Charlie was just a year old.

Grandmother told Charlie, when he was old enough to understand: "Your father was a great man. He had a good job in the white man's world as a truck driver. Your father was Lester Red Tail. He met and married a white woman. Your mother's name was Anna. Lester and Anna had just one child. That child is you. Me and the tribe have raised you since you were a baby."

Yellow Bird taught Charlie, "family is the true measure of wealth." And, through his years of adolescence, Charlie learned of his culture and its values from her and other family members, including his uncles, Ted Tomahawk and Oscar Red Bull.

Charlie had lived through continuing efforts of the white man's government to separate the tribe's family units by placement of children in "Indian Boarding Schools" off the reservation where they cut boys' hair, forbade speaking the native language and wearing Indian clothes, demanding assimilation into the white culture and abandonment of their own. Eventually, for many of Charlie's friends, capitulation to the white man's dictates replaced resentment. Lakota children, who had one foot of heritage in each world, but total acceptance in neither, sometimes quietly, but woefully, accepted a passive existence in the white man's world. There were exceptions. Charlie and Tom Big Horse were two friends who accepted the life challenges ahead, not a muted existence in the white man's world. Tom and Charlie graduated from Crazy Horse High School on the reservation with high grades, many skills, and a real sense of excitement about the future. They had each managed to eventually escape the experiences of forced attendance in an Indian School. Both intended to go to college and attain success in the white man's world.

As graduation from Crazy Horse High School approached, Charlie Red Tail told his grandmother: "Grandmother, you have told me many times about our homelands being wrongfully taken so the federal government could build dams on the Missouri River. You told me stories of the meetings you and my uncles had attended with the US Government's Corps of Engineers. You said they were dog and pony shows. Where no one listened to you. You were very angry and bitter toward the white men for condemning our lands.

"You have told me many times of the Great Spirit's vision requiring someone to seek retribution for the government's flooding our lands. Yesterday you told me I was the chosen one. I will heed the Great Spirit's calling," the grandson pledged to his grandmother as she lay dying, and the assurance he gave her impacted his life thereafter.

As a survivor of the earth's rape and of society's injustice, he with the name of the hawk searched for answers in his life and for several years came up empty. After his grandmother's death, each day he lifted his hands to the sky and prayed to Wakan Tanka for wisdom and to have taken away the bitterness in his heart stirring there for so many years. Charlie wanted to believe the "Great Spirit" would answer him, as it had when the steel door finally swung open and he walked free of false accusations of white men.

On July 4th, 1985, twenty-four-year-old Charlie Red Tail stood at the foot of the earthen dam on the life-giving river and cried. He did not want to see the other side. He dug until he was finished and carefully put back the disturbed, black dirt. Black earth stands for death and a black stone for revenge, according to his learning. He placed the black obsidian stone on the black dirt at the foot of the dam.

Charlie flinched as he remembered as a child in the 1970s when the monsters came and ate the fertile ground that belonged to his people. He could still smell and see in his memory the black plague the invading monsters belched into the air that his people had to breathe.

Then, his mind's eye revisited for a moment the treed island on which he took a deer each year to feed his family. He tasted again the buffalo berries and wild plums on the giving bushes, now inundated with water and long dead. He could taste again the morel mushrooms gathered each spring. He recalled the poem he had composed as he stood in reverence of the flowing waters, braided by years of uncontrolled journey toward another great river. He envisioned once more the inlet where the catfish tested his young warrior learning of how to catch the big fish.

He remembered, but could not now see, the tall cottonwood on the island where the Red-tailed Hawk sat as it accompanied him on his wanderings. And taught him how to attack prey.

The hawk, his elders had taught him, stands for swiftness.

As he now stood at the dam, forlorn and looking to the Great Spirit, Charlie Red Tail also recalled the injustice done to him in the racist white man's court system when he was sentenced to four years in white man's prison for the crime of rape, a crime he did not commit. He was convicted on the false testimony and lies of a ranching family who lived near the reservation.

His emotions were in turmoil as to which wrong he should revenge first—the building of the dam and its flooding of his tribe's lands, or the lies that put him behind the steel door.

Revenge for either grievance was challenging this normally kind and compassionate Indian to accomplish one or the other, or both. And, Charlie had no idea what revenge should look like, or how it should be brought about; his true, peace-loving character seemed to hamper considered thought of the answers he needed.

CHAPTER 1

JUSTICE DENIED

The racism of some "white men" who live near the Horse Creek Reservation is generational and vicious. Provocations of the Indians have historically been many. The Indians are not welcome in this "West" which these "white men" control; those of such ilk run roughshod over all dissent from their self-interest, and they ruthlessly exercise their political power. County government caters to their demands; local prosecutors, elected by the whites, see to it that Indians are punished "appropriately" whenever charged. The congressional delegation in Washington D.C. gives the local governments an ear for their complaints about the Indians' legal rights of equality.

In the eyes of many in the "civilized" white population, Indians are lazy and live off the federal government; they are often viewed as drunks and druggies, and troublemakers, but not as fellow citizens. "They need to remain on the reservation and not mix with the whites" is a prevalent senti-ment in the county. The Indians and the white man gener-ally keep their distance from each other, walking on opposite sides of the streets in town, the Indians kept under close sur-veillance by store clerks, the two races avoiding eye contact at all times—unless a white person wants the disdain in his or her eyes to be noticed by a long-suffering Indian.

If an Indian man messes with a white woman, there is hell to pay. Justice in white man's courts in Indian Mound County, contiguous to a part of the Horse Creek Reservation, is always swift and generally unjust. White man's desired result is always reached. Witnesses always come out of the woodwork. Identification is always certain. And prompted. Juries are solely white—mostly men.

Betsy Stoutwein, age twenty-six, was totally unattractive and uncouth. She was thirty pounds overweight and talked crudely, usually speaking with four-letter words punctuating her loud voice. In her high school she was a leader of the rowdy girls. Her family, though, was proud of her, particu-larly of her rodeo skills and competitive personality. She was the only daughter in the family.

At the Ft. Custer dancehall, off the reservation, on Saturday nights when reservation youth and white youth often attended, Betsy frequently was there and sat on one of the steel folding chairs surrounding the dance floor. Too tight were her Wranglers. She showcased her ample cleavage via a plunging neckline. She wore flashy hand-made cowboy boots, and a big silver belt buckle that she won in a barrel racing event at a regional rodeo, now attached to a hand-tooled leather belt with her name tooled in the back. She drank too much, and was loud and belligerent most of the time. Betsy had been bedded by most every cowboy on the plains.

A few years ago, she had accused an Indian of stealing hay from Stoutwein's ranch. A famous Indian lawyer represented the accused, and his client ultimately found justice in the State Supreme Court, which overturned an obvious miscarriage of justice in the local court. Betsy was livid. Sometime back she had punched out another girl at a local dance, but no charges were ever filed. Her drunk and disorderly conduct engaged in from time to time in Tihay never rose to State charges being filed. School administrators were reluctant to control her disruptive nature in the school, afraid actually of the political power of her father, a former school board president, among other elected positions he held.

Now, she would claim she had been raped at this year's July 4th dance at the Ft. Custer dancehall. Someone was going to pay! And he was going to be an Indian!

Betsy Stoutwein remembered well a year ago, when she had cornered Charlie Red Tail at the dance at Ft. Custer and pressed her body to his. She had invited him to go outside for sex. The son-of-a-bitch had declined! He walked away and left her standing in the corner on the Indian side of the dance floor, embarrassed. Some of the observing Indian girls had even giggled! She then and there vowed to get even.

Her complaint of rape was made to the sheriff of Indian Mound County, Tex Brutkowsky, an elected and many times re-elected enforcer of white man laws and self-appointed guardian of the county, protecting it from unlawful Indians. The complaint was made on July 10th, 1981. Betsy Stoutwein, daughter of one of the most powerful ranchers in the county, busted through the door of the sheriff's office and, filled with hurt and rage began laying out her story to Sheriff Brutkowsky. "You poor girl," said the sheriff in his best understanding voice. "We will get Charlie Red Tail who did this horrible thing to you. And he will be prosecuted and pay for this; you can bet on that!"

The sheriff hurriedly obtained the statements of two members of the victim's family: Jim Stoutwein, the all-around cowboy at the July 4th rodeo where he just won first place in bull riding and first place in saddle bronc riding, thus winning two large silver buckles. He was the alleged victim's older brother. The sheriff also interviewed Mac Stoutwein, the victim's dad, one of the stellar political bosses in the county, a third-generation rancher. These witnesses swore Betsy told them she was raped by Charlie Red Tail, and they told the sheriff all the details given them by Betsy. Their statements were nearly identical and obtained at the same time. In Brutkowsky's mind, their word against an Indian's would be probative in court. Charlie Red Tail raped Betsy Stoutwein— no question about it in the sheriff's mind!

The sheriff called in his deputies, and also the Posse Comitatus members, who "rode as hard" as regular law enforcement. Urgency was stressed by Brutkowsky. A few war-whoops rang out from the eager deputies when Brutkowsky explained the mission to them. The "law" was honored to be assigned the task of finding and arresting Charlie Red Tail. The deputies armed themselves heavily. They were eager to get going and to make clear their superiority and control over the damn Indian who had done harm to one of their neighbors. In total, there were eight armed and ready deputies and four trusted and true Posse Comitatus, those regular citizens the sheriff called on from time to time to make sure a mission was accomplished.

Prosecuting Attorney Tony Jones made sure there was public awareness of the complaint having been made to the sheriff by Betsy Stoutwein. He immediately made the regional TV station and the local newspaper aware of the crime. He sought no arrest warrant from the Circuit Judge, Thomas Remington. Not enough time, really. This was a serious crime. Law enforcement needed to act quickly, whether an arrest warrant was legally required or not! Besides, if necessary, he could obtain a warrant later, after the arrest, as Judge Remington was very cooperative with law enforcement.

There were three squad cars with two deputies in each of them, and one car with two deputies; the posse rode in another vehicle, all together forming a caravan to the reservation. The incident commander was Sgt. Harvey P. Smith, a grizzled veteran of twenty years on the force.

The army left in mid-afternoon from Tihay, a small

town of 750 people and the county seat for Indian Mound County and headed for the Horse Creek Reservation with sirens blasting and red lights blinking, seeking to find and arrest one Charlie Red Tail, a Lakota Indian who raped Betsy Stoutwein. The speed with which they left mirrored the outrage each of them felt toward this no-good rapist who had harmed one of their own. They were enraged as a group, and in varying degrees, as individuals. One officer in particular vowed he would personally find the Indian. He said, "If I am given any trouble, I will kill the scumbag right then and save the county the cost of a trial." No one cautioned him that he shouldn't take such an approach, for Henry Snotberg often talked that way when referring to the Indians. And the rape of a white woman by a "brave" had indeed raised the anger level and resolve of the rest of the caravan.

The route of 66 miles from Tihay to the Horse Creek Reservation headquarters is paved until one comes to the reservation boundary where the road turns to gravel for 18 miles more before one reaches the tribal government center. The road to the reservation passes the dance hall at Ft. Custer, a tiny hamlet with a rodeo arena, dance hall and a bar, near which the alleged crime occurred. Sgt. Smith advised the troops over the radio as they passed, "We will investigate the crime scene after we have Red Tail under arrest. I am afraid he might flee the rez, if he hasn't already done so. Even if he hasn't, I expect some trouble with the tribe as we hunt for him. Be prepared for anything!"

The Horse Creek Justice Center is located in a beautiful valley surrounded by rolling hills—a pastoral setting. The history of the rolling hills includes many years of peaceful relationships between the Indians and the whites who settled a town downstream, but also many clashes of invading white soldiers and the Sioux who had long lived along the mighty river. Not until the reservation system was imposed by the United States government in the 1800s did the Horse Creek Reservation exist; however, even then, the tribe continued to live along the Missouri River, ranching the lands and living peaceably with the other tribes of the area.

All of the tribal government offices are in the valley, as well as a grocery store, a trading post, gas station, hospital, and a community center. There is also a gambling casino owned by the tribe; it is legal because the Lakota nation is a sovereign nation and not subject to the anti-gambling laws of the state and federal governments. At the Justice Center are the tribal court and the tribal police headquarters and, the tribal jail. The heavily used social service agencies are also housed there. The people of the reservation are poor, mostly unemployed, and dependent on the US Government for monthly subsistence checks. Alcoholism and other drug abuse are more than just present, having a negative effect on all facets of reservation life.

Long-time tribal police captain Johnny Many Moons knew Sgt. Smith, for he had several times sought Smith's co-operation on Indian matters occurring off the reservation, though not always with satisfactory results. Still, the two law enforcement men had, in the past, a fairly good working relationship.

Sgt. Smith and his men were dressed in neatly pressed uniforms and polished black cowboy boots, sporting Stetson hats. Johnny Many Moons and a few of his deputies met Smith at the door to the building. They were wearing Levi's, various selections of cowboy shirts, scuffed boots, and horse-hair belts purchased from the local trading post. Captain Many Moons and his men were unarmed.

"Many Moons, one of yours, a kid named Charlie Red Tail, raped one of ours, Betsy Stoutwein, on July 4th, in the trees outside the dance hall at Ft. Custer. Do you know where Red Tail lives or where he is at?"

"No idea where Charlie is at. Just graduated from high school. He lives up Old Woman Creek with his uncle. They do not have a telephone. That's all I know."

"Well, what's his uncle's name, and where does he live? We need your cooperation. Do you know this kid?"

"He a good kid. He smart, a leader. He would not rape anyone. You sure you have the right guy?"

"Yes, I am sure. What's his uncle's name and how do we get to his place? Do you have a map?"

"His uncle's name is Oscar Big Bull. Lives on Old Woman Creek, as I told you. There is no map. We just know where everybody lives."

"Well, how do we get there?"

Captain Many Moons was silent as he thought of wheth-er he should provide the information to Smith. "Head south of here on the main road for about ten miles. Turn right for a while until you get to a bridge over a creek. Go a little further. Turn left for about eight miles until the road forks. Go right and a while later, left at the trees. Go for a while until you come to a big boulder. In that area is where Oscar Big Bull lives."

Standing nearby was Deputy Henry Snotberg. He quickly walked to his vehicle and took off down the main road, siren shut off but red and blue lights blinking. Incident Commander Smith did not notice. Captain Johnny Many Moons did.

"Is this uncle dangerous and likely to give us any trouble?"

"Oscar Big Bull is old," Many Moons answered, irritated by the question and the police car taking off to the south. "You treat him with respect and do him no harm." Smith listened intently and seemed to nod his head in agreement. Many Moons was not so sure.

Despite his many years of training in law enforcement, Sgt. Smith was not much of a detail guy; he took no notes of the directions to Uncle Oscar's house, instead relying on his memory. As he walked back to his blinking police vehicle, he gathered his men.

"Where is Snotberg?" he asked.

"He took off while you were talking to Many Moons," answered one of the men. "He got in the last cruiser and took off up the road. I thought he had been given some kind of instructions."

"For God's sake! How long ago did he leave, and where

was he going?" Smith knew he had a problem. Snotberg had been a problem ever since he came on the force after being selected by Sheriff Brutkowsky. Snotgrass and Brutkowsky are cousins.

"Don't really know. He left while you were talking. Didn't say anything. Suppose he was headed out to find Red Tail."

Oscar Big Bull lived in the grassy, rolling hills above the Missouri River and the Big Bend Reservoir. He was eighty-seven years old. He was much loved and respected by his tribe. The old man had taught Charlie many things when he was a youngster and spent a lot of time with him, knowing the absence of a father in Charlie's life. Big Bull taught Charlie to hunt and fish, how to select quality horses, how to respect and participate in the sacred rituals and ceremonies of the tribe; he introduced him to Charlie's first sweat lodge and emphasized his duty to honor the elderly. The two were very close.

Oscar Big Bull's cabin was small but cozy, not far from Old Woman Creek, and had the luxury of indoor plumbing. A wood stove heated the house in the winter. It had two bedrooms, small but adequate, a little kitchen, a bathroom. Indian crafts decorated some of the walls and a few historic heirlooms rested in various places. The cabin had electricity, and the elderly man had a television that was watched often by him and Charlie, and often by him and neighbors who frequented his cabin when bringing food and niceties. The door to the cabin faced east to receive the morning sun.

A window looked to the west, to Old Woman Creek, with a sweeping view of the beauty of the rolling hills. Looking out the north window, there was a view of the road that approaches and the driveway. The front door to the cabin was on the north side.

This was a tranquil, peaceful place. Trees planted many years before provided needed shade in the summer for this old man, and branches for birds resting, looking, and singing. Kosa, the old Border Collie, provided not only companionship, but also kept the free-ranging chickens from becoming dinner for coyotes. A rusted, battered pickup sat near the house—not much to look at, but adequate for Uncle Oscar Big Bull to drive to tribal council and other tribal events.

"Charlie, quick, come here," the uncle shouted as he watched the television and saw the breaking news announcement that an Indian Mound County white girl had been raped by an Indian named Charlie Red Tail and that Sheriff Brutkowsky had sent deputies to the Horse Creek Reservation to arrest the Indian.

Charlie heard his uncle from outside the open door where he sat in a chair reading the class offerings at University of the West. "What, my uncle?" Charlie said as he went into the cabin. "What's going on?"

"Sit down." The uncle told Charlie what he had just heard on the television.

"This can't be. I have not raped anyone. You must not have heard correctly the name."

"Oh, my son, I did hear correctly. They are coming for

you. Those white men will be here at some time. I know you did not rape anyone. They somehow think you did. But you must go and hide until this can be corrected. Take your rifle and some food and go to Coyote Hill and hide until this is taken care of. We do not have much time, so go." He was shaken. Tears came to Charlie's eyes as his closest relative grasped his arm and looked at him with love, and with fear in his old eyes.

Charlie left for Coyote Hill. It was two miles away on foot, over rocky soil and rolling hills. Deputy Snotberg did not miss the turn at the boulder. The rest of the posse did! As Snotberg turned at the boulder, he noticed the Oscar Big Bull cabin off in the distance. He drove slowly to a few hundred feet from the cabin and noticed an individual on the porch. As he drove closer, Snotberg saw that the man on the porch was an old man, bent over, with long, braided hair and with a rifle in his hands. Snotberg stopped short of the cabin a considerable distance, pulled the bullhorn from his vehicle, and readied his own rifle outside the squad car. There was not a sound to be heard. For all his bravado, Snotberg did not know how to proceed. The man he was looking at was not a young brave who could be Charlie Red Tail. No, this was someone else. "Perhaps I have the wrong place. If I am wrong, I will really look foolish," he murmured. "It must be the uncle. I am going to find out." He blared through the bullhorn, "Hey, put your rifle on the ground and walk toward me with your hands in the air. I will shoot you first should you try to use that gun, you hear me?"

"I not walking nowhere. I will put my rifle on the ground," said Oscar Big Bull. "Don't shoot. Why you here?"

"I am here to arrest Charlie Red Tail for rape. Is he here?"

"No."

"Where is he?"

"Don't know."

Snotberg moved closer, looking, stalking the old man. "I bet you sure do know where the kid is," he hollered as he stood a few feet from the object of his wrath. He struck the old man hard with the butt of his rifle. The old man fell to the ground, dazed. Snotberg hovered over him and yelled, "You either tell me where he is at, or I am going to blow your damn head off—you understand, Indian? Now where is he?" He put the end of the barrel on the elder's chest.

"Ah, ah, told you, don't know. He not here."

As Snotberg raised the butt of his rifle to smash the elderly man again, he heard the whine of sirens, wheeled around, and saw the dust as the army approached after getting on the right road to Oscar Big Bull's place. Charlie was up the first hill from the cabin and also heard the sirens and saw the blinking lights, turned, and saw the dust clouds floating toward his uncle's cabin.

"Wakan Tanka be with me," he said as he immediately knew he must return and protect his beloved uncle. He could see his uncle on the ground as he ran back toward the cabin and felt utter rage at what he knew had happened. His feet flew down the hill as he yelled a war whoop as loud as his lungs allowed. Snotberg turned and fired at the person running toward him. The old man grabbed for the gun! The gun fired again! Oscar Big Bull lay in a pool of blood as Charlie Red Tail and the army arrived at Oscar Big Bull's cabin and saw the old man lying on the ground.

"What have you done?" screamed Charlie as he went to his knees at his fallen uncle and put his hand under his closest relative's bruised head. His uncle was unconscious, with blood flowing from the rifle wound and from his bleeding cheek. The posse was stunned; they stood back as their eyes ranged from Deputy Snotberg to Oscar Big Bull and Charlie Red Tail and back, and at each other—bewildered, but prepared for what might come next unless action was immediately taken. As Charlie was trying to stop the bleeding, two deputies wrestled Charlie away from his uncle, forced him face down to the ground with his arms behind his back, slapped handcuffs on him, and left him in the dirt while Sgt. Smith sent another deputy back to tribal headquarters to summon an ambulance.

"What the hell have you done you, you stupid son-of-a-bitch? You may have just started a new Indian war!"

"The old man went for my rifle. What was I supposed to do?"

"You couldn't fight off an old Indian without shooting him?"

Snotberg didn't answer, just went over to the other deputies, looking unapologetic, and began to explain his version of what happened, exonerating himself from the result. The others were not interested in listening.

Deputy Pearlman rushed to the uncle with a first aid kit and began treating the rifle wound, gave the Indian a drink of water, and exhorted the sergeant to have him loaded into a vehicle and rushed to the tribal hospital. He said, "The man will not live long enough for an ambulance to come and take him there." Oscar Big Bull, fighting for his life, was placed on the seat in the back of a police car, and the driver headed out over the rough road with the old man on the back seat. The roughed-up Charlie Red Tail was placed in another vehicle that followed the first out, while the other law enforcement vehicles followed closely behind.

"Mission accomplished," Sgt. Smith mumbled to the deputy, Roy Kraken, riding with him. "A little messy, but we got the job done alright. I hope that damn Snotberg did not create a big brouhaha for us. We have enough trouble with the damn Indians. But, we got our man."

"It depends, I suppose, whether the old chief dies or not. He's hurting pretty bad."

Charlie was beside himself with worry about his beloved uncle, thinking not about the wrong now being committed on him. Wherever he was headed seemed to Charlie to take forever. Although he was seated upright in the back of the police car, the cuffs were so tight his hands bled, and his arms ached in excruciating pain. The two officers in the front seat threatened him with what was going to happen to him: "You will be hung from the gallows by the good folks of Tihay when we get there, you son-of-a-bitch. And if they don't take care of you, Judge Remington will. You'll be behind bars for the rest of your life, which may be a short one. You can save us all a lot of time if you tell us now how you raped Betsy Stoutwein. You hear?"

Charlie remained silent, his thoughts being with his uncle.

Charlie was unloaded from the deputy's vehicle and proudly displayed to the gathered, hostile crowd. Applause! Shouts, both laudatory for the deputies and derisive toward Charlie belted the quiet air. The historic jail looked like it had come straight out of territorial days—a small adobe building, iron bars on the windows facing the street; it even had a hitching post out front as a tourist attraction, and gallows in the side alley at which hangings had historically taken place. If one did not already know by looking at it, on the front of the building in large letters: "JAIL." The jail was situated next to the Indian Mound County Courthouse that displayed a statute of the area's famous sheriff: "Tom Cassidy—Indian Fighter and Law Enforcement Hero."

Charlie was booked into the jail, a mug shot was snapped, his fingerprints were taken and compared with records, but nothing matched. The historic jail had two cells with rusted bars, iron beds, and metal toilets. An unwashed blanket adorned the cell. Charlie was thrown in the cell that had a small, barred window for light, but no other light; it was next to the sheriff's office itself, which was small and had two desks, two wooden chairs, two leather chairs from a day long ago, barred windows with little light allowed, a wood stove, and two bare light bulbs hanging from the ceiling.

Tex Brutkowsky was a large, lazy, obnoxious man who had been in law enforcement in the West for thirty years, never rising in esteem, but several times elected to a sheriff's office because of his "tough talk" on crime. He walked the talk. He was a "good old boy" who fit in nicely with the influence-peddlers of the people that currently elected him, like the Stoutweins. He frequented the Three Shot Saloon and rubbed elbows with the "big shots" but also with the "little folks," and he held forth with boisterous pontification touching every political subject in the news, and every local issue dealing with the Indians. His wife fixed the meals for the prisoners in his jail and that way made money above his salary—by skimping on the already austere food budget authorized by the county commissioners.

Brutkowsky was quite proud of the fact that his men had captured Red Tail so quickly. He wasn't bothered by the fact that the uncle had been shot, rather choosing to believe his cousin was justified in the shooting and was acting in self-defense. He "humbly" accepted the drinks bought for him at the Three Shot Saloon for the job well done.

As Charlie sat in his cell, head bowed, body aching and desperately looking for a way out, his emotions took him from joy to fear, from aspirations to resignation, from love to hate. *What will happen to me now? Will the white man kill me? Will I be put in white man's prison for life? How can this be happening to me, for I have done nothing wrong!* He could not rid himself of these thoughts as he awaited his destiny.

Charlie was not taken before a judge for several days. When he finally did appear before the judge, the Public Defender was appointed as legal counsel for Charlie. The Public Defender was William (Willie) Thompson. Thompson recently graduated from law school with high grades and had some experience in criminal cases as he assisted public defenders around the state from time to time. The new public defender in Indian Mound County had learned to fight hard on behalf of his indigent clients. He was single and could devote time to his work, but now labored under a strict and often arbitrary judge who pushed a case hard and expected lawyers to follow his burdensome instructions and abide his studied impatience. Defense lawyers and their witnesses were not treated with the same respect as the prosecutors and the state's witnesses, particularly if they were law enforcement witnesses.

Thompson's representation of Indians was limited, and most Indian cases he had handled were misdemeanor crimes. He had never defended a serious felony case, let alone a rape case involving an Indian and a white victim. But when he was notified he had been appointed to defend Charlie Red Tail on a rape charge, he was eager to take it on; he was not intimidated by the seriousness of the case, and he was confident he could do a good job for his client. This case was a big deal to him, although he did not know the added difficulty of representing an Indian on a felony charge in Judge Remington's court; however, he had experienced the wrath of Remington on minor cases, and he was quite aware of the attitude of the whites in the county toward Indians, an attitude he considered to be racist. And, he was also aware the locals were not happy about paying for the services of a lawyer to represent Indians primarily, or anyone else for that matter. Experienced prosecutor Anthony "Tony" Jones, had been born and raised in Tihay. His "old-timer" family still lived there. Old man Jones was a former prosecutor and had been highly regarded for his hard-nosed attitudes in the doing of his job.

At the initial appearance before the court, Tony Jones appeared on behalf of the State and requested that no bail be set. Thompson resisted and argued for a reasonable bail to be set. No bail was allowed, and so Charlie was to await his fate while confined.

Judge Remington set the next hearing for Charlie to be in two weeks, "which will allow his attorney time to meet with his client, investigate the case, and, hopefully, be prepared to enter a guilty plea at the next court appearance."

Thompson arrived at the sheriff's office the next day to interview Charlie. Brutkowsky had little desire to accommodate lawyers in general, let alone Public Defenders who made more money than he does. And he did not need to be reminded of the time in court several years before, court in a fair judge's courtroom, when a Public Defender tore him to pieces on the witness stand, held him up to ridicule when he was caught lying about an important fact of the case, and having the judge rebuke him in front of the jury. No, Tex Brutkowsky had little time for defense lawyers. A long time ago he vowed he would not kowtow to stupid court rules that permitted guilty defendants to go free. Once was enough! But he was smart enough to know he had to follow some of the rules if he wanted to keep his job, such as allowing defense attorneys the opportunity to talk with their clients who were in jail. (Of course, he could generally overhear the lawyer talking with the client, but it was not his fault the cells were close to his desk, although he could shut the door between the cells and his office. In his mind, that would create a safety issue and violate his duty to not allow a prisoner to escape.)

The sheriff carefully eyed Thompson as he walked into the office, and even though he knew who he was by virtue of other jail visits, required him to submit to a thorough search for weapons and contraband before unlocking Charlie's cell and permitting Thompson to enter.

"You've got one hour. If you finish before that, hammer on the bars and I will let you out. No funny business, now."

Charlie watched carefully and considered making a break for it, but thought better of it as Thompson came through the door to the cell. He had no choice, really, as he immediately noticed Brutkowsky held a pistol in his left hand as he unlocked the cell door and stood back a bit.

Willie was a confident lawyer. His personal appearance helped him instill confidence in his clients and because he played by the evidence and court rules, he was trusted by most courts in which he appeared. He was 6'5" tall and a well-conditioned 195 pounds. He carried himself with a good amount of self-assurance, and he was well-spoken.

Charlie's lawyer introduced himself and asked his client to sit on the bed with him; he shook his hand and told him they would need to whisper to each other; he assured him he would work hard for him and he asked Charlie to trust him. The initial interview began, but Charlie immediately interrupted and asked Thompson, "Do you know how my uncle, Oscar Big Bull, is doing? Is he still alive?" The defender could feel the emotion in Charlie's asking, in the unspoken love he had for his uncle. Thompson said he knew nothing about his uncle's condition, but that he would check on him and let Charlie know. In point of fact, the defender did not even know at this time what had happened to the uncle. The interview continued with deepening concern on the attorney's part as Thompson was told the details of what had occurred. When Brutkowsky came back after an hour, William Thompson left with his jaw tightened and his resolve high to fight for Charlie Red Tail. He was shocked by what he had learned from his client. Unless he had been lied to, Thompson was sure his client was innocent. He was also sure that Oscar Big Bull had been unlawfully shot.

With only two weeks until the next court appearance for Charlie, Thompson knew he needed to work fast. First on his checklist of work to be done was the status of the uncle, and so he took off and drove to the tribal hospital, noting the location of Ft. Custer on his way. He would stop at the alleged crime scene on his way back from the hospital. Thompson decided he would talk to the tribal police captain after going to the hospital, and he knew he needed to go to the uncle's home to look for evidence and take photographs. He was beginning to feel a lot of pressure, but not panic. He hurried his thoughts on the drive to the reservation and began to truly sense the gravity of that in which he was involved. The loneliness of a defense lawyer began to set in, but he knew Charlie Red Tail depended on him and that was what now occupied his trained mind.

At the reservation hospital, he found Oscar Big Bull to be recovering from his serious gunshot wound and the blow to his head, but he was still not in the best condition according to the nurse who was attending him. After telling the old man of his connection to Charlie, Thompson quietly told him of Charlie's concerns, got a detailed description of what had happened, and came away feeling somewhat optimistic about the elderly man's recovery.

The defense counsel mapped the roads from the police headquarters to the crime scene; he viewed and photographed the cabin area; he inspected the grounds for physical evidence; he stopped at Ft. Custer on his way back to Tihay, sketched the layout of buildings and trees, and took photos. He hurried on to the jail to give Charlie the good news about his beloved uncle. One of the biggest takeaways from the trip for Thompson was the fact that Oscar Big Bull had acted to save the life of his nephew, at the risk of his own life. Based on all Willie had heard from the uncle and the nephew, love was there at the small house near Old Woman Creek. A deep love, cradled in a deep respect of a young man for an elder, familial love by that elder, and a human need by each for the other in his life.

In preparation for the upcoming court appearance for Charlie, Thompson investigated, researched, briefed, and filed several motions with the Court. He moved for a change of venue to try and protect against the racism he knew existed in the county, filed a motion for permission to take the depositions of the state's witnesses prior to trial, requested that a medical exam of the alleged victim be conducted for the defense and that a medical expert be authorized to work for the defense. He filed a motion to dismiss the charges on the basis that Charlie's constitutional rights were violated because an arrest warrant was not obtained by the authorities although there had been sufficient time to do so.

At the court hearing, with local and regional news organizations in attendance, the motions were heard by the Circuit Judge, Thomas Remington, a jurist fond of his firearms-related namesake. He glared at Thompson and berated him for the filing of "all these baseless motions," and also for "insulting the good people of Indian Mound County by contending they are racist and that they won't give this Indian a fair trial." All motions were summarily denied. Judge Remington proceeded to read the charge against Charlie, advised him of the possible death penalty if convicted, and told him to enter a plea to the charges.

Standing before the judge, Charlie Red Tail said loudly, "Not guilty." The room was abuzz. The trial was set for two months from the date of the hearing.

The trial date was kept on the court calendar despite defense attorney Thompson receiving several death threats from unknown persons; further, a more serious incident happened when Thompson's car was sprayed with bullets when it was parked in front of his apartment. The attorney again filed a motion to move the trial to another county, and alternatively, for a delay of the trial to allow time for the shooting and the threats to be investigated. "Your honor," Thompson argued, "these threats on my life have put in jeopardy my personal safety; this trial should be moved to another county; at least, the Court should grant my motion for a continuance of the trial to allow time to have the threats investigated. My client is being deprived of his constitutional right to a fair trial by my having to personally take steps to protect not only myself but also my client. The sheriff refuses to do anything. He has told me there is nothing that serious about all of my complaints of these matters, and my asking him to do something has fallen on deaf ears. I have talked to the Attorney General and he is looking into all this, but I can't be expected to ignore the seriousness of these episodes and proceed without protection for me and my client being ordered by the Court. I urge the Court to delay the trial until the gravity of the actions by persons in this county is fully investigated by the AG and until the personal safety of myself and my client can be assured."

The Court: "While I agree the shooting, at least, appears to be a serious matter, the anonymous threats can hardly be taken too seriously. The sheriff has advised me the timing of the shooting and the fact that so few shots were taken at your apartment proper indicates it was not a personal assault. I must say, it appears you are hyping the facts in an effort to get the motion for a change of venue granted. You have not presented any evidence that ties these threats to the people of this county. For all we know, the perpetrator could be from out of state or wherever." Raising his voice, the judge continued: "And, as to all this being told to the AG, young man, that isn't the way things are done here. I don't like it one damn bit. We don't need the state taking over law enforcement in this county. This trial will proceed as scheduled! Your motions are denied. I will, however, order our fine sheriff to assign one of his deputies to be your bodyguard during the daytime. Night deputies can do a drive-by at your place every night, perhaps a time or two. Court's adjourned."

The public defenders in the state are State employees and are part of the justice system. Assault on a public defender is a serious matter, no matter the result. Attorney General Richard D. Barth is a no-nonsense AG, experienced in criminal law, dedicated to law enforcement of which he is the leader in the state, and one of the better appointments that Governor Thomas Mick had made. Barth knew the responsibility for protecting a threatened Public Defender was that of law enforcement, not the District Court Judges. When the attorney general was made aware of the terrorist attack on one of the Defenders, he immediately called Sheriff Brutkowski to find out what happened. The lack of an investigation, combined with the sheriff's obviously prejudiced attitude toward the Public Defender's client and his defense client told the AG something was seriously wrong in Indian Mound County. He wasted no time in dispatching a security detail to Indian Mound County to look out for the safety of the attorney after learning of the possible abuse of power by Judge Remington in handling the proceedings against Charlie Red Tail.

A second attack was made on Thompson; the security detail had no difficulty in apprehending the attacker, for the fire from the rifle barrel on that dark night located the assassin for them. Deputy Sheriff Henry Snotgrass was arrested without a fight and placed in the county jail in a cell next to Charlie Red Tail. Charlie did not know Snotgrass. Snotgrass, of course, knew Charlie. As soon as the arresting officers had left, Snotgrass began ranting about Charlie and the alleged rape of Betsy Stoutwein, including the detail that "he, Henry Snotgrass, had tracked you down at your uncle's cabin and I led the capture of you, you son-of-a-bitch." He also made sure Charlie knew he, the nephew of the sheriff, had shot Oscar Red Bull in self-defense. The deputy expected to be out on bail in the morning. "Judge Remington will see to that."

Attorney General Barth called the judge the next morning and requested a delay of the arraignment of Snotgrass in order that an Assistant Attorney General could travel to Tihay and represent the State in the proceedings, the local prosecutor having refused to handle the matter. The judge reluctantly agreed to a week delay after being pressured by the Attorney General. Snotgrass represented himself at the arraignment and plead not guilty. He needed time to hire an attorney. "For sure a public defender will not represent me. They would all be biased against me. I respectively request that you, Judge Remington, appoint a regular attorney to represent me."

Despite the objection of the AG that no showing had been made by Snotgrass that he couldn't afford an attorney, the judge said: "It is so ordered!"

As the trial of Charlie Red Tail for the crime of rape approached, prosecutor Tony Jones was confident he knew what the result of the trial would be. He did not really care whether the Stoutwein girl was in fact raped or whether the sex was consensual, or whether it in fact even happened. He had the sworn statements. He needed to put a troublemaker from the reservation away. A lot was riding on this case. He was up for re-election next year. Jones was elected by the white vote, not the Indian vote. He had been first elected many years before in a landslide, running on a platform of riding herd on the Indians from the reservation when they wandered into Indian Mound County, which had within its borders historical white man-Indian battle sites, many graves of Indian warriors, women and children included, but also many graves of whites killed by the Indians. He'd been elected many times since, without opposition; he was going to make sure he didn't have any. The locals liked him. He held the same attitudes about the Indians as they did.

Sometime back, Jones had been told by a Corps of Engineers honcho that Red Tail's grandmother caused a lot of problems for the Corps of Engineers over the Corps' construction of Big Bend Dam on the Missouri River which was so important to the State for irrigation and for flood control. Jones reasoned that the Corps of Engineers, being part of the federal government, was entitled to cooperation from the tribes, who in his mind were little more than wards of the Bureau of Indian Affairs, which was also a part of the federal government, and which represented the "best interests" of the Indians despite the obvious conflicts of interest in not participating on the side of the Indians who objected to the taking of their lands, resulting in a forced relocation to higher ground. Jones felt he would help the Corps out by this prosecution, as young Red Tail had picked up where his grandmother had left off and he was told the project was "still vulnerable because there was a rumor floating around that Red Tail intended to get revenge for the flooding of the Indian lands."

In preparing for trial, the experienced prosecutor questioned in his own mind whether Stoutweins' doctor performed a rape kit examination at the local hospital, but thought he may have because of "who" was claiming she was raped; however, he was never able to get a report from the doctor, for the doctor could not find the rape kit and did not know whether his nurse or the hospital had performed such an examination.

The doctor fed the same story to Thompson when later contacted by the defense attorney.

Jones also knew Betsy did not report the alleged rape to the sheriff until July 10th. But it was understandable in Jones' mind that a traumatized young woman could not bring herself to go directly or soon to authorities. Sure, Betsy did not tell the Sheriff or him, the prosecutor, what had happened to her, but she had apparently gone to the doctor shortly after the alleged rape, according to both the victim and the doctor. Other Stoutwein witnesses would testify at trial how traumatized Betsy had been for several days, declining any visits from her girlfriends or others outside the family, eating little and crying often. When Jones interviewed the accuser, he could definitely tell she had been severely traumatized. She was very convincing.

In preparation for the trial, Willie Thompson was able to locate one of Charlie's friends who had attended the dance; the friend gave him a list of the other Indians who had also attended and where they could be located.

Charlie tried to interview each of the people on the list; however, Indians are notorious for not cooperating with law enforcement. When a crime is committed on the reservation, whether by a white man or by an Indian, against a white person or an Indian, generally no one is willing to cooperate in an investigation or in court proceedings, period. Is it a code? No, more than a code, perhaps a cultural characteristic of accepting the way of life in which they were trapped: live and let live; die and let die.

Thompson tracked down each of tribal members on the list given him by Billy White Feather and interviewed them; they were not helpful to Thompson; they could not remember anything about the dance; they avoided his questions; they seemed to be lying about different things. None of them were willing to testify for the defense. Thompson sensed they would be unreliable as defense witnesses even if they would testify, although it was one of their own being charged.

Billy White Feather was a good friend of Charlie's. He was willing to address the injustice he saw happening to his friend. "No way did Charlie rape anyone at the dance. I was with him most of the night, and so were Red Bird and her date, Howie Wolf. I do recall that white girl, Betsy, coming over to our side of the dance floor and propositioning Charlie to go outside with her. Charlie pushed her away and walked to join some of our other friends who were there. The white girl cussed at Charlie and walked outside."

The defense attorney tried to interview the Stoutweins, but they would not talk with him. The law did not require them to talk with defense counsel. The defense attorney also interviewed a few whites that had been at the dance, but only learned they didn't care much for Indians, and did not know there had been a rape committed at the dance.

In the old, historical court room in Indian Mound County, the court with the Indian fighter statue in front and the hanging noose in the alley behind, the press-created sensational trial got under way with the Honorable Judge Remington presiding. The old courtroom smelled of the wooden panel that formed the Judge's bench, for years kept up by application of furniture polish, or in the early days, by oil on the walnut wood; oiled paper window shades hung above the two windows, too high for proper dusting above the casement. Two circa 1880 lights hung from the tin ceiling.

Selection of the jury to hear the case, the voir dire, proceeded rapidly, for the judge kept interrupting Thompson when the defender attempted to explore the attitudes of the panel toward the Indians in general and toward Charlie Red Tail in particular.

The trial jury was ultimately seated after Jones, the prosecutor, who asked only a few questions but made many statements, passed the jury for cause and Thompson's "preemptive challenges," those made without having to show any legal reason as to why the potential juror should be excused, were made. The jury, then, was made up of twelve white men, all ranchers. Indians were not included in the jury pool for Indian Mound County from which juries were selected, the exclusion being a surefire issue for appeal by an Indian defendant found guilty.

Prosecutor Jones forcefully presented his opening statement to the jury. Supposedly, the opening statement is to provide the jury with what the State intends to prove, not conclusionary statements of guilt nor instructions as to what the jury should do in the case. Despite Thompson's objections, Jones was permitted to proceed to deliver what really amounted to a closing argument.

Defense counsel Thompson carefully pointed the way to acquittal, addressing the lack of proof and the inconsistencies of the evidence to be offered by the State as evidence of guilt. He could have waited until the State rested before giving the defendant's opening statement, a tactic often followed by defense counsel; however, to wait, he feared, would allow the prosecutor to comment improperly that his not telling the jury about the defense was itself evidence of guilt of his client.

The first witness for the State was Jim Stoutwein. When he was called to the witness stand and was sworn to tell the truth he stood with his chest out with pride, was loud, cocky, and self-assured. In answer to leading questions from Jones, Stoutwein said without hesitation or qualification: "I saw Charlie Red Tail leave the dance with my sister and head for the grove of trees near the dance hall. I saw Red Tail return from the trees with his shirt outside his pants, his belt unbuckled, and dirt on his pants." Jim Stoutwein also testified: "I heard Red Tail tell some buddies at the dance that he had just screwed Betsy."

"When my sister returned to the dance hall she was

sobbing, had dirt on her dress and weeds in her hair. She grabbed my hand, put her head on my chest, and while sobbing told me that Charlie Red Tail had raped her in the tree grove." He testified his sister pointed out Red Tail to him when she returned, and then the brother pointed out the seated Red Tail at the defense table as the same person she had identified to him at the dance.

His testimony regarding the sister's demeanor and actions after the dance was startling. Betsy rode back to Tihay with brother Jim and Jim's friend, Art Smith. "That damn Art and Betsy were getting it on to the point I had to stop and pull over to let them finish. Both were drunker than hell, and I wasn't doin so well myself."

Under cross-examination, the young Stoutwein could not describe the dress his sister was wearing, nor the clothes Charlie was wearing. He couldn't explain why he didn't go after Charlie Red Tail and beat him up or subdue him until the authorities came to arrest him; in fact, Jim Stoutwein at no point in this saga contacted law enforcement about the alleged rape. He had his cell phone with him at the dance and it was in working condition. He could not say how his sister got to the dance; where the dirt was located on the dress; where the dress and the weeds were presently located; the color of her boots and whether she was wearing them when she came in from the grove of trees; whether she talked with any of her girlfriends when she allegedly came back in to the dance hall; whether other people were present when she told him about the alleged attack. In particular, Thompson hit

Stoutwein hard on his testimony regarding the trip back to town and Betsy having sex with Art Smith.

On re-direct examination, Jim Stoutwein tried to explain that what he just testified to under oath regarding the drive back to town might not have been the truth, because he was so drunk he might not be remembering correctly. On re-cross, the young public defender asked: "How many times before trial did you go over your testimony, the questions and answers, with Tony Jones?" Loud objections from Jones and pointed outrage from Judge Remington resulted in the jury being instructed to disregard the question of Thompson. "I should hold you in contempt of court. And if you make one more sophomoric error in this case, I will. Now sit down." The young public defender knew the question was not out of line, but made no retort to the judge for he knew an appeal of this case would be in order no matter what.

Betsy's father, Mac Stoutwein, was the epitome of a western rancher: tall, muscular, weather-tanned, gnarled hands, chiseled face, and a drawl for a speaking voice. He was a leader of the ranchers in the area close to the reservation and was a former elected County Commissioner of the Indian Mound County government. The last time he had run for office, he had been elected with sixty-five percent of the votes. He was a contributor to all of the charity events in the county. Every year he purchased the Grand Champion Steer at the 4-H livestock auction and donated it to the senior citizens' center. Upon being told by his daughter that an Indian had raped her, he was outraged, as any father would be. He was allowed to testify, despite the objection from Thompson, about the details of the alleged rape as told him by Betsy. He also testified over objection as to what his son said he saw at the dance. More hearsay. "That damn Indian needs to be put to death," he forcefully said at the end of his testimony—the jury for sure heard and some nodded their heads. Thompson's motion that the statement be stricken from the record and the jury instructed to disregard it because inflammatory and prejudicial was sternly denied by Remington.

The father did not recall the time when Betsy told him of the attack, and simply testified briefly as to her emotional state that he observed, though no doubt exaggerated. He had little else to say. Thompson conducted a short cross-examination; he was able show that of the few "facts" told him by his daughter, many were contradicted by the testimony of Jim Stoutwein, and would also be contradicted, Thompson suspected, by the coming testimony of the daughter. Betsy had been well prepared by Jones for the trial. She wore a pretty dress, had her hair styled and arranged in an elaborate way; she spoke softly as she described the rape, her voice rising in anger as she identified Charlie Red Tail as the Indian who assaulted her, but quickly recovering to that of a weeping victim on the stand; she sniffled into the kerchief she held in her hand and kept her head bowed for the most part. She had a particularly sophisticated way of dabbing her eyes with the kerchief from time to time.

After ranting and raving before the Court and jury, strutting back and forth with anger not dripping, but rather, surging, from his lips, Prosecutor Jones asked Betsy Stoutwein if her assailant was in the courtroom! Charlie was dramatically identified by Betsy as the Indian who raped her in the grove near the dance hall on July 4th. She seemed to break down when she made the identification, but it was hard to tell as she immediately put her face in her lap and the pretty dress provided a place for deceit. Jones told her, "Take your time, honey, no one is going to hurt you anymore," to which Thompson objected, but the objection was quickly overruled by Judge Remington. No argument on the objection was allowed.

During Betsy Stoutwein's testimony, the white male jury continually eyed Charlie with stern looks and conviction written on their minds. The men eyed the Stoutwein girl, daughter of their friend, with sympathy. She frequently looked at the jury during the trial with "dabbed" eyes and audible sniffles.

On cross examination, Willie Thompson had an impossible task—how could he put a dent in her credibility? Of course, Jones objected to all questions, and the judge repeatedly sustained the prosecutor's objections to Thompson's questioning, more than once stating to the jury, "Defense counsel is badgering the witness." Thompson was well aware of the adage that counsel should not alienate the jury; however, he also knew he needed to make a record of improbabilities and inconsistencies being foisted on the jury by the alleged victim. He went after Betsy tooth and nail until she began "crying" so hard that Judge Remington intervened and instructed Thompson to wrap up his cross-examination.

The State had no more witnesses. The defense moved to have the charges dismissed. The judge quickly denied the motion.

A tough decision for defense counsel now had to be made—should he have the defendant testify? He decided he must let Charlie do so.

When his name was called, Charlie Red Tail rose from his wooden chair, stood erect and without hesitancy. He was wearing Wrangler jeans, a colorful shirt, and had on his scuffed cowboy boots. His friend Roy Big Elk had brought the clothes to him at the jail at the request of Thompson, to avoid Charlie's having to be at the trial dressed only in his jail garb. He walked sprightly to the witness box, sat down, and looked jurors right in the eye. Most looked away.

Charlie forcefully denied that he had raped Betsy Stoutwein, telling the jurors the facts of what actually transpired at the dance. He also testified about his high school scholastic and athletic record, his community service, his family, and his plans for the future. Prosecutor Jones conducted, over objection by defense counsel, but without admonition from the judge, a loud and vitriolic cross-examination, pointing at Charlie, stalking Charlie, cajoling the jurors and mocking Charlie's testimony. He belittled Charlie and with sarcasm designed to elicit agreement from the jury, at times drawing snickers, and tried to put in each juror's head a vision of "nothingness" in the haystack of life for Charlie Red Tail.

One of Charlie's friends who was at the dance with Charlie, Tom Big Horse, testified that Charlie had been with him or on the dance floor the entire night. He was never with Betsy Stoutwein and he never told him he had anything to do with her. Jones began stalking Big Horse, but then suddenly threw up his arms and announced, "No questions of this redskin, your Honor." Objection overruled.

Billy White Feather testified to what he had told Willie Thompson: "No way did Charlie rape anyone at the dance. I was with him most of the night, and so were Red Bird and her date, Howie Wolf. I do recall that white girl, Betsy, coming over to our side of the dance floor and propositioning Charlie to go outside with her. Charlie pushed her away and walked to join some of our other friends who were there. The white girl cussed at Charlie and walked outside."

Jones began stalking White Feather, as he had Big Horse, but then again threw up his arms and announced, "No questions of this redskin, your Honor." He looked at the jury and shook his head, indicating "no." Objection overruled.

Judge Remington was mostly a probate judge, handling the probate of wills and a few adoptions. He had little necessary knowledge of the rules of criminal evidence, so considerable objectionable evidence had been allowed to be offered by the prosecution and be heard by the jury, always over the objection of the defense. The judge seemed pressed for time, and he continually carped at defense counsel Thompson to "get on with it," interfering with Thompson's theory of the defense and making him look bad in front of the jury.

By this time in the trial, the gallery of local citizens was becoming somewhat audible in their thoughts and agreement with the prosecutor. Snide remarks were whispered. The ladies in the gallery were shocked at what happened to poor Betsy. The jurors were aware.

The closing argument made by Jones was theatrical, caustic and hard-hitting. There was no need to be overly concerned with the lack of evidence to substantiate the allegations and testimony of the Stoutwein family. The jury heard what it wanted to hear and acted to protect one of their own.

Defense counsel presented sound argument and what should have a persuasive case for acquittal. No matter. Although he did not need to waste his breath as he knew what the verdict would be, it was important to put another nail in the deceitful coffin of the lies told. He continued in his duty to preserve a record for appeal. Thus, the able defense counsel presented in detail the mistaken beliefs, the falsehoods and the inconsistencies that had been put before the Court and jury by the prosecution. Perjury had been committed. Someday, Thompson believed, justice would be done.

The jury foreman, a ranching neighbor of Mac Stoutwein, firmly and loudly announced the jury's unanimous verdict after the jury deliberated for forty-five minutes, just about the time needed to elect a foreman and take a vote. The vote was required to be unanimous, and it indeed was: "Guilty!"

It was also the year when Judge Remington was up for re-election. Indeed, his grandfather had helped settle Tihay, and there was no question how his late grandfather and his dad had felt about Indians. Judge Remington knew he would be re-elected if he acted accordingly. He felt he had in this case.

Charlie Red Tail's being put away in the state prison for a sentence of four years freed the Stoutweins, the other ranchers in the area, and the Corps of Engineers from the push-back by this rising Indian leader that sometimes complicated their planning for the Missouri river. And the ranchers were pleased that Betsy Stoutwein, the leader of the CowBells, would remain in office.

CHAPTER 2

BEHIND THE STEEL DOOR

Clyde Brown was a big man, tattooed up and down with the colored images typical of criminal gang acceptance—the most important to him being one on his forearm that says "I love you Mama." His huge arms and muscled back were covered with the images only a forsaken soul would choose. He stood 6' 5," had biceps as big around as Charlie's waist, and weighed a "ripped" 250 pounds. His head was shaved. He had a large scar running the length of his left cheek, from ear to chin, obtained in a knife fight that landed Clyde behind bars in the state high-security prison for life. He was now Charlie's roommate.

Charlie quickly learned Clyde was outspoken and hateful toward the federal government, specifically, the IRS. Clyde railed against the "feds" every time he found someone willing to listen, and so Charlie heard it often, having no other choice, really.

"They took my daddy's land, a little acreage Daddy earned by the sweat of his brow! We was poor folks. Only place he had to grow food for our family and farm a bit to earn a little money was on this little piece of land. It was the only place we had to earn a living. None education did they have—in fact, my sister and me didn't even finish grade school. My daddy never did a thing to deserve what happened to him and Mama. He never made much money. At least we kids never saw anything that showed us he had any. Mama worked at a restaurant until it closed. She cleaned houses. The only money Mama and Daddy ever made was just enough to get by on. They just did not have enough left over to pay taxes with. I heard my mama crying all the time after the government came calling. They threatened Daddy and Mama that they had better pay up or they would be sorry—how can poor people be forced to pay taxes to the IRS when they got no money to pay with? The feds continually threatened Daddy and Mama. The feds took Mama's wages from the restaurant. They took Daddy's milk cow, his tools, and his pride. The feds stole our land. They stole our home. My daddy killed himself because of them. But I got even. The son-of-a-bitch deserved to die, he sure as hell did! I cut him up real good, but I have this ugly scar to remember him by. But," said Clyde, "I later got a ranch girl, despite this ugly scar, until I ended up here. She was from a ranching family who lived along the Missouri River in South Dakota—ugly as sin, was a nymphomaniac. She left me when I came in here and stopped coming by to see me. So much for the good life," said Clyde Brown. "I heard she later got mixed up in a rape case and sent someone to prison. Poor guy! She gave it away for free, and no way was the bitch raped by anyone."

Charlie said nothing.

Charlie felt Clyde's pain.

Clyde got to know Charlie pretty well. Clyde liked Charlie. Charlie did not dig into Clyde's personal life, nor did he ask for information from him that showed a bad motive on Charlie's part. Charlie did not look down on Clyde, and when Clyde talked to Charlie, Charlie showed real interest and empathy. Clyde felt Charlie could be trusted. And Charlie liked Clyde also, although they had nothing much in common other than their dislike of the federal government and the "hard times" of life they both knew.

Charlie was locked up behind the steel door of prison for four years. He had gained a clear, first-hand understanding of "justice" for an Indian and the cruelty with which it could be applied. He would often lie awake in bed at night thinking: *How can this be? How can I be locked up here for something I did not do? What am I to do when I get out?* He had no answers, but he did know he had a duty to be done when he got out of the joint—fulfill Grandmother Yellow Bird's vision!

Charlie did not waste his time in prison. He enrolled online in a community college and studied hard. He loved mathematics and psychology. But he also had a strong interest in criminal justice. He wanted to learn how justice should be done. He felt he could someday go back to the reservation and help with the many problems on the reservation—not just the criminal activity, but also the dependency problems caused by booze and drugs. Charlie had good teachers. He read a great deal. He explored online, using the prison's computers. There was nothing in the realm of self-help that he did not immerse himself in, including spiritual topics that appealed to his cultural learning of his place in the world, as taught him by the elders of his tribe.

He did not sound off in prison about what had happened to him. He told no one. He caused no problems. Charlie and Clyde usually talked about a lot of ordinary things, but also about some things that Clyde knew from his life of crime, street-smart things. Charlie knew such knowledge would someday be helpful to him, one way or another.

Eventually, Charlie talked with Clyde of his life while living on the island that was part of the reservation and told Clyde of the strong family emphasis of his tribe. He told Clyde of the Great Spirit, and the teachings he had been given by the animals regarding the weather and survival, and sharing of food. He told Clyde of the reverence of the Indian people for Mother Earth and their knowledge of the earth, wind, and sky. Clyde identified with a good deal of what Charlie told him, for he too had lived in a rural area and he especially identified with the bird and animal stories Charlie shared with him. Clyde seemed to be really interested in the Indian way of life and eventually began, even with his limited education, to read about the Indians and the West. He really liked reading "shoot-em-up" Western paperbacks as well. He sometimes asked Charlie to read to him. Charlie was pleased to do so, for he saw the big guy's need to know more than his cruel world let him have.

Just before being released, Charlie finally shared with Clyde that the reason he had been sent to prison was the false accusation and testimony of the Stoutweins. The night before his scheduled release, Charlie slept little and reflected on his past.

Charlie had become somewhat hardened from being in prison. When he was released, he was uncertain of what to do, had no money, and continued to live with the challenging obligation his grandmother had given to him. He soon drifted from Indian bar to Indian bar and perpetuated on the outside the lonely existence he had inside the prison. However, his mind always returned to his last moments with his dying grandmother. As a survivor of the earth's rape and of society's injustice, he with the name of the hawk, while searching the starry sky on many nights, bit his lip as his heart sought answers in his life. The blood from his lip stained his wool shirt but provided a clear vision of justice. Charlie Red Tail knew what had to be done. He lifted his hands to the sky and prayed to the Great Spirit for wisdom and how to handle the bitterness in his heart. Charlie wanted to believe the Great Spirit would answer him, as it had when the steel door finally swung open and he walked free of the false accusation of the white man.

Charlie learned in prison of helpful contacts in the world of crime and developed a certain mindset for dispensing revenge for the many wrongs his people suffered. Thus, when he left the white man's hell-hole, he had firmly fixed in his mind what needed to be done to fulfill his grandmother's vision. When the steel door opened, Charlie Red Tail had a plan.

However, now, in this time of freedom, Charlie Red Tail could still hear blasting in his ears the bone-chilling slam of the steel door entrance to a dark place and the thunderous clank of a door to a cell at the maximum-security prison that forced him as an innocent, naïve boy of eighteen into the sad, threatening world of prison life and starkly fearsome inhabitants.

CHAPTER 3

UNIVERSITY

Charlie knew he needed to get the education he must have to survive in the white man's world; however, Charlie's goal was not just one of survival in white man's world, but also of learning what he needed to know in order to carry out the vision he had the obligation to fulfill. His problem was that his grandmother had not told him how to seek revenge; she told him only that he would be honored by his people for achieving it.

Charlie was smart. Two universities had recruited him when he graduated from the high school on the reservation, and each offered him a full scholastic scholarship. He had decided to enroll at University of the West. Charlie's expenses not paid for by the school were to be paid by the Bureau of Indian Affairs. The financial help was still available for him.

Four years after graduating from high school, Charlie Red Tail was finally enrolled at University of the West. The university was about 200 miles "as the crow flies" from Charlie's home on the Horse Creek Reservation, a big reservation spreading over 420,000 square miles. It not only lay along Big Bend reservoir, part of the Missouri River, but it stretched far to the south and west, at one point touching the Nebraska border.

Charlie found an apartment to rent at 460 Mulberry Street, so it would be easy for him to walk to campus for classes. He was excited, grateful for the opportunity to go to college, but his view of his future was always darkened a bit by his pledge to his grandmother.

Criminal justice and American History were now of particular interest to him. He decided he would include in his university studies the courses necessary for him to learn the history of the dam system, commonly known as the "Pick – Sloan plan for Dams on the Missouri River in the Dakotas and Nebraska." The Garrison Dam, the Oahe Dam, the Gavins Point Dam, the Fort Randall Dam, and the Big Bend Dam had been constructed in the Dakotas and had affected tribes up and down the river. The Big Bend Dam severely impacted the Horse Creek Reservation and, therefore, Charlie's forefathers' lands located there, including an island in the river. The Oahe Dam impacted the Standing Rock Reservation to the north. Other tribes, in one way or another, were affected as the Sioux Nation as a whole lost a part of what was traditionally theirs and that had been supposedly protected by treaty with the invading white man.

The government's Bureau of Reclamation and the Corps

of Engineers were located in Omaha, Nebraska. Those agencies were in charge of building the dams on the Missouri River, the "Big Muddy." At the time, the public support for the flood control purpose of the dam system was high, and few of the general public knew, or cared, of the effect the dams would have on the American Indian peoples and, in fact, on some of the white ranchers who owned ranch lands in the path of the flooding waters that were to come. Irrigation projects and municipal water supplies added to the flood control ability of the dams were deemed all- important. And the whites were generally paid just compensation by the federal government. The Indians were not!

More than 500 square miles of tribal lands were destroyed by the Big Bend Dam project. Many tribal families on the Horse Creek Reservation were forced to move from the fertile bottomlands to the barren plains above the former river. Their homes, pastures, croplands, timber, wildlife, medicinal plants, and vegetation were wiped out. The Bureau of Indian Affairs did not protect them. The Corps of Engineers did not protect them. The Corps was allowed to proceed until the life-giving waterway was harnessed and brought to heel at the expense of the health, livelihood, and lifestyle of many Indian tribes.

Prior to enrolling at University of the West, Charlie had been told by a medicine man about a Western History professor who was from a long line of "Indian haters." Her ancestors had been on the front line of the efforts of the government to use its army to rid the threat of the Indians to the planned expansion of the white man's lands.

The medicine man told Charlie that if he took her class, he could maybe ask questions about the government's dam project and the government's policies toward his people.

So, Charlie registered in a class taught by Norma Pickenpaugh, who was teaching a Western History class.

Early in the semester, Professor Pickenpaugh announced in a lecture that their study would involve a great deal about the dam system on the Missouri River and the many benefits it provided to humanity despite unwarranted interference from Indians. Charlie smiled. He would be ready for the disinformation he figured would be forthcoming.

In the meantime, Charlie involved himself in campus functions, studied very hard, and found that his fellow students were accepting of him. He loved college! The basketball coach approached him about trying out for the basketball team. Charlie was taken aback by the fact that the coach was aware of Charlie's stellar career in basketball and other sports in high school at Crazy Horse High. He looked forward to the possibility but felt he first needed to address the commands of the "Vision."

Charlie researched the biography and work history of Professor Norma Pickenpaugh. He did not like what he learned. She was born and reared in the East, had graduated from Harvard with a degree in American History, and she had obtained advanced degrees at University of Missouri. Her PhD thesis was on the battle in western South Dakota near Fort Appleby during which the Lakota killed a US

Army general they were fighting. The General's name was Theodore Pickenpaugh. The professor had interned at the Bureau of Indian Affairs in Washington, DC. While teaching at Georgetown University on the topic of the "Western Expansion" in the 1800s, she had angered white students who felt she had unfairly categorized the Indians as "savages" and worse. Demonstrations by the students had brought more than local attention to the university.

When the class sessions on the Missouri River dam project came along, Pickenpaugh taught the lectures with much passion. She lectured on what she considered to be the many benefits to the citizens of the Dakotas and of Nebraska: hydro-electric power serving millions of people; flood control; agriculture's benefits from the irrigation that would follow; recreation on the reservoirs and in the campgrounds that would be built; the benefit of municipal water supplies.

Pickenpaugh taught nothing of the cultural and financial impacts on the white and Indian ranchers and the residents of the reservations along the Missouri. She lectured at length concerning the initial opposition to the project by the Indians living along the river, and in her view, the short-sightedness of the opposition to such a worthy project, pointedly saying, "The Indians opposed the reservation system, until the realization it was to their benefit, and the same would be true about the dam system. Few Indians even attended the hearings; those that did often sat silently, listening, but with nothing constructive to offer. It was as if they didn't understand the benefits of the project. They were selfish and not really caring about the progress that would be encouraged by the dams. And they were not willing to sacrifice anything for the good of themselves and the whites." This general theme was covered over several lectures.

Because the rest of the class seemed to care less about the topic, Charlie was allowed to have the floor to engage the professor. From time to time, he fired questions at her that she could not or would not answer; he called her attention to the real story of the profound effect on the Indian peoples, such as destroying their ability to ranch and farm, hunt, and maintain connection with their homelands. He cross-examined her on an obvious lack of on-the-ground familiarity and knowledge of the project. Charlie called her out on her inflammatory language and her insensitivity to the plight of the Indians. On the final day of the topic being brought up by Pickenpaugh, Charlie told her, "Your family connection to the white man's war on the Indian people tarnishes your objectivity. Your lectures show your prejudice against the Lakota Indians. You should remove yourself from the university. You are unfair to my people and to the truth."

The class cheered Charlie Red Tail. In anger, Professor Pickenpaugh strutted out the door of the classroom and slammed the door behind her.

As Charlie left the classroom, he saw a girl he had talked with once before after class. He went over and talked with her again:

"Do you think I was unfair to Ms. Pickenpaugh in there?"

"Oh, I don't think so," she said. "What I have learned in

her class has made me feel really sad about the historical mistreatment of your people by the government and its leaders during the early years in the West. She showed no emotion when she told of the extermination of the buffalo, such warfare being designed to starve out the Indians. I found the nature and purpose of the reservation system that was imposed to be absolutely deplorable. The implementing of government policies aimed at forcing assimilation of you guys into the white race was repulsive to me."

"What are your thoughts about the most recent wrongs—the taking and flooding of our lands so they could build a bunch of dams?"

"Well, on that, I need to know a lot more. But it didn't seem right when she said the relocation of the tribes from the river bottom to the surrounding hills as part of the Pick-Sloan work was probably justifiable punishment for the killing of whites by the Indians during the western migration. And she implied it was justified when the Indians 'refused to join the progress being made by the United States of America.'"

"Yeah. That was flat-out insulting. And wrong!"

As they talked for a few minutes more in the narrow hallway outside the classroom in Old Main, the girl introduced herself as Johanna Johnson. Charlie introduced himself as Charlie Red Tail.

CHAPTER 4

THE WHITE GIRL

Johanna Johnson lived off the campus of UWest in an apartment on Mulberry Street. Mulberry Street runs into Sycamore Street, the street creating the south border of the UWest campus. Her apartment was at 360 Mulberry, to the south from the Ranch House Fraternity at 260 Mulberry, and a block north of Charlie Red Tail's apartment.

Johanna had never wanted for good grades or friends. She was smart, athletic, quite pretty, and sexy, with a wholesome personality. Her high school education was at a top-notch private school in the East where she learned how to be a lady—a smart one. She did well there and made many friends from throughout the country who, like her, were developing strong opinions about contemporary issues, and looking forward to their independence by going to college. Despite her Eastern schooling, after graduation she longed to return to the West, for her family was there, and her best friends had stayed there after high school and were attending colleges in South Dakota and Wyoming. So, she enrolled at University of the West in Three Creeks, South Dakota, near the Black Hills.

Johanna's parents are still alive, but she had rarely visited them the last year since returning to the West and going to college—not since she and her father had fallen out big time, primarily over their respective environmental views. He had no time for her "protect the environment" positions, and she denounced the "polluters," even the coal industry in which her father had spent a lifetime, and where he was highly regarded by the other industry leaders and by government leaders. He cut her off from a hefty allowance, and they had talked little since then. Johanna was able to draw on her trust fund for most of her school-related expenses. It was not her father's money, for her grandfather on her mother's side had set up small trust funds for all his grandchildren.

At University of the West—renowned, and many would say reviled—for its natural resource curriculum, she decided instead of pursuing a degree in petroleum engineering, or geology, as her father had pushed her to do, she would seek a degree in Environmental Sciences with a minor in elementary education. University of the West was well endowed by the coal, oil, and gas companies of the region. Johanna's decision to study environmental science, and attain a minor in elementary education, did not sit well with her father. Not only did she want to study the environment, she wanted to help protect it from the destructive energy industries that poured money into the university.

Johanna loved Western History; she joined the adventure clubs at "UWest"—she skied, snowshoed, and climbed. She worked with the environmental studies department out in the fields and forests; however, she also attended hearings protesting the environmental policies of the Bureau of Land Management and the US Forest Service. And, particularly when it came to coal mines in the West, polluters in her and her friends' opinion, she joined with other environmentalists to protest against the "earth-degrading industry."

CHAPTER 5

ENVIRONMENTAL PROTECTION SOCIETY

Johanna enjoyed college life, dating when she wanted, and she was frequently asked for dates. She first met Carlos Madrid one night at an offbeat cafe near UWest following a protest rally. She was seated, enjoying a cup of coffee. Madrid came by her booth. He was dressed in 501's, a smart-looking, pressed white shirt, and wore Birkenstocks. He wore a digital watch on his left wrist, an Indian bracelet on his right wrist, and he had a diamond stud in his left ear lobe. He seemed confident and engaged in purpose as he asked her if he might join her. She hesitantly said, "You are welcome to do so, but I am short on time and might need to leave soon."

He sat in the booth across from her, in full light under the overhead fixture. Johanna took note of his olive-colored skin, flowing black hair, piercing eyes, and his Spanish accent as they exchanged introductory pleasantries. He told her he was a junior at UWest and was originally from Spain. Carlos' looks and demeanor showcased what she was later to learn was his elitist upbringing and his family's extreme wealth. By US standards, he was perhaps someone entitled to respect and attention, she thought, as they momentarily looked at each other.

After they talked for a few minutes about university classes, their likes and dislikes, Carlos said to Johanna: "This country is so much like Spain. Our heritage, like yours, has always been one of exploration and exploitation. The goal of life is greed, permitting the rich to get richer and the rest of the people to scramble for the crumbs left on the economic table. However," he said, as he looked straight into the eyes of innocence across the table from him, "I will see to it that the rich exploiters of Mother Earth pay a price for the degradation of the environment. That would be a good start to setting the record straight on good and evil. It is up to us to see to it that the evildoers are punished and Mother Earth protected."

Johanna was taken aback by the strident tone and the substance of Carlos's words. She wondered if she were in danger and looked across the table one last time before quickly leaving.

Carlos' eyes trailed after her. He hoped he would see her again.

Carlos Madrid was bold, if not considerate; he was pushy and not inhibited. He managed to be at the same locations

Johanna visited during the next several days.

He was quite irritating to Johanna. He entered into her conversations with others, and often disturbed her quiet study time at the library. But she was interested in his diatribe about the energy industry when they first met. She decided to accept a date with him if he asked.

He did.

During the spring semester, Johanna and Carlos dated off and on. On one date, they lay on a blanket on the warm sand along the beautiful blue water of Lake Deepwater. The lake was close to Three Creeks and was frequented by college students from UWest. As they enjoyed the springtime and the warmer sunshine, they talked and shared poetry, which they both enjoyed. Johanna commented on the plight of the American Indians and the disgusting professor she had in American History. But mostly, they talked at great length about the poor people living next to the disease-belching refineries around the world.

"It is so sad what the big corporations have done to people, and particularly the people living close to their death discharge of pollutants into the air and rivers," Johanna said to Carlos.

"It is up to us to stop them!" exclaimed Carlos. For the time being, the subject was not pursued.

Johanna and Carlos laughed and flirted and enjoyed the beauty of the earth on which they lay. His accented words inflamed her passions for the environment. He did most of the talking, however, and came across as very self-centered. She was OK with that for the time being, but she knew it was a warning flag that would need to be addressed further if she continued to date Carlos. Time would tell. She felt she had met someone in her life that shared her environmental passion.

After several fun dates and coffee meetings, Johanna was comfortable with Carlos. They always talked about the environment and the big energy companies, the desecration of Mother Earth, and how to stop the polluters. On one date, Johanna wondered out loud how she could make her father and those like him abandon the path of destruction they were on. Carlos replied, "They do what they do for one primary reason, the pursuit of money and power. I hate to speak ill of your father; however, he is one of the leaders of an industry that is the principal contributor to industry's attack on the ozone layer and one of the principal causes of global warming. They must be stopped!"

On one occasion, Johanna and Carlos walked to the edge of a bluff outside of Three Creeks and looked down on an oil refinery, the Sand Hills Refining Company. It was near the town. In fact, when the wind was just right, the townspeople and the students could smell the emissions coming from the refinery. It was still operating after having been attacked by eco-terrorists who destroyed a portion of their pipeline supply. Johanna had heard about it; Carlos did not want to talk about it and changed the subject when she brought it up.

When Carlos asked if she would like to go with him to an

EPS meeting, Johanna asked, "What does EPS stand for, and what is the meeting about?"

Carlos explained that he was working with a group known as the Earth Protection Society. "We are the front line of the war against the cannibalistic corporations who destroy the very earth from which they take their valuable bounty. It is not enough that corporations, like the Sand Hills Refining Company down there, tear up the landscape, pollute the waters, and scar the horizons with their derricks, goosenecks, and belching pumps. They also control the political landscapes. The energy whores protect only their own interests and ignore the cries from the people for protection of Mother Earth herself as she fights to provide for the needs and enjoyment of the many. We must fight and destroy the tormentors of the earth's soul so our people may reclaim that which God has provided to them—a sustainably healthy and productive environment, free of pollution and earthly degeneration." He continued for at least another ten minutes, his rage focused on the energy companies and their leaders.

"You bet," Johanna answered. "I will go with you." She thought this must be a group of college students who protest against environmental harm and lobby for good legislation to prohibit continued ruin of the environment.

She promised Carlos she would keep secret what she learned of the EPS and the people there, as she was told by him she must do. "I look forward to meeting your EPS friends and learning more about their mission. I will see you next week outside the place of the meeting. Did you say this is a 'cell' meeting?"

"Yes," Carlos replied. "We are a small group of seven guys, including me, and two girls. We are a 'cell' because we are a part of something much bigger, but we are not controlled by the bigger organization. We make our own decisions and set our own timetables. Our only real connection with the other cells is that they or we can provide to one another technical assistance that may not otherwise be available to a particular cell. I believe we are the foremost protector of the environment and of the species who share this earth with us. We have worked hard through various means to stop the juggernaut called 'progress' that is promoted by the energy development going on in this country today."

"What projects have you been involved with?" asked Johanna.

Carlos refused to be specific. "We are involved with projects that are outside of the ordinary, and I'm not at liberty to describe them to you until you have been accepted into our cell and you have signed on to our principles and goals. You must meet certain standards before you can join us."

Johanna was okay with that for the moment, but immediately questioned in her own mind what could be so important to be that secret and to be kept from her if she was being invited to the cell meeting. Johanna quickly realized there was much she needed to learn before becoming committed to the passion to which Carlos seemed totally wedded. She thought, *Maybe I don't know this guy well enough to be feeling the way I am feeling toward him.* She was not being as mature as she liked to think she was, and was a little bit afraid of her judgment at this time.

But Johanna could not help but notice the passion as well as the anger possessing Carlos. She knew this was a guy who meant what he said and who could persuade others to help him. She decided to go to the cell meeting and learn more.

CHAPTER 6

RACISM, AGAIN

Charlie was flustered a bit by Johanna Johnson's boldness several weeks after his taking on Professor Pickenpaugh in the Western History class when he saw Johanna on campus and she asked him to accompany her to Heck's, the main coffee shop on campus.

"Sure."

From Charlie's observations, only white people hung out at Heck's. There, Charlie believed, the privileged churned their incessant babble of meaningless observations and ideological opinions while playing what they considered sophisticated card games. It was not a place where he felt comfortable.

As they approached the coffee shop, he definitely noticed her flowing, blonde hair, her beautiful, long-legged body, proudly displayed in tight jeans and a low-neckline top. But he was a little uneasy. Charlie's uneasiness lessened a bit as Johanna and he slid into a vinyl-covered booth in the far corner of the social swirl. He felt vibes of sincere interest by this white girl in this Indian. He did not look her in the eye, a trait he has retained from his Indian culture; he shyly glanced at her as they began to talk.

Johanna took note of Charlie's braided black hair, his high cheekbones and rust-colored skin. She thought to herself, *What a strong, handsome face.* She noted, however, his sad eyes. She loved his quiet voice and felt warmth from seeing his erect, muscled body and boyish smile. She felt no measure of superiority toward or pity for him. She felt very comfortable being with Charlie Red Tail.

"Charlie, I have been thinking about Pickenpaugh's class and our talk after the last class. I would like to know more about the dam project you were grilling her about. I find what you said very interesting. She had no right to be curt and crude toward the Indian people, and certainly no right to strut her stuff out of the classroom and not engage you in discussion. Care to share?"

"Sure." Silence.

"Well, what about it?"

Charlie then told Johanna a brief recap of what had happened to the river and how it had affected his people.

Johanna wanted to know more, but she sensed she should change the subject.

Johanna asked about his life in high school and now his life in college. Charlie answered her in short replies.

"What does your dad do?" she asked politely. He did not answer. "Charlie, what does a reservation look like? What was it like to grow up on a reservation? From what I can tell from class and other studies, it was not very good. It seems you guys were forced onto reservations and were located where the lands were not very good for making a living. Is that true?"

Charlie became silent again. He hurt inside from being reminded of the past. He looked out the window at the big pine tree and the flowering bushes. The images became blurred. His heart pumped and pumped. His breathing was labored.

Johanna did not probe any further, as she could tell that Charlie was carrying something in his heart that was not yet ready to be revealed. She reached across the table and squeezed his hand. Charlie and Johanna sat facing each other in the booth. Feelings of warmth and respect inched along the invisible line of communication needed by them both. Something had sparked a flame between them.

"Shall we leave and go for a walk?" Johanna asked.

They did.

"Hi Johanna, where did you get the buck Indian?" hollered Jim Stoutwein from the table of rednecks near the door as Johanna and Charlie walked by his table.

Johanna sure knew Jim Stoutwein. He had been after her a few times for a date; he lived in the Ranch House Fraternity on Mulberry Street she often passed by when walking to the UWest campus. She had seen him on the lawn on many occasions. Catcalls and whistles often rang out as she passed by. Stoutwein usually strutted his stuff wearing a big belt buckle, pressed jeans, boots, and a cowboy hat rolled high on the sides, giving him a slick look with his greasy black hair. The hat had an Indian hatband around the crown.

Johanna wheeled around and fired back loud enough so Stoutwein as well as all in the coffee shop could hear as she and Charlie reached the door: "You! You son-of-a-bitch! You have groveled at my feet for a date more than once, but no way will I ever go out with a make-believe cowboy who is ignorant, obnoxious, and ugly! You need to grow up! Date a skunk, if one will have you!"

The redneck table howled like sick dogs and followed with lust the swinging ass in tight jeans as Johanna closed the door. Others in the coffee shop took notice, some by hoots or whistles. As Johanna and Charlie hurriedly left through the door, Stoutwein turned red and shouted for all to hear, "I will find that redskin and hang him from a tree alongside his white bitch. Nobody talks to me that way, and no redskin will ever have her."

Charlie flinched and then tensed to a point of anger amid vivid flashbacks in his mind of a time past.

As Jim Stoutwein left Heck's that day and walked back to the fraternity house, he suddenly recalled the face of the Indian with Johanna at the coffee shop: *His face was thinner four years ago and he was really wild in the eyes. That brave has been a problem for my family and our neighbors for a long time. His people agitated at the hearings on the dam project and were always claiming the lands along and in the river were rightfully theirs. This guy was one of the feisty ones who argued with me and my buddies at the public dances on or near the reserva-tion. I remember one time when this Indian was dancing with a pretty Indian girl and I tried to cut in and dance with her. Of course, I was drunk, but I would have kicked this Indian's ass if his friend, Julie Thorson Star, had not interfered and told me to leave. I sure told the redskin off before leaving and no doubt scared him so he wouldn't interfere with me again. I also told him he would regret this night.*

That was all Jim Stoutwein remembered about the Indian as he walked back to the fraternity house after Johanna and Charlie left Heck's.

CHAPTER 7

THE VISION BURDEN

Charlie was determined and committed to obey the "vision." His best friend was Tom Big Horse, who knew about the vision. They had known each other since Indian School. Tom could be trusted. The Indians believed that friendship was the real test of character, the true mark of a man. After graduating from Indian School, Tom went to college and had already graduated. He now worked in an architectural firm in the Billings area. He had done very well financially. Married. Three kids. A devoted wife. Charlie decided to take a drive to go see Tom.

Tom and Charlie had been through a lot together, growing up in poverty, forced to attend Indian School, helping each other in fights, suffering whites' harassment, sharing their innermost thoughts and dreams. Tom and Charlie's grandmothers were friends, and Tom's grandmother had also suffered the loss of "Big Muddy" bottomlands. Tom's uncles and Charlie's uncles together worked a small cattle ranch that had to be relocated to the higher grounds overlooking the "new river." The two young Indian boys had talked of getting college learning and even of a willingness to go back to the reservation to share their knowledge and care for their people. They agreed to always be proud of their heritage, even in the white man's world, and to earn trust and respect by the white man while remaining proud of who they are: Lakota Sioux.

"Tom," Charlie said as they sat near a cedar bush on a hill overlooking their former island. "I have something to share with you that is consistent, I believe, with my grandmother's vision she received from the Great Spirit. I know I can trust you. I have not shared the vision nor my plan with anyone else."

Tom looked at his lifelong friend, nodded his head in acceptance, and leaned forward to eagerly hear what Charlie was planning.

The sky was clear, no clouds overhead. The smell of the cedar was intoxicating. Charlie's emotions were turned on high. This would be the first step in following his plan for revenge against the government for the bad treatment of his people and the taking of their lands once again for the benefit of the white man, this time for the building of dams on the Missouri River.

Charlie began slowly: "Tom, I had a lot of time to think while I was behind the steel door. As you know, Grandmother told me her vision before I was sent to prison. She explained to me as we walked along the Big Bend reservoir one day that I was to speak and act for the tribe and those who went before us; I was who the Great Spirit would empower to successfully seek revenge for the flooding of our lands under the waters of the flowing Missouri, no longer flowing freely, as a spirit flowing free, but rather, chained to the whims of the white man; she told me I would need to decide how to cause revenge to happen, but I should know the tribe expected it to happen, and as the red-tailed hawk hunts, to make it happen in a swift manner."

Charlie told Tom of the enormous pressure he felt and the loneliness of his heart, as he put his hand on Tom's shoulder and cried.

"You tell me what to do, and I will do it for our people," Tom said. Tom Two Horses and Charlie Red Tail then grasped each other's forearms so the interior of their arms touched on the scar made when, as little kids playing together, they foolishly cut their own arms and melded them together, tied rawhide around the arms, and became blood-brothers. They were one. The tribe was their family.

"I will keep secret what you tell me, my brother. What is it that is so heavy on your heart?"

Charlie told Tom how he had come to know Clyde Brown, who was in prison for murder and that Brown would not ever be released. "Clyde shared with me a hatred he had in his heart for the United States Government because of what the government had done to his parents, and he told me some of his experience from the world of crime. In particular, Clyde told me of his experience with, and the availability of, explosives. He told me how to use them.

"A person can apparently buy explosives from the people that Clyde gave me the names and contact information of. But it is expensive to purchase not only the goods but also the silence of the sellers. I have no money. I have committed to memory the people I could contact. They are not from around here. One lives in Denver and the other in New Mexico. Clyde warned me these dudes are bad people. Don't cross them, Clyde warned me. But I am not even sure I will buy any. Tom, you remember the dynamite stored in the Black Hills that we found several years ago? Maybe it's still there, but I think I will explore going to Denver to see the guy Clyde told me about."

"I have a quite a bit of money saved," Tom said, "and I can access some more. How much do you think you will need?"

"About $5000, I suppose. I really don't know. That's a lot of money. I am not sure I should let you use yours for this. Perhaps we should rob a bank or steal a car and sell it," Charlie said jokingly. "What do you think, Tom? Maybe if we need more than five I could get the tribe to loan it to me, so long as they would not know what I needed the money for."

"No, Charlie, we are not going to rob a bank or steal a car or go to the tribe to get the money. We are not that kind of people. I have it and it is yours." Tom paused. "Why is it you need explosives?"

Charlie did not immediately answer. He did not want to involve Tom any deeper than he now was. "You will know when you read of it in the paper. The entire tribe will know, for it will directly affect them. Trust me until then."

Tom nodded in understanding.

"Be safe, my brother."

Charlie Red Tail left his close friend, secure in knowing Tom would not share their talk with others and he embarked on a journey he knew was fraught with peril, but also with the potential for much satisfaction. He was not afraid, for his judgment, he felt, was well honed over the time he had been looking forward to fulfilling what was expected of him. He would be brave and his people would be grateful. He would be honored.

When Charlie left Tom Big Horse's, he did not know what to do next. He went back home to the reservation, where he felt at peace. He wanted to go visit his uncle again. Though a graduate of the white man's indoctrination classes at the Indian School, Charlie most often sought learning from his sense of place and the elders of his tribe—particularly the elder who was his uncle and who had lived long in the Indian world. He was the one who knew the medicine man the best, who talked with the spirits the most, and who taught his people how to live. Oscar Big Bull had lived through the early 1900s army mop-up of the Indians, the demanding years of the reservation system, still imposed on the Indian people, the stealing of Indian lands with the US dam project beginning in the 1960s, the massacre at Wounded Knee in the 1970s, and he was now too old to fight again. So he taught others how to survive and live as an Indian.

Lawyer Thompson had visited Charlie while he was in prison on more than one occasion. He kept Charlie aware of his uncle's recovery from the gunshot wound and conveyed to the beloved man Charlie's wishes.

The minute Charlie set foot on the Horse Creek Reservation, he felt at home despite the run-down government-built homes, the barking dogs running free, the junked cars, and the clothes hanging on the outdoors clotheslines. He knew his uncle would put him up for as long as he stayed on the reservation. Sharing is a deeply held virtue of the Indian people. The extended family always provided for its members. Charlie knew he would not stay long, in any event, but he came to listen and share with the wise elder of the tribe, for despite feeling at home, his heart was heavy due to the task bestowed on him by his grandmother. Charlie needed a better understanding of what was expected of him.

He did not find it on this trip to his homeland, for Oscar Big Bull was in the reservation hospital again and failing. Charlie talked with him as best he could and then decided to go to Denver.

CHAPTER 8

BIG BILL

Bill Jesser, known to all others as Big Bill, was as tough and mean as a man can be. And all who worked for him knew just how mean he could be, for each at one time or another had received his unleashed fury. A white man, Big Bill seemed to identify mostly with minorities, so his stable of whores, network of drug runners, and selected goon squad were all from a minority of one kind or another. He boasted of himself being an equal opportunity employer, for he had Chinese, Mexicans, and Blacks under his control. His only exception to his preference for recruits were the Indians. Indians were too accepting and non-violent for Big Bill. He couldn't make them do his dirty work despite beatings, drug dependency, and extortion. Big Bill despised the redskins because he couldn't control them. He had used one once in recruiting Indian girls for his stable, but even the females seemed somewhat principled and unmanageable. They were clannish, something Big Bill could not have if he were to totally control the minds and the bodies of those trapped in his web.

Big Bill found his enterprises of prostitution, drug dealing, and extortion paled in comparison to his profits from the illegal sale of firearms and explosives, both from a revenue standpoint and pure job satisfaction. Murder was not his bag, for the penalties if caught were too severe, although he had, on occasion, been forced to use it as a tool in his enterprises. On the other hand, the illegal sale of firearms and explosives carried less harsh sentences upon conviction, and getting caught was rare. Bill Jesser and Clyde Brown made a lot of money peddling the big bang weapons, primarily dynamite, for each had learned a lot about their use and destructive power before their dishonorable discharges from the Army. They were of the few in modern army training who knew how to blow up a bridge, for example, for most warfare now would use smart bombs, drones, or something similar. At the same time, dynamite was still being used to take down tall buildings, blast rock, and for similar projects. Big Bill not only knew where to get his hands on the stuff, but he prided himself in "advising" customers of the quantity needed to accomplish a particular job. That way, he felt he shared a piece of the action.

Big Bill and Clyde had worked well together; however, Clyde sought out an IRS agent who had harassed his mom and daddy, and he killed the guy. *Goodbye, business partner, you slime ball*, a disgruntled Big Bill thought at the time. He knew that a good thing could not last forever. Clyde was good at what he did but had no couth. But Big Bill thought Clyde in prison would perhaps lead to some "referrals."

When Charlie telephoned Big Bill Jesser from a pay telephone, he had more than butterflies in his stomach. He was scared to the point that his speech was uncertain and weak. He had taken a long time to build up the nerve to make the contact by dialing a number in Denver given him by his cellmate Clyde, Big Bill's buddy. All Charlie knew was that Big Bill could help him blow something up with dynamite, an explosive about which Charlie knew nothing. He did know of its destructive power by having seen some of the Forest Service's use near the reservation, and, indeed, he knew of the potential use at an earthen dam because he had watched in awe as the Corps of Engineers blasted along the river.

Charlie's going to see a man like Big Bill Jesser made him physically ill. Charlie's going there was so contrary to his upbringing and sense of justice. Yet he knew he must be loyal to the Great Spirit and the vision relayed to him by his grandmother, even though he did not feel totally comfortable in his role or at all certain that his plan, if carried out, could be successful, let alone amount to justice for his people. But he wanted to do what was expected.

Clyde had assured Charlie that Big Bill would be available to help him with anything he needed, and that he should tell him that he had been a cellmate of Clyde's in the "big house." This Charlie did when the gruff voice as the other end of the line answered in a deep, gravelly voice: "This is Big Bill and youse best have a good reason for callin." Charlie stuttered when he told Big Bill that his buddy Clyde had told him to call him whenever he needed help with anything. Charlie was interrupted at that point and told to get off the line but to meet him at a park in Denver in three days—alone! The name of the park was Bloody Gulch. Big Bill said he would be wearing a black cowboy hat and a red bandana around his neck. Big Bill slammed down the receiver. Charlie hung up the telephone.

Bloody Gulch Park in Denver was beautiful beyond description. Unfortunately, it was also the most dangerous of places for those who didn't know which locations were safe. Charlie traveled there after three sleepless nights. He was afraid and concerned. Should he borrow someone's gun? Carry a knife, which he knew well how to handle? Have someone come with him, which Big Bill had made clear was not allowed?

Charlie almost did not go to meet Big Bill. He had been having a great deal of uncertainty as to whether it was smart to go to see the thug. He was not sure he wanted to be getting together with the criminal element Big Bill represented in Charlie's mind. Of course, he had already been exposed to criminals—that is, Clyde and the others in prison. He knew Big Bill and Clyde were in frequent contact despite Clyde being behind bars, for they still planned and schemed by using a "family visitor" at the pen on visitation days, which were once a month. This was the way, unknown to Charlie, that Clyde made Big Bill aware of Jim Stoutwein's false testimony that put Charlie in prison.

It was a Sunday afternoon. It was hot in Bloody Gulch, crowded at the pool and the picnic areas. People strolled on the rolling green hills. Songbirds entertained those willing to listen. The big oak trees offered cool spots to avoid the blistering heat. Charlie saw a big, bald man wipe his head with a red bandana and then wrap it around his neck. He wore cowboy boots and a black hat. He wore sunglasses. His muscles were ripped, his biceps huge. Charlie was close enough to see two other men who seemed to be enjoying the park, one standing several feet away from the bigger man, perhaps guarding him or acting as lookout, and the other farther away near the grove in which Charlie stood. The one was about five foot five inches tall, looked like a body builder, and wore an oiled black cap. The other was taller and not as muscular but looked more dangerous. He wore a railroader's cap, sweat-stained and dirty. He had a bulge in his back pocket. He was closest to Charlie. Charlie felt like he was having a heart attack, and his breathing was heavy. The big man could not see Charlie. Charlie knew from the island how to move without detection or noise, although it was difficult without more trees or foliage. He had tracked many deer. The grove of trees did provide him some cover; the wind in the branches provided some sound covering; the sun was such that he had a narrow runner of dark shade. This Charlie thought. Suddenly, he was aware of an object sticking him in the back and the husky warning: "Do not move, or you're dead." Charlie froze.

He was taken to the big man, Big Bill.

Big Bill did not only look big, he looked mean. With Big Bill's sunglasses off, Charlie was able to see a patch over the left eye. It had skull and crossbones on it. His t-shirt was without sleeves, fit tightly, and had the inscription "Rosie's House of Sin" prominently displayed. Tattoos were all over his arms and the sides of his neck, as if climbing up to a better place. His Levi's were dirty and worn. He had a several-day beard. His cowboy hat was cocked sideways on his head, had a tortured look, and carried the dirt from many a location. His leather belt displayed a big belt buckle made of silver, featuring a big piece of turquoise shaped like a serpent. Big Bill's one-eyed stare was practiced and intimidating. There was no smile. His teeth showed only when he talked, revealing gold fillings, irregular bite, and gaps of the missing. He pulled a plug of tobacco from his pocket, strategically placed it in his mouth, and grunted before he spit. There was no rush for anything, only an overriding air of superiority and confidence.

Charlie knew not to speak until Big Bill spoke. The two guards moved away. Finally, Big Bill turned his attention to Charlie. "Youse say youse are a friend of Clyde's. I know that. He says I can trust his friend. How's Clyde doin these days?"

"When I left the joint, he was in solitary confinement for having a fight in the yard. He said he would get even with the squealer. He was in good health, although his scar was causing him some problems because it was still red and festering. He told me to say hello to you."

"Yeah, he sure took care of that bastard, but that cut was bad. Clyde tell me youse were in because some broad and her no-good brother told lies at trial and youse was convicted as the redskin that raped the white gal. Is that true?"

"Yes, it sure is. Their names were Stoutwein, redneck whites who lived close to the border of the Horse Creek Reservation in South Dakota. He is no good. The brother's name is Jim Stoutwein."

"I don't like bastards who lie. Putting a man in prison, fur somethin he didn't do, is the baddest of crimes. He should pay fur what he did to youse. Tell me where the son-of-a-bitch lives."

"Well, he ranches near Upper Goose Creek, South Dakota, which is on the edge of the Badlands," Charlie said. "But he's not the reason I need your help," Charlie murmured. "I need to buy some dynamite, and Clyde told me you could get me some."

"What the hell do youse need that fur? Youse goin blow something up?"

"Yeah. A control tower of a dam." Charlie had forgotten the advice he had received from Clyde to not tell Big Bill why he wanted the explosives.

"How big?"

"Here's a picture." Charlie knew it was big, because anybody could see the part of it that is above the water. Charlie did not really know the particulars but had read some of the Corps of Engineers' brochures. "Here's a pamphlet that gives the dimensions."

Big Bill did not look at the pamphlet. Charlie thought, *He cannot read!* But Big Bill did stare at the picture. He kept staring. Finally, he said, "How in hell do youse expect to blow up that monster? Da youse want a nuclear bomb? Youse don't know what youse need, and I got nothing that I can give youse that would even remove a wart from the face of that beast, let alone blow it up." There was silence between them for what seemed like an eternity to Charlie. A small bag hung at Big Bill's side. It was green, with a flap, but was not fastened. It contained something. Big Bill reached inside the bag and pulled out a plastic bag filled with crystals. "Here, put this in your Indian pipe and smoke it. We is done talkin. Come see me again when we can talk about drugs we can sell on the rez. Then we can do business."

Charlie was disappointed in not securing a source for the dynamite he needed. As he drove home to South Dakota, he began to consider his strengths and his weaknesses. He was confident he could sneak into any place he wanted, despite the tough security clearance checkpoints. It would take him awhile to decide how to get into an area such as the Corps of Engineers office in Omaha, the Big Bend administrative offices at Deer Creek, or the control tower that raises and lowers the locks of the dam. Yet, he also was somewhat reluctant to commit violence ever since he knocked the hell out of a bully at a bar. He remembered how bad he felt at the time, but also remembered how good it made him feel when the group he was with gave him their high-fives. In his mind big time was the steel door he had supposedly recently walked away from, but which frequented his dreams—or nightmares. He was not interested in going back.

"Well, I will have to give this whole thing a lot more thought before heading off toward a box canyon from which there might not be any return," Charlie said out loud. He drove on.

CHAPTER 9

THE COAL DAD

Peter W. Johnson, Johanna's father, had been a proud leader in the coal industry, a superintendent of the largest coal mine in the Powder River Basin of Wyoming for many years before his retirement. He had been influential in the industry's effort to have authorized and built a coal-slurry pipeline to transport coal to the southwest part of the country. The plan would have drawn large quantities of water from the Ogallala aquifer, with controversial effects. The huge aquifer underlay large pieces of Wyoming, South Dakota, and Nebraska. The plan was defeated, primarily due to the opposition of ranching interests and environmentalists that joined forces to save the water of the aquifer and avoid the environmental degradation, which, they argued, would have been caused by the proposed project.

The coal executive was now involved with the industry's push to have a shipping terminal for coal built on the West

Coast, the coal to be shipped by rail from the mines in north-eastern Wyoming to the West Coast for transport to Asia.

Peter "Pete" Johnson was no wallflower. Since his time as head of the powerful coal giant, Far Horizon Coal Company, he had continued to be involved with the challenges of the coal industry, forced by new environmental concerns of global warming to change its way of doing business, seek more global markets, and continue to fight the environmentalists for coal's survival as a leading producer of energy in the US and the world. He was one of the most effective industry lobbyists and was well known in legislative and regulatory venues.

Mr. Johnson felt strongly that the environmentalists were ruining this country and throwing monkey wrenches into every otherwise viable energy project needed for the continued progress and move toward energy self-sufficiency for the United States. "I have never met an environmentalist worth a red cent," her dad had told Johanna more than once. "They have thwarted every major coal, oil, or gas energy initiative in the country, save their pet projects that won't light more than their own homes." That statement pretty well summed up his attitudes and opinions. When Johanna proudly proclaimed hers and that she was an environmentalist, Dad had his second heart attack. He blamed it on his daughter and began the process of cutting her off from his money.

However, in recent years, Mr. Johnson's feelings toward his daughter had softened, and his heart ached over the strained relationship that had developed between him and his only child. Now in his failing health and aging body, he began to acknowledge what it was that drove Johanna from his home and life. He knew he had not been willing to listen to his daughter's opinions regarding the environment and about the coal industry's pollution. Pete admitted to himself that he had not spent enough time with Johanna as she was growing up. But he had been so terribly busy with career and other obligations. He knew he had been too intolerant of her brilliant mind, too self-centered and demanding of her, although he remembered many happy times with the family. Pete Johnson knew he had to mend fences and fight his way out of the hole he was in. He also knew he loved his daughter.

He talked with his wife, Donna, about his thoughts and concerns regarding Johanna. No words, though softly expressed, hit home more deeply than Donna's saying: "You have been distant from Johanna. At an age when she really needed your understanding and love, you cut her off. It is not Johanna's fault, it is yours, that you have no relationship with her, and it's up to you to make amends and just love her for who she is and despite what she believes. And quit being so stubborn and mean!"

They met at the coffee shop on campus, as Johanna did not want to meet with her dad at her apartment. Her dad was uncomfortable, as was she.

"Daddy, are you feeling OK?" Johanna asked. "I haven't seen you for so long. I have missed you, Daddy. I'm glad you came to visit me. How is Mom?"

After a little chitchat back and forth, her dad had watery eyes and spoke rather haltingly. "I am truly sorry for being so strict with you and for not understanding your feelings about the energy industry and the environment," her dad said with a lump in his throat. "I love you dearly and I know I hurt you when I withdrew not only my financial support of you, but also my time and affection. I am not too religious a man, as you know, but I ask you to forgive me. I want to be your father again. Can we begin anew?"

Johanna could not look her father in the eye as she heard what he said. She knew in her heart that Daddy loved her, and she never stopped loving him. But the hurt from their failing relationship had taken a toll. Her sorrow had caused her not only heartache, but it also fostered some crazy, rebellious behavior. She could not immediately clear her mind of rejection and longing for her dad. She had stayed in contact with Mom, so she knew of Daddy's health problems and of a seemingly changing attitude from him toward her.

"Daddy," Johanna finally whimpered, "there is nothing to forgive. I have missed you terribly, but more importantly, I have never given up on receiving your understanding. I have done a lot of growing up during this period and have realized the bigger pictures of life are important to consider. I have deeply held beliefs about the coal industry and global warming, for example, but I also now understand the role coal must play in the future energy needs of this country, although I remain adamant that the industry must work harder to cause less carbon pollution. That said, Daddy, I want for us to begin anew and enjoy each other in non-confrontational ways. I have learned so much from you about life and giving back to others and this country that I will always want to do what I think is right."

Her dad listened intently to what Johanna said. He fought back tears, this big, tough man.

He held his daughter's hand. "What are you going to do when you are out of school?" her dad asked. "Do you have a job yet or are you still looking?"

"Daddy, I am still enrolled at the university. My grades are great. I will probably qualify for a scholarship if I go to graduate school. I have decided I ultimately want to teach elementary school. I need to pick up a number of education courses. And, I have a job while here at school, but I am not at liberty to tell you yet what it is. But I know you will be proud of me. Now let's go get a burger and I will show you around campus and the town. Can I come home for a couple of weeks?"

Now, her eyes were watery.

CHAPTER 10

UNDERCOVER

Johanna felt like she had been "born again" after the meeting with her father and the relief from the strain of the hurtful behavior of the past given by each to the other. She had a new job that no one knew about, and about which she could not tell her father—undercover for the Justice Department's task force on "ecotage" terrorism. Her role was to help prevent destruction of energy facilities and infrastructure by environmental terrorists. Although still passionate about the environment and the obligation of all to protect and preserve it, she never believed in harming someone's property, and certainly was not ever interested in terrorism. This day she reflected on what had happened one night as she was walking home after a cell meeting, when a well-dressed man in a suit got out of a black sedan and stopped her. The man spoke to her on the sidewalk near her apartment. "Johanna," he said, "you are hanging out with the wrong people. I have been tailing you for some time. I am with the Justice Department's task force on eco-terrorism, and I could perhaps arrest you right now and have the book thrown at you. What are you doing getting involved with the EPS?" FBI Special Agent Rex Anderson asked rhetorically.

"How do you know what I have been doing?" Johanna answered in a strong voice. "How do you know my name?"

"It doesn't matter how I know the things I know," the agent said as he showed her his badge and raised his voice as he told her she was already in big trouble, as far as he was concerned. "If you want a chance to avoid my taking you in and charging you with aiding and abetting a terrorism enterprise, then let's talk and you can explain to me how involved you are with this group of misfits and terrorists. I will give you 24 hours to think about this, but if you tell anyone about my contacting you, I will find out, and you will be behind bars before you know it. There are some steps you can take to make it right. Here is my card. Call me when you have thought seriously about this."

With that, the agent got back in the black sedan, and it drove off.

Johanna walked hurriedly to her apartment. She was not sure of how she felt—afraid, scared, disbelieving, perplexed, but, strangely, excited! She felt she had done nothing wrong by going to the Environmental Protection Society meeting with Carlos. After all, she knew nothing really about the meetings or the people attending, although she had questioned in her mind what the cell group was all about. She knew Carlos, of course. She was uneasy after the last meeting when Carlos and his group were talking in seemingly guarded terms and words, particularly when they talked of a federal entity, the exact identity of which was not mentioned or she did not hear. She had gone home that evening and doubted she would go with Carlos to any further meetings. When the fellow from the justice department task force on eco-terrorism now came into the picture, her need to understand what the cell group was up to seemed incredibly important. If the agent was correct, the EPS was a dangerous organization, plotting to do something dangerous and extreme. No doubt, she thought, their agenda could include doing something against the very interests her family had been involved with, and which she had recently recognized as an important part of energy development so necessary in this country.

Johanna could not identify the reason for her excitement. She knew there was a difference between excitement and meaningful purpose. For sure, Joanna was threatened by the fact that she apparently could be arrested for her having attended the EPS meetings, although she was confused as to why. But it was obvious to her now that she had been dragged into something illegal and under investigation by the authorities. She was scared of being so close to having been arrested; she was scared that she was being asked to do something dangerous; she was scared because she did not know what would be expected of her and whether she had the ability to carry such things out; and she was scared because of the uncertainty about where this all might lead. However, she had interest in the possibility of undercover involvement that she could not put into perspective. Johanna knew she needed to contact the federal agent and find out from him what the EPS was being investigated for and what he expected her to do if she were to agree to what he was asking. She also knew she needed some advice from someone she could trust.

John Wilson was a respected lawyer Johanna knew from her reading the local rag during her time at University of the West. She had never been to see a lawyer; she just knew she had better see one now. Her appointment with Mr. Wilson was quickly granted when she called him at his home late that night. He met her at his office on Oak Street the next morning. His office was quite well-appointed, Johanna felt, with nice furniture, light colors, and Western art on the walls. There was also on the wall in the waiting area a plaque proclaiming Mr. Wilson was honored as a Best Lawyer in America in the field of criminal law. There were other plaques and certificates, each indicating this was a lawyer of favorable recognition and considerable accomplishment. He invited Johanna to the inner office.

"Please, sit here," he said as he directed her to the side chair next to a working desk. Behind the desk and on the sides of the large room were law books of many sizes and varying colors. Soft light hung over the desk and there were soft lights on the walls and recessed lighting, dimmed, over the bookshelves. The floor was of planks with a large Navajo rug under the side chairs. The air was fresh and not stale.

Mr. Wilson did not sit behind his desk. He sat on the other side chair beside Johanna. She noticed he was a man in his sixties, graying hair, fit condition, and spoke with a soft, confident voice. "Johanna, I appreciate your calling me. What can I help you with that is so urgent?"

Johanna blurted out, "I was stopped outside my apartment last evening by an FBI agent who said I was running with the wrong people and I could be involved with eco-terrorism. He said I could avoid being charged with a crime if I cooperated with him. I understood him to be telling me I was running with eco-terrorists and the FBI was investigating some of the people in the cell that I had been associating with," Johanna told him in a panicked tone and high-pitched voice.

"Now calm down, Miss Johnson; there is nothing to be worried about right now," Mr. Wilson told her in a calming, reassuring voice. "Everything you tell me is strictly confidential. I will not tell anyone what you tell me unless authorized by you to do so. I am going to ask you a number of questions, and it is important that you tell me exactly what has happened. I need to know about your background, your family's background, your education and schooling. Specifically, I will need to know the names of the people you have become friends with that may be involved in the activities that the FBI is investigating and what you know about them. Now, just tell me about yourself and about the matters that I have just mentioned to you."

Johanna did what he asked and laid it all on the line. She told him her background, about meeting Carlos Madrid and his inviting her to a meeting of the Environmental Protection Society, her attending a few meetings with him but not learning anything really about what the meeting was all about. Her narrative was interrupted at times by tears falling from fearful eyes and by Mr. Wilson's asking specific questions and requesting clarification.

When she was finished, he offered her a cup of coffee. She gladly accepted. Johanna and her lawyer sat quietly for a few minutes. Then, Mr. Wilson went behind his desk and removed from the shelves a law book that Johanna noticed was labeled "United States Code." He spent a few minutes finding particular sections of the book, studying those sections, and he then closed the book. He turned to Johanna and said, "From what you tell me, I do not believe you have committed any crime. The applicable statutes require a specific intent to commit the crime that is proscribed in the statutes. I rather suspect that the FBI agent was scaring you in order to obtain your cooperation and that he, not knowing all about your involvement, believed you were mixed up with something illegal and that you no doubt had committed some crime. Obviously, the FBI has information that indicates the Environmental Protection Society is a terrorist organization, and that is why the agent was immediately suspecting you of some illegal activity. He also no doubt knew you had attended only a couple of meetings with the group, and so he probably viewed you as a recruit to the group rather than a person that had previously been involved in a terrorist activity. Such groups are known as cells.

"I know something about these cells, because earlier in my career I was a federal prosecutor. In fact, I know the current United States Attorney, and the FBI agent identified on the card he gave you. Of course, I do not know what information they may have about you specifically, nor about this Carlos fellow who has involved you in something you should not be involved with, or on the other members of the cell. I believe you should make the phone call to the FBI agent. Do not tell him at this point that you have consulted with me. I am guessing he will make arrangements for you to meet with a task force that is investigating ecotage, at which time you will learn more about the cell group and the expectations the FBI might have of you. Should the task force or the FBI agents at any time indicate to you that you are being charged with a crime, you should stop listening to them, advise them that I represent you, and get up and leave the meeting. I do not think they would arrest you there, because if you are telling me the truth about your involvement, they clearly do not have enough probable cause to arrest you for terrorism, and probable cause is required under the law. "Probable cause" means the authorities must have evidence that a crime has been committed, and that you probably committed it. If they do not talk further about you being arrested or in further trouble, my best advice is for you to cooperate with them, no matter how scary that might seem to you. They would fully prepare you for what you would be expected to do. At the same time, if it reaches the point where you agree to cooperate with them, then you need to ask for some assurance, in writing, that you will not be charged with any crime. If the task force will not agree to provide you such an assurance in writing, then my advice to you is to excuse yourself from the meeting, advise them at that point that I represent you, and that although you want to cooperate, Mr. Wilson has counseled you to get assurance in writing that you will not be charged."

Johanna left emotionally spent from the meeting with her attorney. Her meeting with him had lasted for over two hours. Although she felt less afraid, knowing Mr. Wilson would represent her, and although she immediately had confidence in him, she still felt very afraid. She left the law office to make the phone call that could forever change her life.

At her apartment, her hands shook as she dialed on her smart phone the number she had been given for contacting the agent. Her mouth was dry. She had to dial the number a few times before getting it right. When the agent answered, he seemed to know the number from which she was calling and who was calling him. He instructed Johanna to meet him at university library, in the periodicals section, the next morning at 8 o'clock, and then he hung up abruptly.

The University of the West library was a beautifully designed and decorated building with considerable glass, several floors, inspiring views in all directions, inviting Western designs many Western scenes in paintings, bright colors, and

Indian artifacts displayed.

As Johanna entered the library, she tried to look confident and not be noticed. In neither attempt was she successful. "How are you doing, Johanna?" asked Fred, an acquaintance from one of her classes. "You look rather disheveled. Did you have a hard night?" he asked mischievously.

"I'm doing just fine, thank you," replied Johanna as she moved quickly toward the periodicals section. She found a desk at which no one was seated, nor was anyone close. She looked at her watch and it said she was two minutes early. She dared not move or look around and sat motionless with her mind racing and her heart beating at a rapid pace. Joanna was sweating and her hands felt stiff. She felt like she was about to cry.

A man stepped behind a chair in front of her on the other side of the table. She recognized him as the federal agent, Rex Anderson, who had stopped her on the street in front of her apartment. His manner was serious, as his eyes were fixed on her without blinking. The skin of his face was drawn tight around a full set of teeth that normally would be attractive, but to her seemed threatening, like those she had seen in a snarling wolf picture. Johanna did not speak and for a minute or two, Anderson did not speak to her. Finally, the agent sat down across from her and in a nonthreatening voice said: "I am glad that you came to meet with me. You have done the right thing. I have no doubt frightened you, but I assure you I will shoot straight with you and give you all the information you need to do what we expect. You will be protected and safe."

Johanna gulped and looked at the man through teary eyes, but at the same time, she felt somewhat relieved and less threatened. "I want to do what's right. I don't want to go to jail. I have not done anything wrong, and I cannot understand what it is you're asking me to do. All I did was go to an environmental group's meeting with a friend. They did not tell me what they were meeting about or share with me any details about their activities, nor whether they were plotting to do something illegal. You must believe me!" Johanna told him, raising her voice, but then realized where she was, not wanting to be noticed or overheard.

"I cannot give you many details at this point, but I will reiterate, you will be doing an immense service to law and order in this country. It will be necessary for you to come to our offices in Indian Falls and meet with a task force on eco-terrorism. The government will pay your expenses, and I assure you that you will be safe on your trip, and you will be asked to do nothing of which you're not capable."

"Can't you tell me anything about the EPS and what they are up to?"

"I can only tell you that they are plotting to either burn or blow up something that they feel is threatening to their cause of eliminating energy projects that, in their view, destroy the environment and benefit the rich at the expense of the rest of the country. Now, that is all I'm going to tell you at this time. Here is an airline ticket you can use to take you to Indian Falls and back. I will meet you at the airport and take you to a hotel and later to the meeting with the task force, at which time you will be fully briefed and told what you are being asked to do."

Johanna was not as concerned now as she had been and felt that tinge of excitement she had experienced earlier at the prospect of being involved in such an important matter.

CHAPTER 11

FBI TASK FORCE

Johanna's flight from Three Creeks to Indian Falls was in the evening hours. Included with her airline ticket was a reservation for a room at the Holiday Inn for two nights. Johanna was surprised that she would be in Indian Falls for that length of time but packed a bag and told no one where she was going. She took along her laptop and her cell phone, although she now was scared to use her phone for anything, thinking the FBI probably tapped her phone. She packed a business suit and shoes and appropriate accessories, feeling she needed to make a good impression, but traveled in jeans and sweatshirt. The sweatshirt was one her father had given her and had an inscription proclaiming, "Coal is Cool!" It was one she had never before worn.

At the Indian Falls airport, she recognized Agent Rex Anderson as he approached to greet her. The agent quickly escorted Johanna through the terminal to a waiting black vehicle that was at the curb. The driver wore dark glasses. Johanna thought it strange and was a bit intimidated at the driver wearing dark glasses this time of the evening. He was dressed exactly like Agent Anderson, not as a chauffeur— Brooks Brothers suit, tasteful tie, and polished black shoes. Agent Anderson motioned to Johanna to get into the backseat, and after she had, he also sat in the backseat.

Agent Anderson spoke to her in a soft voice. "Don't be afraid. We are taking you to a nice hotel where you can eat dinner and spend the night. We will pick you up at the front door promptly at 8:00 a.m. tomorrow and escort you to the federal courthouse where the federal task force on eco-terrorism has its offices. There you will be briefed on what the task force is asking you to do. You will meet the other members of the task force and you will be given an opportunity to either cooperate with the task force or not." He did not say what would happen if she chose not to cooperate, but she recalled the threat of being arrested at their first meeting and knew the high stakes of what was about to take place.

"One final thing," Agent Anderson said. "Do not attempt to contact any of your family or any of your friends to tell them where you are or for what reason you are here."

The agents had already done Johanna's check-in at the hotel. She went to her room, sat on the bed, unpacked the few clothes she had along, and then went to the café. She viewed the menu at the hotel café, but nothing looked good; however, she knew she needed to eat, so she ordered a club sandwich and coffee. She ate a little of the sandwich and drank the coffee. She stared around the nicely decorated café, not knowing what she was doing in this situation and what was going to happen to her. An element of fear began to creep back into her thoughts: *What if I take off and hide someplace—on the reservation, perhaps? What would they do to me? This whole thing is crazy! How could Carlos get me involved in something so wrong?*

Back in her room, as she got ready for bed, Johanna began to weep. She felt terribly alone, sad, afraid, and threatened. Matters were moving too fast for her. "I need to talk to Charlie," Johanna whimpered, without knowing why it was he with whom she wanted to talk. She cried until sleep overcame her exhausted state. She was too restless and disturbed for restful sleep but made it through the night to face the day and what was happening to her.

Promptly at 8:00 a.m., Johanna stood at the front entrance to the hotel and was met by a black vehicle with a driver wearing sunglasses. Agent Anderson stepped out and quickly directed Johanna into the back seat.

"How was your sleep?"

"Terrible."

"Not surprising, I suppose. Did you have breakfast?"

"No. I did have a cup of coffee. How could you expect me to act like nothing important is happening to me and I am not here by my choice?"

Nothing more was said as they drove to the federal building downtown, a short distance from the hotel. They entered a parking garage under the federal building and came to a stop in front of an entrance. Lighting was dim. Agent Anderson got out of the back seat and asked Johanna to do the same. He held a card to the mechanical scanner. He escorted her to the elevator. He pushed the number three. They got out of the elevator and went directly to a large conference room, which they entered. It was filled with a number of men and women sitting dourly around a large conference table. Only a few looked up and at her. The conference room was austere, lacking in any color or warmth. The furniture was government-issue, cold gray and metallic. Lighting was good, however, and windows allowed daylight.

Johanna felt she was going to faint. She was bewildered, her eyes were wide open and watery, and she felt weak. She had a dry throat. She felt flushed.

Without saying a word, Agent Anderson directed her to a chair at the middle of the table on the right side. She sat down. All eyes now seemed to be staring at her. Anderson offered her a glass of water that she accepted. The chair was hard, not well padded; it had arms, and a straight back.

"An inquisition?" she asked. There was no reaction from the solemn faces.

After a minute or two, but it seemed longer, Agent Anderson spoke. "Members of the task force, let me introduce you to Johanna Johnson, whom you were previously advised has been attending cell meetings of the Environmental Protection Society in Three Creeks, South Dakota. You will note from the file you were given that we have had her under surveillance for the past few weeks. She is a student at

University of the West. She has no criminal record. The extent of her involvement with the cell is not known. We do know she has attended the cell meetings with a person who has been under investigation by us for several years and who has past involvement with terrorism, including the sabotage of the pipeline in the sand hill country of Nebraska last year. His name is Carlos Madrid, an undocumented who is also enrolled at University of the West. Miss Johnson's detailed background information is in your packets. She is voluntarily appearing here today to meet with this task force."

Then, in a forceful and direct voice, "My name is Paul Carbine. I am the agent in charge of this task force on eco-terrorism. I want to inform you why you are here, what the Environmental Protection Society is about, and what is expected from you. Should you decide to not be cooperative with us, you could be charged with obstruction of justice and perhaps other crimes, although you certainly have free choice in the matter. You need to understand that this is serious business! Should you attempt to assist the EPS or any of the cell members by disclosing this meeting, the content of this meeting, or any of the details you learn here, we will find out, prosecute you for obstruction of justice and being engaged in a terrorism organization, and prosecute you for those crimes. Do you wish to help us? I trust you have had time to think about this and have decided you want to cooperate—is that true?"

In a composed, confident manner, Johanna replied, "Yes, but you must understand I have not done anything wrong.

I have not committed any crime. Now, what do you expect of me and what is this EPS all about? I do not understand why I am here. I need to know how it is that I have become involved with you people."

Carbine continued, "The EPS, we believe, is plotting to blow up a railroad installation used in connection with transporting coal from eastern Wyoming to the West Coast. Eco-terrorists have set fire to oil company properties in other areas of the country, destroyed industrial complexes, and have caused some $200 to $300 million dollars of property destruction, so we know they are dangerous and capable, although we don't know which cell was responsible for those attacks. We believe the cell you are involved with destroyed an oil pipeline in the Sand Hill country in Nebraska. We need to find out what their current plans are and stop them before they act again. The FBI believes eco-terrorism to be one of the most serious domestic threats in the US today."

Johanna paused. "Oh my gosh!" Johanna then exclaimed, "This doesn't involve me! This is not anything in which I am involved! No way would I do something like you have described!"

Agent Anderson said, "We need to infiltrate the cell. We know that to be a difficult task. These underground cells are loosely organized; they have no particular leader; they are very secretive; they strike their targets and then move on, disappearing into the underground world of eco-terrorism. They look like you and me. They have no dues, meet anonymously, recruit to specific activities, and then disband.

For someone to belong in the overall movement, he or she must totally believe in the eco-terrorism movement. The new members must do some destructive act in the name of Mother Earth or provide the cell with useful information in order to belong to the cell. We need for you to infiltrate this group and tell us of their plans. We believe Carlos Madrid is recruiting you for involvement with the group."

Johanna was flabbergasted. She went silent for a few minutes before speaking. "Carlos has certainly expressed strong opinions to me concerning his hatred for the energy companies and what, in his view, they are doing to the environment. But I have had no inkling that what he is planning with others is to destroy property or harm others. I have no knowledge whatsoever of his plans, or for that matter, I have no knowledge of eco-terrorism. This is all news to me, and it is quite shocking! I have been to only a few meetings with Carlos, and he is the only one I have gone to a meeting with, and the people there have not disclosed to me any intentions or details of planning something terrible. I have asked some questions about what they have been involved with in the past, but Carlos has told me he cannot give me any specifics about the past or the future until the group has accepted me. I haven't even told him I am interested in joining! I thought this was an environmental group that protests in the streets, lobby decision-makers, and that sort of thing."

Agent Carbine said, "Carlos knows your father was a bigwig in the coal industry. He no doubt believes you can obtain important information from your father that is needed for their plans of terrorism. We believe what they are after is to know the route to be taken to transport coal to the West Coast from the Powder River Basin coal mines in Wyoming, so they can sabotage the project. You are being recruited to the cell, but by no means are you in. If what we are thinking is correct, we believe the terrorists will ask you to get that important information from your father, to find out the haul route that is being planned and when it is to begin. We want you to be in the cell and work undercover with us. We want you to get information from your father and provide it to the cell."

"But I don't know anything about infiltrating a criminal activity. What if I am discovered as working undercover for the FBI? What if Carlos is violent and dangerous to more than property? I might be in great danger to my person, and what about my father? Will he personally be in danger of being hurt by these people?"

"You will be kept under constant surveillance, as will Carlos Madrid. All we want to learn through you is what they are planning and when it is to take place. And we will give you instructions from time to time that will ensure you are not detected. Agent Anderson will be your contact. No one outside of this task force will know you are involved. Miss Johnson, you will be doing something honorable for the good of the country. These people need to be stopped before they do more damage. So far they have not killed anyone, but who knows what they are capable of doing." He paused. "Have you told anyone about our having contacted you?"

"I have talked with an attorney, John Wilson."

"Yes, we know you did. Actually, we know John Wilson and feel he will represent you well by giving you good advice. We have not talked with him about you, but we know he understands a great deal about how the FBI operates, and also, a great deal about ecotage."

"Mr. Wilson advised me to have in writing that I will not be charged with a crime if I cooperate with you. If not, I am to leave this room. Will you put this is writing?"

"Yes, we will have the United States Attorney draw up such an agreement and send it to Mr. Wilson. I am sure he will be in touch with you in short order."

CHAPTER 12

A REUNION

A week or so after returning to campus from spending some time at the reservation, Charlie went to Heck's, the coffee shop across from campus, in hopes he might see Johanna again. That was where he and Johanna had gone once during last semester, the last time he had seen her. Since then, Charlie had often thought about Johanna, how nice she was, how easy she was to be with, and how principled she seemed to be.

Johanna was seated in a booth, looking a bit forlorn. It was the same booth in which they had sat together that first time. Charlie felt she was preoccupied with something. He felt he should not interrupt her. But she looked very beautiful as he eyed her, and he couldn't look away from her as he stood near the doorway to the coffee shop. As he finally turned to leave without speaking to her, he heard, "Hey, Charlie! Come and say hello." He did. "Join me for a cup of coffee." He did.

"How have you been?" she asked with a smile on her face.

"Oh, OK."

"Well, I went to my best friend's wedding in Santa Fe. I was her maid of honor. That was fun. I had never been to Santa Fe. It is really neat. Have you ever been there?"

"No," answered Charlie, somewhat uncomfortably.

"So, where is home for you, Charlie?"

"Oh-h-h…on the Horse Creek Reservation," Charlie replied in a barely audible way. "Actually, after we were removed from the island that was our home, we lived near Joe Creek, but Horse Creek Reservation is what the big area is called. It's near Big Bend Dam on the Missouri River." Charlie could not believe that he had told Johanna all of this. He usually doesn't speak much, and when he does, it is not to a beautiful white girl. He kept his head down in embarrassment.

"How far is it from here?"

"About 200 miles."

"What's it like?"

Charlie did not answer for the longest time. Then, softly, he began to tell her. Johanna noticed how engaged he became, how his eyes widened and his voice raised. She could tell he was willing to share his place with her, with pride. This was different from when she had asked him such questions before. She was relaxed and glad.

"Well, it's a place where I feel free, where my people live without much fear, where the animals are respected, and the elders of our people are looked up to and cared for. The earth, wind, and sky are our teachers of life as they guide us through our place on this earth. It is a simple place that is peaceful, but where we live without many nice things. The government involves itself in too much of our lives, and many of our people have come to rely too much on it, causing them to become lazy and living without meaning. Young people learn to respect Mother Earth and take care of it and the animals. There is little future for them, because they cannot find meaningful work. But for the most part, all our people are happy because they are close with each other. Our families are important to us. Even extended family. And friendship is a true mark of a man. I hiked and hunted. Rode horses. Camped a lot. We always had enough food and water, and if we were short, others would share. We shared a lot, even if we had little."

Charlie became uncomfortable with his talking so much. He again became quiet. His hands were sweaty.

Johanna wholly identified with the values he was sharing. She leaned forward somewhat, more into Charlie's space. After a minute or two of silence, Charlie said, "One did not dare to date a white girl. Bad things could happen. I couldn't even be in a group of white buddies who were with white girls. Cops and white ranchers were always watching me and my buddies and waiting for an excuse to get rid of one of the Tribe." Charlie paused. He mumbled in barely audible words, "One time they succeeded, and I paid a huge price." Johanna did not hear what he mumbled. Their conversation continued, Johanna taking the lead while looking at Charlie with caring eyes. She realized Charlie was somewhat uncomfortable talking with her, but she could feel the warmth of his eyes as he looked at her. She felt tingling in her being as their eyes met.

Suddenly, Charlie blurted, "Would you like to go to dinner with me sometime?" Now, he truly felt embarrassed. He had overstepped his bounds, for sure.

Surprisingly to Charlie, Johanna put her hand on his and said, "I would really like to do that. When shall we go?"

Charlie looked into her big, brown eyes, and spoke in a halting way. "Let's . . . go . . . tomorrow night. I will meet you at the Owl Inn at seven—if that's OK." He hurriedly excused himself without hearing whether the time and the place were OK, and left, stopping at the door for a second as he looked back at his first date with a white girl.

The Owl Inn is not a showcase. Romantic it is not. It is somewhat dark, a bit small, with oiled tablecloths, used menus that need replacing due to the dropping of one thing or another on them that could have been wiped off, but wasn't. It had wooden chairs, a counter at one end of the room, and tables toward the back and one near the entrance. Cheap lights, colored, hung from a cord over each table. The table farthest from the entrance, however, had a window looking out on the street. A couple of audio speakers were situated on shelves circling the room and held artificial flowers that, along with framed Western posters on two walls, provided "ambiance." The kitchen added sounds of a different kind, but it all blended somewhat to create a college town eatery different for sure from the cafeteria on campus.

They arrived at the same time. "Seat yourselves wherever you like," ordered an elderly woman, perhaps the owner. Her eyes belied her welcome as she followed an Indian and a white girl across the old, carpeted floor that had obviously been vacuumed many times, perhaps not always thoroughly.

Johanna was wearing a short skirt. Her boots were leather and high on her calves. Her blouse was colorful. She wore a tasteful silver necklace with a turquoise pendant. Her hair, thick and flowing, was strawberry-blonde in color. Pretty turquoise earrings dangled from her pierced ears. She had a scarf around her shoulders. She wore little make-up, for it was not needed.

After they were seated, Johanna saw that Charlie had on a bolo tie, beaded in beautiful colors of blue, red, yellow, and orange. The bolo had sections of varying lengths, but uniform, and matched side to side. There were dangling fringes at the two ends. The sliding centerpiece was a design created by someone with great artistic ability. What seemed to her a flower or a desert plant commanded her attention as she gazed on this beautiful work. She did not know whether she should ask who made it or simply compliment him just then. She complimented him.

In a nervous voice, Charlie blurted out, "Johanna, you really look nice." The ice had been broken. He felt relieved in a strange way. He felt more confident all of a sudden. She was a really nice person, he could tell. He was very happy!

Johanna sat straight in the chair. Her hands were in her lap. She was somewhat formal due to her upbringing and teaching. Her words had been somewhat stilted. She thought, *To hell with it*, and placed her elbows on the table and leaned forward. Her boldness heartened her, as it did Charlie, who noticed. The ice had been broken for her, too. She had been nervous about this date.

The conversation began to flow, although Charlie talked mostly in short sentences with deliberation, while Johanna gushed with enthusiasm and comments and questions. They ordered food and learned much, each about the other. They enjoyed what they were hearing from the other. Johanna liked Charlie very much.

When they were finished eating and talking, Johanna remembered a late meeting she was to attend and suggested they end the evening and leave the café. Charlie was OK with that but wondered to himself whether he should ask to see her again. He had no contact information for her. How would he get ahold of her? He decided he would not ask these questions, for he knew he could track her down again.

Johanna held his hand and told him she had a really nice time with him and perhaps they could see each other again, relieving him of his hesitancy to suggest the same thing. She hurried away and Charlie stood wondering if seeing her again would ever happen. He also noticed a changed demeanor in Johanna after the dinner and as she headed for her meeting, but could not tell for sure what had changed about her. He decided to say nothing.

Johanna and Charlie each went their own way that night, but not before the guy seated unnoticed at the table near the entrance had abruptly left ahead of them.

CHAPTER 13

CHARLIE AND EPS

After leaving her dinner date with Charlie, Johanna immediately went to the first cell meeting she was attending after meeting with the task force. At the meeting she paid particular attention to a discussion of the "when," although she did not hear anything about the "what" nor the "where." Carlos was a leader in the debate of the members. He seemed to be urging an earlier action. Others did not seem to agree. Johanna dared not ask the cell group what they were planning. She hoped to be able to get the information from Carlos after the meeting. For now, she was content to listen and make mental notes. Carlos did not include her in the conversation nor ask her for her thoughts, as he knew he had sufficiently kept her in the dark that she could not offer anything of value anyway. But when Carlos became increasingly angry and loud, frequently referring to the "feds" and at one time to the "FBI," she became very disturbed. It began to sound to her like they were discussing a time for some criminal activity!

She knew she needed to be careful. Following the meeting, Johanna told Carlos she needed to go to her apartment to study. She hurried away from the meeting.

As Johanna later sat in her apartment and thought about the meeting. She was disturbed not only by the content, but also her being told by Carlos afterwards, before she hurried away, that last winter an Indian had been brought to one of the meetings. Carlos told her the Indian was outclassed and ignorant of the important work the EPS does. Carlos said, "he only seemed to want the society's help with some project of his own involving a river, of all things, and the plight of the Indian people. The brave should have been coming to us with an offer to help the EPS with its projects, not the other way around. Of course, what would you expect from a redskin?"

Johanna flinched at what Carlos said and was taken aback at his expressed prejudice and arrogance.

"Was Charlie the Indian at the EPS meeting? Why was Charlie at an EPS meeting?" Johanna asked herself. If Charlie had been at an EPS meeting, she reasoned, he must be up to no good. This troubled Johanna a great deal; however, for now, Johanna knew she must focus on the EPS and learning more about their plans, and the only way she would find out the plans would be from Carlos. But her attraction to him was no longer present. Carlos was exposed to her for what he really was—a terrorist!

Her life was becoming increasingly complicated, for she now connected the undercover assignment with the possibility of Charlie being involved. Johanna knew that whatever the case, she needed to get away from Three Creeks and UWest to have time to sort out her suddenly even more complicated life. She could not think of anyone she could talk to about how she should proceed, and more importantly, how she felt about Charlie. She felt terribly lonely. She wondered if the FBI was aware that Charlie had attended a meeting of the EPS. Her mind was aflame with denial of the possibility that simply because he attended a meeting, she had to spy on him. But why had he been there?

CHAPTER 14

ON THE TRAIL OF THE UNKNOWN

Charlie had never been to Omaha. He was headed there after his dinner with Johanna because in Omaha was the headquarters of the Army Corps of Engineers who had designed and built the dams on the Missouri River. As he looked at a map, he knew it was a long trip to Omaha, though he did not yet know whether his going was preliminary or exploratory. Since meeting with Big Bill and thereafter considering more carefully blowing up the dam, he realized his ability to do anything against the authorities was really going to be hard, if not nearly impossible. His options for having meaningful revenge all by himself, he acknowledged, were limited even if not nonexistent. Each day that he thought about the "vision," he increasingly thought about it as a burden, not an honor. He was experiencing more uncertainty and an increasing lack of will, but the shame he would experience if he did nothing he felt would be unbearable—his honor destroyed, and his life could become meaningless and without any purpose whatsoever. He thought about Johanna and his thoughts mixed in with the mission and the already difficult challenge that he realized was becoming even more complicated.

"So why am I driving to Omaha?" he asked himself. He couldn't answer the question—he just was. He had to do something. He couldn't think clearly anymore. He was consumed by this task. He was depressed. Perhaps he should end it all by his own hand, he thought. But there was Johanna. The only bright star in his sky was Johanna.

He drove on. Across the Indian reservations of Dakota he drove, seeing the Indian world set in the white man's arena—the run-down houses, the abandoned, dilapidated vehicles near as lawn ornaments, the hitchhiking young and old, the weathered stores next to substantial government offices, the thriving crops belonging to someone else, and the graffiti of the hopeless. He drove on.

"I thought those brothers and sisters were why you were getting educated and planned to come back to the reservation," he said out loud. "How will doing harm to someone and something as revenge for something done years ago to our people solve anything? Getting caught and going back to prison would not be worth it." But no one was listening. He drove on.

He headed east and south from Three Creeks toward

Omaha. He knew he had to cross the Missouri at some point, but he had not been on this highway before. It seemed he would never get to the Big Muddy, but finally, as the road climbed up a big hill and began down the other side, he saw the Gavin's Point Dam! The reservoir looked spectacular, the trees lush, sitting under the big, blue sky. Charlie thought, *this is a lot different from Big Bend Dam sitting on two reservations that have no farm country or growing crops adjoining on both sides, and irrigated from the river.* He saw barges hauling goods below the dam in the free river, and fishing boats and fancy pleasure boats, houseboats plying the waters of the reservoir. People were camped in the campgrounds along the water. And he saw the ubiquitous power lines stretching like a spider web as far as he could see. Charlie felt he had much to ponder as he drove down the hill to the visitor center.

The visitor center had the usual promotional displays, and some educational, proclaiming the enormity of the dam system, the untold benefits of the system, and some historical information. Charlie could not help but notice how little was said about the Indian inhabitants, nothing being said about the taking of Indian lands, and of course, nothing about the morality of the "progress" supposedly accomplished by the taming of the Missouri River. Charlie's mission became clearer as he steamed inside himself over the one-sided presentations of the promotional displays he read. The Corps of Engineers knew how to blow its own horn, for sure. At the same time, Charlie was learning a lot more about the dam project than his grandmother had told him. His thoughts analyzed what he was learning and he considered the pros and cons of what he learned. "There certainly are some benefits to the dams," was increasingly on his mind.

By studying the handouts at the visitor center, Charlie learned there was a visitor center at each of the five dams on the river except at Big Bend. Sabotaging a visitor center at a dam other than Big Bend Dam would leave his "homeland" free of the destruction and perhaps divert attention from the Horse Creek and Lower Brule people as the perpetrators of the carnage. Charlie studied the center inside and out, and took notes and photographs. There were no guards or security other than a security camera that he had noticed when he first arrived. He avoided it. He decided he would travel now to other visitor centers and not to Omaha. He was at the most southern of the dam sites. He decided to travel north until reaching the upper dam in South Dakota, the Oahe.

As Charlie traveled north on the east side of a stretch of the longest waterway in the country, he drove by the planted fields of small grain and the row crops growing in the irrigated fields. He admired the clean, prosperous towns set among the fields and smiling faces as he drove through. Charlie could not help but compare with his homeland what he saw, the different lifestyle they had and the lack of modern conveniences and equipment for his people. He began to debate in his head the taking of his people's lands along the river with the obvious benefits others had reaped from the government's having done so. He recalled the quiet, nurturing environment in which he grew to manhood, his tribe's ethic of helping each other, sharing with others, and worshiping the Great Spirit that revealed itself in everyday events. He thought again of the sky, wind and water, the rightful place of all animals, plants, and birds of the air—the mutual respect of each to the other and the reverence that instilled itself in his people, and in him. Charlie thought, *how do I reconcile the two worlds?* From his education and teaching he knew that times change, that "progress" sometimes creates benefit at the same time as loss. He was experiencing at the university the white man's world of plenty, its education system, its medical institutions, its churches. He had experienced the feeling of love when he came to know Johanna Johnson. He talked to himself. "How can I continue to live in both worlds? How can I fulfill Grandmother's vision when I see good in the change brought about by the damming of our life-giving river? Why was I chosen? How am I to take on the federal government, and why should I? For principle? For what? How can revenge on such a small scale have any meaningful significance and benefit to my people?"

Charlie finally brought himself back to thinking of something else, that something else being Johanna Johnson.

CHAPTER 15

WAPITI BAR

The Wapiti Bar possessed none of the dignity of its name-sake, the majestic elk. It was dirty in condition as well as mission, dimly lit, had old furniture in various states of repair and various materials. It was an institution of ill repute due to its close proximity to the reservation where liquor was illegal, where the addicted and pitiful wasted away their humanity with others of similar misfortune, and where sex could be obtained for little price or more liquor. It is one room, no porch, had steel bars on the windows and doors and smelled of smoke, beer, and sawdust that was on the floor as a keeper of all that was spilled, dropped, or knocked down. This was a sad place.

Big Bill and his cohorts had ridden from Colorado to the border of the Horse Creek Reservation on their Harleys and stopped at the Wapiti Bar when they saw Indians, both male and female, leaning up against the outside wall of the building and one woman lying on the gravel to the side of the building. Also, they saw the beer signs. They were thirsty. They parked. They went in. They ordered beer from a grizzled, middle-aged man behind the bar. He was stout, mean-looking like them, and grunted but did not talk. Big Bill immediately noticed a short baseball bat behind the bar. As they drank their beers, Big Bill saw a white man in the corner of the room with an Indian woman. She was drunk. The white man was too. The man was big, dressed with a big belt buckle, cowboy boots, jeans, and a cowboy shirt. The drunk woman was heavy but not old, dressed in a skirt and moccasins, and her blouse was open. The bartender called out, "Hey Stoutwein, do you want another beer?"

Big Bill stood outside the dilapidated, dingy bar on the Southern border of the reservation and schemed. Big Bill had not been willing to wait for Charlie to contact him with ideas for distributing drugs on the reservation—the starting of a new place of addiction and despair, and potentially a very profitable enterprise couldn't wait. No matter; Big Bill knew how to spread the evils in his dastardly inventory and he cared nothing about the suffering that always accompanied his lucrative, illegal efforts. Big Bill, however, was not without all principles. He wanted to carry through with the rage he had internally experienced when Charlie Red Tail told him of the white man, Jim Stoutwein, who had lied in court, along with his sister, about her being raped. He had vowed then, as he did now, that he would make things right for the friend of his friend, Clyde.

Big Bill was not alone. He had with him some of his henchmen, part of his organization—his force of evil. Big Bill motioned to his men, and they left the Wapiti Bar. They rode their Harleys over the border of the reservation a short distance where they could observe the bar, and they waited. The afternoon turned to dusk. Jim Stoutwein left the bar and started his Ford 3500 diesel pickup with dual wheels, black in color; he pulled out and drove off across the reservation boundary. Jim Stoutwein was headed home to the ranch not far away and just off another boundary of the same reservation. The Lazy Bar C had been homesteaded in the 1800s by Jim Stoutwein's grandfather. Since then, the Stoutweins have added more land, expanded their Hereford cattle herd to one of the largest in the area, and had maintained the finest horses. The Lazy Bar C employed a good many cowboys who were known not only for their skills, but also their troublemaking. They were fortunate that Mac Stoutwein wielded enormous political clout in the county; that had saved some of them many times from earned punishments for their behavior in the nearby towns.

As Jim Stoutwein drove home, he noticed a few motorcycles followed him but thought nothing of it, as at this time of year many motorcycles were in the area, headed to a rally in the Black Hills. He thought about the sexual satisfaction he had just had, the chores to be done at the ranch, and the return to college next week where he was president of his fraternity, his brothers all from rural America like him. He was happy and satisfied, except for recurring thoughts about

Johanna Johnson and her Indian brave.

The Lazy Bar C bordered the Horse Creek Reservation on the west. Stoutwein turned off the main road onto the gravel road that led to the ranch headquarters. He no longer saw the motorcycle lights behind him.

But Big Bill now knew where Jim Stoutwein lived. He and his gang continued on to the town several miles on the other side of the reservation, where they had rooms reserved in a motel that welcomed bikers headed to the motorcycle rally in Sturgis.

When they arrived at the motel for the night, Big Bill told Horny Al, Hairy Harry, Bill Braun, and Jerry Pinnelly to pay attention. "I don't want youse to get in trouble here. This is an important trip we is on. Youse got to keep low profile. I want to find out the lay of the land--where Injuns live, pick up their government checks, and when that happens. We is only investigating. Youse all will come back here later when we want to sell dope. Tell me what youse see for law people and where at. Youse have two days. You SOB's better not get in trouble! And, we have another job to take care of. We are going to get that Stoutwein scumbag. We will do that in two days and then leave the country and go back to Denver. He will be comin out of the ranch after the weekend and we will get the lying son-of-a-bitch. OK? Do you idiots understand me?" The men all nodded affirmatively, without hesitation.

Two days later, Big Bill and his henchmen hid their cycles in the grove of oak trees near the turnoff from the reservation highway to the Lazy Bar C. It was Sunday night. It was dusk.

They put fallen branches, big rocks, and sagebrush on the ranch road and a short distance from the main road. They waited. He came.

The seizure was fast and the purpose quick. They dragged him from the pick-up without saying a word to him, broke his right arm immediately, smashed up his face, beat him to a pulp, but not unconscious. Big Bill was out of control. "Youse swine! Youse lying bastard! Youse white scum! If you ever do wrong to an Indian again, youse will wish you were dead." With that, Big Bill and his men left Stoutwein in the road, removed the debris, and headed out. As they rode their Harleys past the Wapiti Bar on their way back to Denver, Big Bill gave the bar the finger salute and laughed.

CHAPTER 16

THREE IN THE PARK

Johanna went to the next EPS meeting. She sat next to Carlos, who reached for her hand, patted the empty chair next to him, and brightened when she sat beside him. The meeting was just getting started. The room was the same smelly, dismal place she had been in for the other meetings. She was not sure the guys and gals there were the same ones as the first meeting, because she had not paid much attention to them and had not been introduced. This time she paid attention.

Carlos started talking. "I have told all of you about my girlfriend Johanna Johnson." Johanna winced. "I vouch for her as feeling strongly about the environment and about the bastard companies that are destroying it. She knows first-hand about this, because her dad is one of the kingpins behind the coal mines that are destroying the ozone layer and are huge in causing global warming." Johanna winced again and recalled what Agent Anderson had told her of his belief that Carlos wanted to get information from her about her father and the shipment of coal to the West Coast. "I strongly believe she should be invited to join our efforts if she can do as we ask. She could be big in getting us the information on the proposed shipments of the black devil from Wyoming to the West Coast." He paused when Thor Graham stared at him and frowned. "Uh-oh—perhaps I have said too much."

"Johanna, we thank you for coming. We now must have our meeting and must ask you to leave. We will be in touch with you," Thor Graham said, after drawing deep on his joint.

Johanna nodded, but before leaving the room asked, "What are you planning to do? I have been here a few times before and still do not know what the plans are. Last time, Carlos, you told me there was an Indian here. What is he all about?"

Carlos spoke up. "Johanna, we cannot disclose to you yet what we are planning, for you have not met our tests. I will tell you after the meeting what is expected of you. As to the Indian, he is not yet one of us. As I told you before, he was here trying to get us involved in some crazy idea on the reservation because the government had taken their lands illegally. We may contact him later."

Johanna left.

As she walked, she started to cry, then began bawling. Tears ran down her contorted face and made wet her coat. She sat down on a bench in a little park near the building where she had attended the meeting. She was fearful in a way she had never been before. The fear she felt and the overwhelming emotion within focused on the undercover expectations the FBI had put on her, but eventually those pressures gave way to clouded thoughts about Charlie and what she had just learned about him. Her sobbing became verbal as she quietly murmured, "Please, God, don't let Charlie be a member of the EPS or involved with something bad. Please. Please."

Suddenly, she felt a hand on her shoulder. She froze, not knowing who it was. It was Charlie! "Are you OK, Johanna? Why are you crying? Has someone hurt you?"

Johanna could not help herself. She stood and hugged Charlie for a long time. She stopped shaking and crying. She no longer felt alone. They sat down in the quiet of the park, not knowing what to say. But then, no words were necessary.

Charlie knew Johanna had gone to an EPS meeting. He had followed her as he was concerned for her safety. He felt panic as his thoughts turned to the possibility of Johanna being part of the group called EPS. He had been to such a meeting and didn't know much about them, but his thoughts toward them were not good ones.

"Do you want to get a cup of coffee, Johanna?" Charlie asked softly.

"Yes, I would, Charlie," Johanna softly answered.

As they strolled through the park toward the coffee shop they heard, "Hey, Johanna, wait up a minute!" It was Carlos Madrid!

When they stopped, Carlos thought he recognized Charlie. "Don't I know you?" he said. "We met someplace not too long ago." He couldn't immediately place where he had seen Charlie. "What are you two up to, Johanna? I need to talk to you about something."

Johanna's pulse raced. Her eyes blinked rapidly. She stuttered when she spoke. "This is-is-is Charlie, Carlos. Charlie and I take a couple, a couple, of classes together. As I came by the park, Charlie saw me, he saw me, and invited me to have a coffee with him. I know we need to talk, Carlos. Let me give you a call tomorrow."

Carlos looked bewildered and a bit angry. He looked at Charlie and Johanna suspiciously, but after a pause said, "Of course, that will be fine. I will wait to hear from you." Carlos turned and headed back to the EPS meeting, pausing to look back just once, trying to remember where he had seen the Indian he had just met.

When Charlie and Johanna sat in the booth familiar to them both, they looked deep into each other's eyes, but said nothing at first. They were alone in the place, except for a guy seated across the room near the door. He was bent over on his table, had a cast on his right arm, and he had severe bruises on his face; he limped as he went to the door and left. But both Johanna and Charlie failed to notice him, as their thoughts were elsewhere.

Charlie spoke first. "You know, that guy that stopped us at the park—he, he, was at a meeting I went to, to ask for help with something. He never spoke but was sure there."

"What meeting was it, Charlie?" Johanna knowingly asked.

"Well, I don't recall the name exactly, but I had heard about it from a guy I know on campus. They met in a stinky room where I think you just went; just a few of them were there. I am not sure why I went there, but I had been told this was a good group of guys interested in my people. I had been complaining to my friend that the government had wronged us by taking our lands for the dams on the great river, and I was thinking of trying to make things right."

"What were you asking help to do?" quizzed Johanna, questioning Charlie more than once.

Charlie did not answer at first. He sat head down. Finally, he answered, "I can't tell you that, because I did not know myself what I wanted them to help me do."

"Charlie Red Tail, do you now belong to a group that the guy who stopped me in the park belongs to?" Her voice rose a bit.

"No, I don't belong to any group, and I haven't been back to that one again."

Wanting to get out from under Johanna's questioning, Charlie blurted, "Why were you at a meeting with that guy? How do you know this Carlos guy?"

Johanna flushed a bit at the sudden change of direction in the conversation. "I met Carlos here on campus awhile back. He asked me out a couple of times. I did go on a couple of dates with him. Now, he seems to think I belong to him, and he probably wants to ask me again for a date. I will call him tomorrow and find out what he wants. It is no big deal."

She had not answered Charlie as to why she had been at a meeting with Carlos on this night.

The espresso she and Charlie ordered quickly came. They sipped their drinks and eyed one another, not suspiciously, but in a way that showed each was a bit uncomfortable at the moment. "I am so grateful you came by while I was in the park. Thank you for your caring and your warmth."

"You don't need to tell me why you were crying," Charlie told her. "But I want you to know you can talk to me any time about anything. I am a good listener, and I can keep a secret. I too get sad, and even afraid, sometimes. It is really tough to feel alone."

Johanna thought: *How does he know I was feeling so alone and somewhat scared?* She paused her thoughts. *I would really like to know this man better.* With that, she told Charlie, "I really must go now. I have some studying I must do for class tomorrow. Would you mind walking me home? It is not far from here."

It was a spectacular night: clear sky, full moon, and millions of stars. The huge oak trees' shadows were painting a picture of how beautiful life could be at times. Johanna felt very safe being with Charlie, and she let her perky personality play through the heaviness in her heart caused by the expectations of her from two competing sides of life—the sinister and the brave. She knew which side she wanted to be on. She just did not yet know how to be there. She again took Charlie's hand. Her heart beat faster as she felt a firm grip given back. The walk was too short, she thought. Their words were light and happy. She was playful.

Mulberry Street had somewhat narrow sidewalks lined with huge oak trees; bushes lined many yards; the rich aroma of fall was pleasing to those walking by. Johanna's apartment was upstairs in an older, two-story Old Dutch home, facing Mulberry Street, about six blocks to the south of the campus coffee shop. A dim streetlight was on the corner, some thirty yards to the north. The row of older homes provided many apartments, mostly for young students attending the university. The only real blight on the neighborhood was the Ranch House Fraternity located one block north of Johanna's apartment, at 260 Mulberry. The frat boys were wild and rowdy, and well aware of the many girls living in the apartments to the south on Mulberry Street.

At 360 Mulberry, Johanna Johnson said good night to Charlie Red Tail and watched as he walked south. She'd had a wonderful time with someone she liked more each time she was with him. Her thoughts added to the attractiveness of this handsome man. Secretly, she wished she could invite him to talk and laugh into the night, perhaps sip a glass of wine as they shared deeper thoughts than known of each to date. But she was bothered by the fact he was at an EPS meeting and by what Carlos had told her as to why Charlie was there -she did not invite him up. She wanted to see Charlie again and said so; at the same time, Charlie blurted that he would like to see her again.

Charlie kept walking, noticed the dark, deep purple color

in some of the berries on the bushes along Mulberry Street, and found himself fondly recalling the many treks he had taken on the island called home in the Fall when he picked huckleberries. He loved eating them right off the bush. He loved the deep color of the berry. It reminded him of the color of blood, as his grandmother often told him it was blood from the Great Spirit when he brought to her the overflowing buckets; most of all, though, he loved the jam his grandmother canned, and the warm flatbread she put under the berries for him to enjoy. He picked off a bush several berries and popped them into his mouth. He misses his grandmother, but the memories of her make him very happy. He still thinks often of her flowing, grey hair tied in a ponytail with a beautifully beaded band she had made. She always had a pretty, long dress on, a colorful belt around her tiny waist, and stood so erect, like a goddess. She had given Charlie a sense of calm, of caring, and of having confidence. Charlie thought of her this night as he walked Mulberry Street and he thought, *Johanna has a lot of the qualities of Grandmother Yellowbird.*

Carlos Madrid walked in the direction of the EPS meeting after talking with Johanna near the park. He was a bit jealous. He had been anxious to tell Johanna what the group expected her to do in order to become a part of their mission, although he was not ready to describe to her the mission. He was following the rule of the cell and not saying too much until a new member had proven worthy of being involved. Yet, he was bothered more by the fact he had just seen Johanna with the Indian who he just figured out had come to a cell meeting some time ago. "Why was she with the redskin and what were they talking about; I had better find out what is going on with them. I don't want her to be with that Indian!" Madrid did not go directly back to the EPS meeting, but instead followed Johanna and the Indian to Johanna's place. He would later demand an explanation from her. But not now. He needed to get back to the cell meeting.

CHAPTER 17

HORNY AL'S VISIT

Carlos Madrid also lived on Mulberry Street. His place was to the south of campus and was in the high-rent district. He lived not far from 360 Mulberry, at 510 Mulberry Street in a spacious house he had purchased in order to live comfortably while attending UWest and pursuing his passion of justice for the environment. His house had 2500 square feet, a nice study, a fenced backyard, and was furnished with heavy Spanish furniture. He had maid service.

Johanna did not know where Carlos lived. She knew, of course, where Jim Stoutwein lived, for she had hurried by the frat house many times when Stoutwein and his buddies let her know they were watching her by shouting their catcalls and rude language. Since she had put down Stoutwein in the coffee shop when she was with Charlie, she had given little thought to Jim Stoutwein. She had seen him this semester on one occasion only, when she walked to the U. He was on the lawn with some of his cohorts, sitting on the porch while the others passed a football. She had noticed the cast on his arm, but nothing else, as she walked faster. That time she heard nothing from him. She was always relieved when she got past the frat house at 260 Mulberry Street.

Jim Stoutwein was obsessed about Johanna and the Indian. Not only did he have to deal with his frat brothers reminding him of being put down by Johanna when she and the Indian were leaving the coffee shop, he also was having to deal with his injuries and what the thugs who beat him up said about lying and harming Indians. What was the bastard referring to? Did he know about the "rape" of his sister and the lies that he and his family told? What were they doing in cowboy country? Jim Stoutwein was deeply troubled, and again vowed he would "get" the Indian.

When back in Denver after the trip he and the boys took to the reservation, Big Bill thought about the Indian, Charlie, whose full name he couldn't remember. Despite having taken it upon himself to get the ball rolling, Big Bill was still interested in the possibility of the Indian being the man for opening a crack cocaine distribution network on the reservation. "The Indian must know lots of people on the rez," he said one morning to Horny Al Gonzales. "The kid needs talkin to. I mean talkin to, and convinced to help us with our business! The Indians gets money once a month. No jobs. They is on welfare. Worthless already. Many of them already on drugs or booze, according to the info youse dug up there.

There ain't no law enforcement. It shud be easy pickins. I want ya to go see Indian Charlie. It ain't gonna be a social call, you understand. Al's not asking, but sure telling. If he gives youse any trouble, youse know what to do, and youse better do it!"

Horny Al Gonzales was a pitiful sight—long, dirty hair, homely features, never clean-shaven, with disturbing twitches in his face. Big ears. Narrow eyes. But he wasn't wimpy, for sure. He stood about 5'10" and heavily muscled, and although not slim, for he weighed 225, he was quick with his fists and feet. The tattoo of "mother" on his right forearm said little about his demeanor. He was one tough SOB, as mean as they come! He got his nickname from the gang because of his many sexual assaults and his frequency at the whorehouses of Big Bill's enterprises.

Not knowing Indian Charlie's full name, Albert Gonzales knew he needed to do some investigation and find out not only the name but also the Indian's address and perhaps his hangout. So, Al left on his Harley the next day and headed for the Horse Creek Reservation, stopping first at Milo's Gun Shop to pick up some more rounds of 7mm ammunition. Horny Al took the same route he and Big Bill, Hairy Harry, and Pinnelly had taken the prior summer. He enjoyed the rolling hills, the wide-open spaces through Wyoming and Western Nebraska, and the bars, diners, and dives in the small towns in the rural areas along the route. He really did not have a care in the world as he cruised along on his

Harley, except he was getting his fill of Big Bill and the lack of action in the crack business. He was convinced he could do better and make a hell of a lot more money on his own.

It didn't take him long when he was on the reservation to find out where "Indian Charlie" was living: "Somewhere at University of the West in Three Creeks." The exact address, no one could or would give him. Horny Bill did not worry about that, for he knew he could track the Indian down once he got to University of the West. He found Red Tail's apartment without difficulty after bribing a young man working at the registrar's office.

In order to get from the campus to Charlie's apartment, Horny Al had to pass Carlos Madrid's house on Mulberry Street. A bright red Corvette was parked in the driveway. Lights were on in the house, but looking through a large picture window, Horny Al saw no one inside except a dark-skinned girl in a robe. He moved on.

This night, Gonzales left his Harley Davidson motorcycle around the corner from Mulberry Street, on Pine Street, in a no-parking zone. He had no license plates on the cycle. The serial number had been scratched off. Officer Nick Spencer passed by, thinking nothing about the cycle being in a no-parking zone, for illegal parking in this college town happened frequently. He did notice, however, as he drove closer that the cycle had no plates and he thought it strange, so he investigated further and found the serial number had been scratched off. He called dispatch and asked that the cycle be confiscated. As he was examining the cycle more closely he heard on his police radio that there was a fight going on in a bar downtown. He hurried there, and on the way again contacted dispatch and suggested that the cycle be dusted for fingerprints.

The kingpin in Big Bill's crack-cocaine operation was soon inside the outside door of Charlie's apartment house. It was getting late in the evening—after classes. He was inside the vestibule, seated on a small bench, waiting for Charlie to come home. He had rung the bell for the apartment labeled "Charlie Red Tail" but received no answer. Horny Al sat there for a long time with glassy, red eyes. His speech was somewhat slurred as he talked to himself. His eyelids drooped. His goatee was red, sharply pointed. His oiled cap partially covered red hair hanging past his big ears. He wore high leather boots with his pants tucked in.

When Charlie came through the outside door, he was startled to run into a guy in the vestibule whom he did not know, but who looked strangely familiar. There were other apartments besides Charlie's on the second floor, so Charlie assumed the guy was there to see someone else. "Who are you wanting to see?" Charlie politely asked.

Horny Al made it clear that he was there to see Charlie. "List'n, you savage, I want some info. Big Bill sent me. You know Big Bill. He don't mess around. I don't neither. We are goin outside and talk. Understand? Don't you give me no shit. Understand?"

Horny Al had Charlie by the arm in a strong grip. Charlie thought for a moment that he would try to take this guy out by punching him in the face but thought better of it for the moment. Horny Al forced Charlie outside on the wooden walkway at the front of the house. Charlie was taller, just as muscular, and, he thought—a lot tougher. Charlie was wrong; he broke Horny Al's grip on his arm, swung his fist with speed and force, and threw a punch at Horny Al's face. It landed with power on his nose, and Gonzales was staggered and started bleeding. As Charlie started to follow up the blow with more of the same, he was met by a flurry of fists to his face, was knocked down, and received a barrage of feet to his face and stomach as he lay on the steps and the ground.

Horny Al's voice rose to a scream, his fists clenched as he stood over Charlie. "Ya dumb son-of-a-bitch. If ya wants more, jest let me know. I will put ya out and stuff your red skin in a trash container! Don't mess with Horny Al Gonzales! Understand?"

Charlie did not answer. He was stunned and dizzy. He felt like his face and back had been run over by a truck. He struggled up. He stared but said nothing. Gonzales continued his rant with a raised voice and a fist ready to deliver more blows. "Listin, you punk, I want'a know on what day of da month you bastards on the rez receive your government checks. I know ya get money ev'ry month. I w'nt to know da day of the month and where ya are when you get it. Understand? Do ya get cash or checks? And give me the names of five redskins who could make a fair amount of money working for Big Bill."

Charlie still said nothing. In his foggy state, he remembered Big Bill saying something to him in Denver about selling drugs on the reservation. Charlie finally figured out what was going on, but he wanted no part of it. But how was he going to get away from this beast? Thoughts of escape rushed through his head. He knew he had to do something fast. He was about to run, when he saw a police car on Mulberry to the north of them slowly driving toward them.

Horny Al saw it as well! "Ya not seen the last of me. If ya says a word to that cop bout this, we will hunt you down and cut ya up. Understand?" He quickly ran from the front of the house and into an alley at the back. He ran south. He did not go to the Harley. He had noticed before that the red Corvette at 510 Mulberry had the keys in the ignition. He helped himself. The red car raced out of the neighborhood.

Charlie quickly went into his apartment and locked the door. He was shaking and bleeding. His face and ribs hurt really badly. He was stiffening up, was weak and disoriented. He collapsed on the bed.

Horny Al had always wanted a sports car, so he had fun driving the red Corvette on the back routes to Denver. It would do 120 miles per hour without breaking a sweat, corner like his Harley, but ate gasoline like there was no tomorrow. Still, the trip to Denver to report back to Big Bill was a sweet dream for Al. He knew he had some explaining to do about not getting the cooperation of Red Tail but thought he could make Big Bill understand what happened and why he could not yet get the information they needed to set up the distribution network for crack on the reservation. Besides, there would still be time to get the information before the winter set in, the felon figured. He wasn't going to worry about it just yet, for he had miles to go before meeting up with Big Bill in Denver. The only thing really on his mind was whether he could come up with a plan to keep the Corvette and not let Big Bill know he had it. He would think about that and come up with a plan before he hit the Colorado line. "I have a friend who can git rid of the serial number and other identifying information for the 'Vette and hide it for me until I decide to sell it," Gonzales reassured himself. He would go straight to the friend's place, and Big Bill would not know the difference. But he would need to get himself another Harley before he could see Big Bill. He knew that would be easy.

The Denver thief did not know that Officer Nick Spencer had seen the red Corvette racing out of town and had run a license check on the car. The license check was being run while the Corvette sped away. No worries. Officer Spencer was familiar with the owner—one Carlos Madrid, the smart-ass rich kid who lived on Mulberry. He would be caught next time, for there is always a next time for rich kids who have only a sense of entitlement and little work ethic or common sense.

Officer Nick Spencer did not think much more about Carlos Madrid until a few weeks later when he passed by Madrid's house on Mulberry Street and noticed a new, black sports car in the driveway. *I wonder if the rich kid's dad bought*

145

him a new, fast car? This Porsche would outrun that red Corvette anytime, he thought. The license plate check confirmed the owner was Madrid. *I'll be darned,* Officer Spencer thought. *He must be damn rich or involved in some enterprise that pays him well.*

CHAPTER 18

FIRST AID

Having thought about the night of the dinner date with Charlie, their meeting at the park bench, and the endearing walk home, Johanna was anxious to see Charlie again. After Charlie left her at her apartment last night, she spent a lot of time thinking about him, and her heart spoke loving words tempered with caution. She realized she really did not know Charlie very well, but she felt safe with him and adored his looks, his manners, and his kindness. He seemed a gentle person. He was someone she could talk with and who seemed to care about her and understand her. Johanna worried, though, about not knowing for sure why Charlie had been at an EPS meeting and what he might have had in mind that would involve this cell she was now infiltrating for the FBI. She was very concerned and bewildered.

She kept telling herself it didn't really matter. Her inner self seemed to not really care about that part of Charlie's life, at least for now. *But if not now, when will I know? What if he is a terrorist? What could he be up to?* ran through her mind over and over again. Her judgment told her she needed to find out, if her relationship with Charlie was to go much further. *How will I find out? How can I believe him if he tells me he is not involved with something illegal? Why would he need the help of the EPS? Did Carlos know what he was talking about when he told me the "Indian" was asking the cell for help? Do I need to turn him in to the FBI?* These thoughts and more ran through Johanna's mind throughout the night as she searched her beliefs about right and wrong, and the leanings of her heart. She knew trust must exist for any relationship to survive. She became distraught and finally found sleep.

The next morning, Johanna set out to find some answers. She was hopeful she would run into Charlie on campus and they could talk all this out. She knew, however, that she could not share with Charlie her work for the FBI. When Johanna saw Charlie in front of the student union, she was shocked to see his bruised face, closed black eye, and his cautious steps.

"My gosh, Charlie, what happened? Who did this to you?"

"Oh, no one. I fell down the damn steps at my apartment building last night. No big deal, other than I hit my head on the step and bunged up my ribs a bit. No big deal. I will heal up right away."

"I am so sorry, Charlie. You look like you had a run-in with a bulldozer. Will you be OK? Can I do anything for you?"

"No, I will be alright. What are you doing? Where are you headed?"

"I was headed to the Coyote Den for a cup of coffee, but not now. Let me walk with you," Johanna insisted. After Charlie faltered for a step or two, Johanna took Charlie by an arm and helped him to his apartment. Nothing was said by either of them on the way; however, for Johanna, her fears and concerns were taking a back seat to her growing love for this guy who perhaps was more complicated than she could handle.

At 460 Mulberry, Johanna noticed blood on the outside wooden walkway as it led to the apartment in a two-story white house. She said nothing. At the vestibule, she took note of the inside stairs—just four of them that went to the second level. *Hardly a lot of stairs to fall down and get hurt this badly*, she thought.

She said to Charlie, "Which apartment is yours? I am going to clean your cuts and bruises and heat some tea or coffee for you." Charlie started to resist, but the effects of the beating forced him to reluctantly accept. He knew he needed something to calm him down, although it had been many hours since Horny Al had confronted him and beat the daylights out of him. He mumbled that it was OK for her to go up to #1, the corner apartment that looked over the yard to the south, the alley in back, and the sidewalk in front. A small landing at the top of the stairs served three doors to three different rentals.

Charlie's apartment was stark, Johanna quickly noticed,

with flowered wallpaper on the walls—a version of long-out-dated wall covering; a low ceiling with one hanging light fixture providing dim light; a kitchen with two metal cabinets, one on each side of the old fashioned sink, and a table with chrome-plated table legs; a rusted toilet and a shower, with corroded head and handles; one hanging towel in a broken rack; a cracked mirror over a sink; and a small writing desk with a gooseneck lamp containing one bulb. There was an overstuffed couch with a tear in it, a twin-sized bed with a colorful Indian blanket, an old chest with drawers that looked out of the runners, and an open bar suspended by wire from the ceiling on which to hang clothes. It had three hangers with a shirt and a pair of pants hanging. The floor was wood. Oak. Johanna noticed drops of blood on the floor that had not been cleaned up. The cheap window coverings were thin and frayed on the south-facing window, hardly giving privacy. A floor grate vented the forced-air heat.

"Remove your shirt and pants, Charlie, and lie down on the bed, face up," Johanna instructed. Charlie looked at her for a long moment, and then slowly removed only his shirt and lay down, face up. Johanna put some warm water in the lone bowl from the cabinet and looked for a washcloth, retrieving one from the bathroom. She slowly applied the warm cloth to Charlie's face and stomach, bathing the cuts and bruises with gentle dabs. She looked at Charlie's closed, swelled left eye and murmured softly, "Charlie, who did this to you? How did this happen?" Charlie did not reply. She asked Charlie to turn on his side and there she saw the bruising and the open wound. Johanna's breath was taken away, for one of the bruises was in the shape of a boot. She applied pressure to the open wound to stop the minimal bleeding. She bathed the injured back in warm water. Johanna bent down and kissed Charlie on the cheek. "Did you call the police? Charlie, please answer me." Charlie opened his eyes and grimaced as he tried to get off the bed, but fell back where he had been.

After a rather long silence, she said, "Charlie, I really care about you and want to help you in any way I can. If you decide you want to talk about this, I will be here for you. But for now, I am going to fix some tea. Do you have any?" Johanna asked, trying to get Charlie to say something. Charlie said nothing. "Why can't you talk to me, Charlie?" Johanna pleaded, becoming emotional, for she felt so bad for him. "You are safe here. I want to help you like you helped me when I was hurting in the park. Please talk to me."

Charlie mumbled something to her, but the only words Johanna could clearly understand were "Denver" and "drugs."

"What are you saying, Charlie? Are you involved in drugs? You need to tell me, Charlie, or I can't help you. At least I can listen." Then she realized she shouldn't push so hard with so many these questions and needed to back off. Charlie was not in any condition to tell her what had happened.

Johanna fixed the tea and walked to Charlie and helped him sip some of the tea through his swollen lips. Charlie soon fell asleep. She became quiet and slumped down on the couch and gazed over at this man who was such a mystery to her, but to whom she knew she was feeling romantically attracted. Johanna sat, lost in her thoughts. She looked at the muscular, ripped guy with the handsome face as he slept on his bed and wondered…wondered what could he be involved with that he got beaten up the way he was, why he was at an EPS meeting, why, why, why—over and over again.

When Charlie woke up three hours later, Johanna was still there. He sat on the edge of the bed. She came to him and sat beside him. She held his hand in hers. She spoke to him softly. "How are you feeling, Charlie?"

Charlie did not answer immediately, and then said, "Johanna, thank you for your kindness. I cannot tell you right now what happened. I don't want to involve you in anything. I like you a lot. I am sorry." With that, Charlie put on his shirt, stood up, and asked Johanna to leave.

For the next several days, Johanna was consumed by her concern for Charlie's condition and by her thoughts that Charlie might be involved with illegal drugs. Her imagination ran rampant. She thought, *Charlie is a drug dealer who had a deal go bad; he is selling drugs on campus; he is in financial trouble; he is running from the law; he is an addict; he may want to get me involved,* and on and on. She lived in mental turmoil. She couldn't sleep, was irritable with her girlfriends, and was afraid—not for herself, but for Charlie. She knew Carlos was looking for her. He had left messages on her cell phone. She had not contacted him yet but knew she must, sooner rather than later. What would Carlos want? What was she to tell him as to why she hadn't been in touch? What should she tell him when he asked her again for a date?

A week passed and Johanna wanted to talk again with Charlie. She walked on campus looking for him and resolved that if she did not see him on campus, she would go to his apartment. She walked to Heck's, where she had gone before with Charlie. As luck would have it, Charlie was sitting alone in the same booth where they had previously sat together. He had his head down. He had his hands around a mug of coffee. He sat not on the end of the seat in the booth, but further to the inside, and away from the window. He suddenly looked up and was staring straight ahead. She could see his face had healed up for the most part.

Johanna slid into the booth across from him. "Charlie, I have been looking all over for you. How are you? You look much, much better than when I saw you last."

Charlie gazed into her eyes for a moment and then said haltingly, "Johanna, you should not be seen with me. I am not sure myself what's going on. I don't want you to worry about me. I can take care of myself. I need to go back home for a while and be alone and with my people. I don't know what to tell you. I do care for you a lot, but I am no good for you."

Charlie looked away. There was silence. Then Johanna said in a whisper, "Charlie, you must tell me one thing—are you in trouble with the law? Because if you are, I need to know why. You said something to me about Denver and drugs when we were at your apartment. What is that all about? Are you involved with drugs?"

Charlie looked Johanna in the eye. "I am not," Charlie said firmly. But he did not say anything more.

"Charlie, I want to believe you, but you need to tell me why you were beaten up and what it has to do with drugs and Denver. Why should I believe you when you say no? And while you are at it, tell me why you were at an EPS meeting," she said, her voice rising. *Oh, what have I done to him with this distrust and lack of understanding. He doesn't deserve this.* Then, for the first time since Johanna had known him, he put her hand in his, and held it. Although bruised and swollen, much larger than hers, and callused, Johanna felt his warmth and her heart pounded more rapidly? He leaned forward and said softly, but firmly, "I have nothing to do with drugs. I am not involved with anything to do with drugs. I tell you the truth. I will tell you what has been going on when the time is right. I will share with you. You need to trust me. I care so much for you. I will not do anything that isn't right with my values, and I think with yours."

"But what the heck is going on with the EPS? I know you are wondering why I was there too. I told you, I had dated this Carlos and he invited me. Other than that, I can't tell you much, because I don't know much about it. He told me you were there and asked for help. Is what he told me the truth? Charlie, you have to tell me what is going on. I can't continue to see you while wondering about this all the time," Johanna urged excitedly, but regretting it as soon as she said the words.

"Well, I can't continue to see you either, if you are involved with that bunch. Are you doing something illegal? And how can you see me when you are seeing that Carlos?" Charlie said forcefully, with a bit of jealousy invading his tone of voice.

For several minutes, Charlie and Johanna sat in the booth looking deep into each other's eyes but saying nothing. Neither knew what to say next. They just looked at each other. Longingly. With love. Finally, Charlie told Johanna he must go. He stood up. He slid out of the booth and left. He did not look back.

Johanna quietly wept, while fearing she would not see Charlie again.

CHAPTER 19

HOME VISIT

As Johanna walked to the EPS meeting and the inevitable strain of being with Carlos, she wondered again what she had gotten into. Carlos continued to press her to go to her father and learn what the coal industry's plans were on delivering Wyoming coal to the West Coast port in Washington for shipment overseas. It had become clear to Johanna that a prerequisite to her being admitted to the EPS cell was not only her providing information on the routes from Wyoming's Powder River basin and its coal mines and the coal mines in Southeastern Montana to a port on the West Coast, but more importantly, whether the industry was discussing with companies in Canada the possibility of shipping through Canada to the West Coast. From what she could gather, and what she had relayed to FBI Agent Anderson, the EPS was planning to blow up some kind of railroad facility or structure on the route. If the route ultimately went through Canada, it would open up several opportunities for the EPS, including collaboration with a cell group in Southern Canada.

The task force was working on disinformation she could feed to the EPS so as to gain the full confidence of the cell, but the information was not yet ready. In the meantime, she needed to make excuses at the meeting as to why she did not yet have anything to report to them; however, the cell members were getting impatient, and Carlos was increasing his pressure on her.

"Should I go to my father and ask for the information the EPS wants?" Johanna asked of Agent Anderson after the meeting. "If I do get information from Dad, do I give it to the cell, or do I give them false information?"

"You need to get whatever information on the route you can from your dad, because that is being required in order for you to become part of the cell and to be privy to the actual plans they are in the process of making. If the proposed route includes part of Canada, we are well positioned with the Canadian provinces to involve them. We know of the Canadian cells. We just need specifics of what they are up to, in order to do what may be necessary to stop them."

"I know Dad is going to British Columbia next month, but I don't know what for, or whom he may be meeting with," Johanna replied. "I plan on going home in the next week or so, which would be before he goes to BC, so maybe I can get some details of his trip."

"That's great," said Agent Anderson. "Just be sure you report to me what you learn from your father, and that you do not give any information to the EPS until I tell you what to tell them and when."

"OK," Johanna replied firmly.

Johanna's relationship with the FBI task force remained very frank throughout, businesslike, and no warmth or encouragement. Johanna was glad to have it that way.

Since it would be a week or two before Johanna could get away from school and her classes to go home and see her folks, she decided to make a greater effort to locate Charlie. She missed him more and more as time had passed without seeing him, and she was troubled about their last meeting and the way it ended. *I really need to talk with Charlie and find out what is going on with him, but he will insist on knowing what is really going on with me as well, and I can't tell him. I would have to lie to him and I hate to do that. Perhaps I can sidestep the EPS entirely, as I did before.* Johanna went to Charlie's apartment to see if she could find him there.

When Johanna got to Charlie's apartment, she knocked on the door and a girl answered. "Is Charlie here?"

The girl at the door asked, "Charlie who?"

"Charlie Red Tail," Johanna replied.

The girl told her, "There is no one living here by that name, but he could have been a previous tenant. My boyfriend and I moved in about two weeks ago."

Johanna left and headed to the administration building on campus to see whether she could find out where Charlie now lived. At the administration building, she was told

Charlie had left school and they had no forwarding information. Johanna was shocked! Johanna cried.

Johanna went to see her folks. As she and her family sat down for dinner that first night she was home, in the elegant dining room in the house in which she grew up, Johanna knew what she had to do. In the time since her visit to the administration building, she had reversed her thinking about Charlie and was now satisfied that he was indeed involved in some way with illegal drugs and that he was not somebody with whom she should be involved. Anyway, she knew she had more important things on her plate: she needed to work her way out of the EPS mess, get her graduate degree in education, and find a job—a job far away from the problems she was having, from the people in her life, and from her fondness for Charlie Red Tail, which she couldn't deny.

"You look wonderful," her mother repeatedly told Johanna over the few days Johanna slept in her old bedroom, went to familiar places with her friends, and had long talks with them about her plans after graduation. Johanna loved her parents very much, but now was not the time for "touchy-feely" words and wishes.

Johanna needed to learn information from her father that would satisfy Carlos and the other creeps in the basement that had begun to seem like hell itself. She wished over and over again that she had not gotten involved with Carlos Gonzales and all that followed, but she could not undo what had gone before and that had turned a great college experience into a fearful duty of civic responsibility.

When alone with her dad, Johanna said, "So Dad, how is your coal project going? Are you having any success in getting agreements to ship the stuff to the West Coast for delivery in Asia? It sounds like a big project that probably will be hard to accomplish. Why is it taking so long?"

"Thanks for asking, my dear. It's been a lot more difficult than I ever expected. With all the politics being played, the money issues, and environmental issues, in some respects it's been a real nightmare. On top of that, we've got a federal government that is waging a war on coal and wants to make it prohibitive for the coal companies that have long been providing the fuel to power this country to continue in business. This administration and the environmental organizations want it to be replaced by clean energy, whatever that means. I know the feds want 'clean energy' to be the power source for the new America, and for that matter, the new world order, free of coal's air pollution and carbon footprint. But there is no way that change can be brought about simply by putting coal companies out of business. It's not going to happen any time soon; I am sure of that. This country needs electricity and power. Are we going to turn off all the lights in this country and live by candlelight?"

Johanna and her dad had overcome their decidedly opposite views on the environment and neither wanted to go back to the quarrels, hard feelings, and animosities that had developed over the years, but put behind them at their loving reunion earlier in the year. Their détente allowed them to now talk about environmentally related matters without further estrangement. Johanna's heart had not changed, but her maturity permitted civil discussion with her dad.

"Why are you headed up to British Columbia next week?" Johanna asked. "Does it have anything to do with the coal project? As I understand it, Montana also has some interest in shipping coal. Are they involved as well?"

"Sure are," her dad grumbled, "but we even have trouble with the Indians in Montana who are fighting our plans. They contend we would be damaging cultural sites and the environment. And so it goes."

Her dad was more than willing to share information about the project with his daughter. Most of the information he was privy to had been disclosed to regulators, after all. But he and only a few were involved in one particular planning aspect of the proposed project, and that part had to do with the route or routes from the mines to the coast. What made this part of the project so private was that alternatives did exist, and which alternative was ultimately chosen would largely determine the opponents of the project and other obstacles. This was no small concern.

"The coal companies know certain environmental groups are opposed, as well as some small towns and quite a few ranchers and farmers. The farmers and ranchers are really opposed if a new railroad line is to be constructed, which probably needs to be the case. If so, it would interfere with their agricultural operations.

"Small towns do not want dozens of coal trains coming

through at all hours of the day. The local governments make no money off it. There might be some jobs for the people, but not likely. The small-town residents do not want their peaceful existence taken away from them.

"But the environmental community is what the coal companies fear the most, due to their combined political power, the coalitions that they could form with the small towns, the farmers and ranchers, religious groups, medical groups, and who knows what others. Included within the environmental concerns, however, rests the biggest threat to success faced by the coal companies and states supporting the project—the eco-terrorism movement that could be so destructive and expensive to combat. They have already done so much damage in this country, from blowing up pipelines to stopping logging in certain forests. They no doubt would like to add a railroad to their list of possible targets."

As her dad told Johanna of these concerns, she became uneasy, for obvious reasons. She badly wanted to tell her dad everything, but knew she couldn't, at least not now. For now, she had to trust the task force and Agent Anderson.

"Well, between you and me and the gatepost," her dad said, "I am going to British Columbia to firm up a Canadian route. I will be meeting with the ministers of BC responsible for permitting, and with a Canadian railroad board that is interested in transporting some of the coal along their border with the US. The province will earn a lot of money from the railroad fees imposed on the railroad company. No one here in the States is currently thinking of or discussing this potential northern route. The part of the Canadian route we will use has few bridges or other infrastructure that makes it vulnerable to sabotage. If we can keep this quiet, we think we can get the jump on any eco-terrorists so that their planning would be frustrated and delayed until the permitting process is complete. Then we could protect the vulnerable sites along the route, for the coal companies then can secure the route, including bridges. Terrorists may know odds and ends about all this—and even, perhaps, about the possibility of a Canadian route for part of the hauling; however, they cannot plan or act until they know for sure what the route is. We know. They do not. It's as simple as that. We have the planning completed and under wraps; permits for the coastal facility are pretty much in hand.

"Since we will have the route finally decided soon after my trip to Canada, the transportation route will be finalized. It will be the track that runs from Turning Point to Red Top. We can handle whatever efforts anyone makes to abort the project. Be sure and keep all this under your cap, Johanna. Only the FBI knows we have a Canadian route for a portion of this project. The feds are interested in cutting off any group who has eco-terrorism on its mind and that might try to attack this project. Now, as I said, don't tell anyone about this. OK?"

As Johanna returned to the university after visiting her parents, she did not know how to handle what she had now learned from her father. If she disclosed to the EPS this information her father had asked her to keep secret, she would be betraying her father and the trust he was placing in her, and she would be putting the project in jeopardy. Surely, if she told this information to the eco-terrorists, they would take action to in some way sabotage the coal industry's plans. In doing so, they would sabotage not only the coal industry's plans, but also the states of Wyoming and Montana's positions on this most important project that would yield so much in revenues to those states.

If I don't provide this vital information to EPS I will still have uncertainty about the FBI'S threat to prosecute me hanging over my head, and any hope I have to answer my heart about Charlie. She shuddered at the options that seemed to be so limited in her mind.

CHAPTER 20

THE CAVE

Charlie stopped at his uncle Oscar Big Bull's cabin on the reservation near Old Woman Creek and gathered up his camping gear, his backpack, his knife, and his rifle. Because he could no longer adequately care for himself, his uncle no longer lived there. He had moved in with Charlie's other uncle, Ted Tomahawk. The cabin had been vacant since that terrible day when his uncle had been shot and Charlie had been arrested. After gathering his belongings, Charlie headed for the Black Hills and the trails he knew so well, that playground on the horizon that had intrigued Charlie since he was a kid. Charlie and Tom Big Horse, and many times Charlie alone, had hiked and explored the Black Hills, Ȟe Sápa, so named by the Lakota long ago and told to him to be a spiritual place for the Indian people.

The times in the forest—hiking the animal trails, swimming in the lakes, seeing long distances from the mountain heights—had been peaceful, fulfilling times for Charlie. He was able to talk with the spirits, dream of places and people beyond, and allow his heart to imagine finding joy with a beautiful mate in the future times. Charlie knew of the waterfalls, the birds, the deer and elk, and the blessings of the earth located there. He had long studied them before painting them on paper. He also studied the surroundings, home for the animals, and the seeming reverence of it to the inhabitants.

The young Indian with the name of the hawk had often sought refuge in the forest from the stress that sometimes occurred on the reservation, but mostly because of the beauty he saw there and the excitement he experienced. He knew the Black Hills was forest lands taken by the federal government from the Indian people despite the treaty of 1868, in which the United States agreed to the rights of the Lakota and other Indian tribes to keep this spiritual forest free of the aggression of the white man, and to protect it for the Indians. The 1868 treaty of Fort Laramie was but one of many broken treaties of the white man. Not long thereafter, the gold rush began in the Black Hills and the United States Government stood by and let it happen—perhaps encouraged it.

Charlie thought, *I know the animals, the trails, the waterfalls, the meadows, the mountains themselves- places I can hide and not be found. And, the place where the white man keeps hidden things. I know where the US Forest Service stores dynamite.*

Charlie had been to the underground cellar many times.

He had seen with his own eyes the stacks of boxes, some opened, housing the violent red sticks, and the snake-like cords for the lighting of the destructive power. Charlie was curious as well as frightened whenever he visited the stash of destruction. He had no use for such things—until now, perhaps. Charlie had thought for some time that he shouldn't have gone to Big Bill when he did and before he figured out for himself how to destroy a dam, or at least severely damage one, or perhaps before he even decided to use the dynamite hidden in the bunker located on the land sacred in the eyes of his people.

Charlie left his pickup behind some trees and boulders near the Battle Mountain trail, remote by all standards and not used by many people, but it was his favorite route to high country and one used by his ancestors in their escape from the fierce battle at Deer Creek. He knew the trail well. Far up the mountain near a waterfall, Charlie and his friend Tom had found a cave. In the cave, they found messages on the walls and a stone pipe that became a part of their fantasies. They left the pipe there and told no one of their find, so no one else knew of the secret place. Charlie was now headed back to the safe place of comfort and peace. It was but a day's hike from there to the "red sticks."

It was a strenuous hike through dense forest with lots of downed timber, narrow game trails, many fruit-bearing bushes and aspen trees, as well as creeks wide and deep at the lower elevations, but mostly trickling and musical in the higher places, brooks finding their way to the meadows below. The boulders, fallen trees, and wildflowers added the creator's beauty to the canvas of scenes so enriching to Charlie. The scent of the pines capped the sensory wonderland Charlie so loved.

He hiked the many miles, stopping only now and then to watch the scampering chipmunk or the acrobatic squirrel as they left their busy work for places of safety. He liked seeing the Pine Marten, so hard to spot, but particularly handsome. There was nothing heavy on Charlie's mind now as he walked along and climbed higher to his sense of "safe place." Not even Johanna worked her way into his thoughts as he lost himself in the enriching place called Black Hills.

Charlie had covered the entrance with branches and other slash his first time there alone, and each time after, as he sought the quiet hole and its surroundings. He removed the debris and looked at the sun to see how much time he had until dark. The cave was not big, but suitable for a couple of people to camp within its walls. The entrance faced east, as Indian dwellings did, to receive the rising sun at the start of a new day. Previous times at the cave provided wood for a fire if necessary, thatch for him to place leaves on for bedding, and a few utensils for water and some cooking. His bedroll from his backpack would provide warmth in the cool night. His knife, given him as a gift from his uncle when Charlie "became a man" according to his tribe's ritual, was always with him for protection and various uses. He was very skilled with it.

Porcupine Creek runs near the cave. It provides the drinking water and water for cooking. It also gives Charlie the opportunity to catch fresh trout and big frogs for dinner. The three-piece fly rod attached to Charlie's pack would come in handy when the first hatches appeared in the mornings and the evenings of his stay.

Charlie found the wild raspberries were plentiful, and mushrooms were thriving in the creek's wetlands. Jerky that Charlie had made from elk meat killed last fall would be a treat later on in his stay. He knew that if he wanted, he could also add to the menu a squirrel or two, for he had his rifle along. Charlie made all of these observations, but in all honesty knew he could also eat the freeze-dried foods he brought along, cook in the camping stove using the butane fuel, and cook in the aluminum pans and bowls he had recently acquired. He thought, *Am I becoming a white man?*

When Charlie awakened with the sunrise the next day, he set about hiking this area so familiar to him. He headed straight for the underground bunker hiding the dynamite. As he hiked the miles to the bunker, he was deep in thought about what he would do when he reached the bunker, but he was also deep in doubt as to whether he should take the red sticks and pursue his plan to blow up a portion of the dam near his people's lands. To take out even a part of the dam would be to unleash the fury of the river and no doubt would bring hardship to his people living below and near the reservoir. This troubled him deeply. Was his personal honor worth the carrying out of the vision?

When he reached the bunker, he stood a long time before the mostly hidden entrance. He knew what was within, for he had come by the bunker years before, forced the door partially open, and seen within. Now he balked. He sat for a long time. Now he questioned himself, more than his thoughts before this time. Now his mind flashed with the face of Johanna. Now thoughts came to the fate of his brothers and sisters if Big Bill and Horny Al were successful in spreading their evil to those already suffering in one way or another on the reservation—alcoholism, other drugs, unemployment, medical problems untreated, the total breakdown of extended families, the mainstay of the cultural and familial life of the tribe. Charlie sat there for a long time. Then, he walked away.

Charlie spent the next several days thinking about what he should do. His sleep was restless. He had little appetite. He thought often about the challenges he had before him and that were magnified in his mind. Was he a coward? A traitor to his people? He didn't know if he could live with a decision to not fulfill his obligation of revenge that so long had tormented him. "But what do I do with my education and with my people?" he asked himself. "I promised myself to come back and help my people by being a leader and by teaching them a better way to live in the white man's world. And then there is that thing with the crooks in Denver and the drugs and the guy who beat me up. I can't let that threat to my people happen, but who am I to stop it?"

His sense of self was saddled with sadness, guilt, and re-morse, the remorse relating totally to the way he had rejected Johanna's reaching out to him at the coffee house; the guilt eating at him caused by his Indian teachings of the impor-tance of honor—the fulfillment of the duty he had to fulfill the vision and his leaning toward not doing it; the sadness of not knowing how to handle his warm feelings toward Johanna, a white girl.

He thought, *Am I in love with her? Can I truly trust her if I share my fears with her? Do I have any right to burden her with my problems? Would a strong warrior of the tribe do that? Do I really care whether one would or not? Maybe I should go back to the university and see if she will talk with me again, and maybe I should be a bit more honest with her about what is going on with me. Or maybe I should just forget about her, and the "vi-sion" as well, and build myself a cabin on the reservation and live there the rest of my life.* A long time had passed since Charlie gave much thought to the other wrong requiring revenge—the wrongful imprisonment he had suffered after the false accusation of rape, and his conviction based on the perjured testimony of the Stoutweins. Hatred toward the Stoutweins had haunted him ever since the accusation had been made, but now he felt it had been too long stuffed away in the back of his mind. Maybe revenge against the Stoutweins would be a more honorable action to take, rather than blowing up a dam. His mind began to race with thoughts of how revenge against the Stoutweins could be carried out, so much so that even the fear of going to prison again did not detour his mind. He could easily find the liar at UWest and use the knife his uncle gave to him, a little justice for the beating of his uncle by the authorities initiated by Stoutwein's lies; he could sneak into the frat house and kill Jim Stoutwein at night; or he could follow him to his family's ranch and do him in there, or on his way there; he has a good rifle and he could shoot Stoutwein from afar, and then escape back to the reservation; he felt Jim Stoutwein was nothing more than a pile of garbage.

Charlie knew that when he went down from the cave to the other world, something had to be done. He could not abide his indecision any longer. And he knew that whatever his decision going forward was to be, the taking of tribal lands and the building of the dams was not just another past wrong inflicted on the Indian people by the powerful white men, but an ever-present wrong that would continue to dominate his thoughts as the struggle for justice would go forward, perhaps only in the courts of the land.

CHAPTER 21

SURPRISE

Carlos Madrid contacted Johanna on the Monday she returned to campus after visiting her folks. He told her his comrades in the cell were getting more and more impatient with her and if she was serious about joining them, she had better hurry up. Carlos seemed to be a bit angry when he talked to her, and it was upsetting to her when he said, "Besides, I have my doubts about you anyway. You seem to have this thing about that Indian I saw you with, and I know you have seen him several times. Are we finished? Why won't you go out with me anymore or have coffee or whatever? If you are not interested in me, I take it you are not interested in our movement to save the environment. We have a cell meeting this Friday night and you had best have some explanation for why you have nothing to report to us. And, by the way, I want to have dinner with you after the meeting."

Reluctant as she was, Johanna nevertheless answered,

"That sounds fine. I will be there, and dinner afterwards works for me."

"Thank goodness!" Johanna exclaimed when Agent Anderson called her on the Thursday night before the cell meeting on Friday. She had been trying to figure out how she was going to explain to Anderson that she couldn't be involved anymore with the undercover assignment.

"I don't think I can go through with this," she anxiously said to Anderson. "The only information my father has given to me--" she gulped, did not finish the sentence, had tears running down her cheeks. "I am not willing to betray his trust. Not only would I be betraying his trust, but I would also be enabling the EPS to do the very thing we are trying to prevent—terrorism—and it would be against my father's interests and his company, and I cannot do that to my father, no matter what the consequences might be for me, and if you want to charge me with some crime—I know I am not guilty of any crime—then go ahead, and I will fight you all the way. I will not betray my father and you cannot make me do so," Johanna said, now sobbing uncontrollably.

"Now calm down, Johanna. You meet me tomorrow morning at 8:00 in the library where we met the first time. We will talk more then. In the meantime, get yourself together. Do not, I repeat, do not, do anything foolish! You need to meet me at the library at 8:00 in the morning," said Agent Anderson, and he ended the call. Johanna sat in a chair, exhausted, and continued sobbing. She dreaded the next meeting with Anderson.

Charlie Red Tail did not know the group he was meeting with for the second time was an eco-terrorism cell. Before the first meeting with the EPS, an Indian friend he met on campus had told him the group was interested in the environment and in social justice. Based on what he was told, Charlie had concluded it was a group of students that would understand his issues and perhaps help him and his people. They had excused him after a few minutes the first time he went. Now, he did not know whether he would even get in the door. He reasoned, however, that the purpose of the group must not be bad, because if it were, Johanna would not have gone to meetings there. For some unknown reason, at the urging of one of its members named Carlos, on this Friday night they agreed to let him speak, but only for a short time.

Johanna also went to the EPS meeting, arriving a bit late. The meeting was in progress when she entered the room. As her eyes and ears adapted to the darkness and sounds of the meeting, she quickly realized the voice of the person talking, who was seated on the other side of the room with his back to the door and addressing the cell group was, incredibly, Charlie Red Tail! Johanna felt weak.

Charlie was talking in a raised voice. "I don't believe anyone in the white man's government cares about the bad treatment of our tribe by government—they never have," said Charlie, leaning forward in the small basement room, discolored by time and smelling of too much weed, spilled beer, and farts. "If you truly believe the dams are for the good of all people as well as the river itself, you can sit on your butts and do nothing. But you should know better! The Missouri River is an important water source in this country and has lots of historical meaning. The river was castrated by the construction of the Big Bend dam, and my people were once again victimized."

Charlie went on: "As I told you before, our soul was flooded out by white men and we have been slowly dying since." Charlie fumed. "If we don't act now, the will to free the river may be forever lost and my people will know nothing but walleye fish and government campsites. Let's join together, and I can get some of my tribal members to help raise hell in the halls of government, arguing for what is fair. The government needs to take down this damn dam."

Thus, Charlie felt he was urging, cajoling, seeking help with action rooted in fairness and demanded by future generations. He did not know, however, what he would do if the group said "yes" to his plea for help. If they said "yes" he would have to deal with it, but he felt it was at best a long shot for them to get involved.

Predictably, their response to Charlie was not encouraging. He had watched the reactions of the cell members and their obvious indifference to what he was urging. His cause was more personal and limited than the goals of the idealistic dropouts from the university he was talking to, who were no doubt talking of saving the world from global warming.

Charlie knew this was a group not committed by blood to a common purpose; rather, he judged they were joined together only by excitement, privilege, and self-importance. They seemed to have no leader. They no doubt lived in frat houses. They would not likely join him, who was ignorant of their cause, whatever it was, and which Charlie did not even know. More than one of the assembled members, including Carlos Madrid, told Charlie: "Absolutely not. We are not interested in trying to bring justice to your people." He was again asked to leave.

Charlie stood up, abruptly turned around, and left. He did not see Johanna standing in the dark across the room as he left. Charlie's eyes were filled with unspoken rage, his mind inflamed with emotion. He was later relieved they did not agree to help him, for he knew he could not explain to Johanna why he was there anyway, if she found out he was at the meeting.

Johanna was stunned and unable to speak. The pit in her stomach was deeper than any coal mine could be. She fought to gain composure and address the questions required for her membership in the cell directed to her by its members, questions led by Carlos Madrid. Eventually, after some time, she was forthcoming and shared with the group of terrorists the secrets of her father and the plans for trains through Canada. Ezekiel was the first to offer congratulations to her, followed by the others, but with lukewarm enthusiasm offered by Carlos. Johanna could not help but notice what Carlos said or didn't say, and therefore regretted even more their dinner date, and what no doubt would include questions of her involvement with Charlie, ensconced in the palpable jealously of Carlos.

Johanna's dinner with Carlos was even more uncomfortable than she had imagined it would be. They met at the restaurant where she and Charlie had enjoyed a wonderful evening together, where they had moved closer to knowing each other and wanting to know more. Now, Johanna wondered in her own mind whether the tenderness of that evening was real and sincere, or whether the strident diatribe of Charlie's at the EPS meeting was the true Charlie. In her bewilderment at what Charlie had said and was planning, she was even more puzzled by the discussions she had with him previously where he had assured her he was not involved with anything illegal.

When Carlos brought up "the Indian," Johanna told him, "There is nothing between Charlie and me. He has wanted to date me more, and I have not wanted much to do with him. As far as I can tell, he is a guy out of his element here at UWest, looking for friends and looking for someone to help him attack a white man's wrong against his Indian people. Let's forget about the Indian and talk about the plans for attacking the trains full of coal."

Carlos said, "Good!" and told Johanna how the information she gave the cell of EPS at the meeting would allow the plan to move forward. Carlos became very excited! He told her she was now an official member of the cell. He offered a salute with the beer in his hand. She gulped.

CHAPTER 22

POST-MEETING BLUES

Meeting with Agent Anderson Friday morning at the library before the EPS meeting that night had allayed Johanna's fears of betrayal of her father; she was comforted to know that her father was aware of what she was doing with EPS, and why. Knowing that her father was aware of her undercover assignment made Johanna feel much braver.

She had actually been somewhat excited about her mission before attending the cell meeting that Friday night. Charlie's being at the meeting took all her excitement and confidence away. She did not know what Charlie had told the cell members before she arrived. Was his being their somehow illegal? She had not betrayed her father, but now must she betray Charlie?

Johanna had no one to talk to about Charlie—no one was that close to her in whom she had the kind of trust where what she now knew of Charlie could be told. Her searching for a confidant finally ended; she made an appointment with John Wilson, the attorney who had advised her about the FBI's task force on eco-terrorism and the Bureau's demands made on her.

Without much emotion, in fact in a rather detached way, Joanna told John Wilson all that had happened since her last conference with him, including the fact that Agent Anderson said her father was aware of Joanna's involvement with the FBI and with EPS. She shared with the attorney that Agent Anderson had also related to her how he had worked with her father to concoct the story about the coal industry using a route through Canada to transport coal to the West Coast. She told Mr. Wilson of how she had dreaded the meeting with the EPS even though she knew she did not have to betray her father; however, in a most emotional way, Johanna told Mr. Wilson of what had happened at the EPS meeting last Friday night—that she had been late, and when she arrived she saw and heard Charlie talking to the cell group. With tears, Johanna told Wilson what she recalled of what Charlie had said.

"Do I have to turn in Charlie to the FBI?" Johanna blurted. "I know Charlie is not capable of a criminal act. He is too kind, too considerate and too levelheaded. I was aware of his hostility toward whites because of the taking of their lands by the government, for he expressed such in a history class we took together, but he did not make any threats of violence or retribution toward the government or anyone else. What am I to do—what is my obligation?" Then Johanna realized she may have let the cat out of the bag about Charlie. "You won't disclose this information to anyone, will you? What I told you is protected by attorney-client privilege, is it not?"

"Well," Mr. Wilson began, "there is nothing you have told me that indicates Mr. Red Tail is about to commit some crime. If he was saying he was going to do such things, then we might have a problem. But not at this time. What I heard you saying is that Charlie was at the meeting asking for help in some way, but not in doing a specific act or acts other than demonstrating an exercise of free speech rights. At least that's all you heard, apparently. One can't infer from what you have told me that he intends something that would raise the ethical question of whether that 'something' takes away the confidentiality privilege you have with me. Have you told me everything you know about Mr. Red Tail and why he was at a meeting of an eco-terrorism cell?"

"Yes, I sure have; however, I also know he has had some violence done to him. He hasn't told me anything about it except in one of our conversations he mentioned the terms 'Denver' and 'drugs.' I know he is not capable of using or dealing drugs, so I am without a clue why he mentioned them in connection with some injuries he had sustained a while back. I saw his injuries, but he would not tell me who had attacked him or why. He just mumbled something about Denver and drugs. I did not press him about what I thought I heard."

Attorney Wilson methodically questioned Johanna, and Johanna truthfully answered, about all she knew regarding

Charlie, including all meetings she had with him, all social get-togethers, all telephone calls, all physical contact, exhaustively making Johanna recount the entire past between her and Charlie.

At the end of the session, Wilson encouraged Johanna to find out more about Charlie, if that was possible, and then he asked, "Are you in love with him?"

CHAPTER 23

BODY AT THE DUMP

"Body of James A. Stoutwein Found in Landfill," proclaimed the *Freedom Leader* on April 1st, the county newspaper for Indian Mound County. The article reported: "Stoutwein was identified by his sister, Betsy Stoutwein. Her brother was a member of the prominent Mac Stoutwein family, longtime residents of Indian Mound County who ranch near Upper Goose Creek, and young Stoutwein was a student at University of the West. His unclothed body had evidence of trauma to the body, a knife wound at the neck." An autopsy would be performed, the paper reported. No suspects were in custody, according to the article. The newspaper had not yet learned that Stoutwein had been scalped.

The next day, the *Freedom Leader* ran a story that the Stoutwein family had been victimized once before when their daughter was raped by a reservation Indian named Charlie Red Tail. The paper did not say that Charlie Red Tail had killed young Jim Stoutwein, but the speculation that he had done so began circulating throughout the region in print, on television and radio. And all news outlets now reported that the victim had been scalped. Outrage reigned throughout the West over the revelation.

Indian Mound County law enforcement personnel immediately suspected Charlie Red Tail. It was known by law enforcement Charlie had been released from prison. And he was listed as a sex offender living in Three Creeks after he enrolled at University of the West. The local sheriff and the State Division of Criminal Investigation entered the picture immediately as the manhunt began to find Charlie Red Tail.

The University of the West campus newspaper, *The Sly Coyote*, learned of the homicide and reported in its weekly newspaper that a member of the Ranch House Fraternity, to which the victim belonged, reported to the *Coyote* that an Indian who had harmed the Stoutwein family before could be responsible. The fraternity member did not know the Indian's name, according to the student paper.

The news reports of the murder spread quickly throughout the West. The case had all the fodder necessary to spur public interest: A prominent ranch family member murdered near an Indian reservation; a spectacular location where the body was found; few clues as to "who-done-it"; the victim scalped; however, the rumored, incredible fact was that an Indian from the Horse Creek Reservation who had been convicted of raping the murder victim's sister several years before was the prime suspect. Although no factual basis was being reported for suspecting the Indian, the press covered his guilt as a likely fact, and the hyperbole added to the story by the sensational press outlets went a long way to convince the outraged public that the scenario was probably true. After all, as one national news pundit reported, "It certainly appears the Indian from a South Dakota Indian Reservation may be the murderer, based on the reporting of the campus newspaper at University of the West where both the Indian, one Charlie Red Tail, and the victim were attending, and based on interviews with Stoutwein family members and the facts of the rape conviction of the Indian recited in the victim's hometown newspaper."

Thousands of tips from self-proclaimed investigators poured in to the law enforcement agencies soon after the body was found. For many of those reporting, the guilt of Charlie Red Tail was established. The ranchers near the Horse Creek Reservation even began discussing the need to form a vigilante group if justice was not promptly done. They would find the Indian who raped Betsy Stoutwein and murdered Jim Stoutwein, and justice would be "swift."

Supervisor Paul Carbine, who headed the task force on eco-terrorism that included FBI Agent Rex Anderson, also headed the office of the FBI that had the responsibility to investigate the murder of James Stoutwein. Carbine knew there would be a lot of publicity surrounding the case because of the gruesome facts that were known, and particularly since an Indian from the Horse Creek Reservation might be involved. Carbine knew Anderson enjoyed some good-will among Indian tribes due to his handling the murder of an Indian girl years before. For those reasons, Carbine felt Anderson should be the agent to lead the investigation in the Stoutwein murder case.

Rex Anderson was an experienced, decorated agent of the Federal Bureau of Investigation. He was known to be hard-nosed, dedicated, but also fair-minded, and he was scrupulous about following the law. Perhaps his most famous investigation was years before the murder of James Stoutwein. He successfully found the "perps" who murdered an Indian girl along a road off, but near, the Morningstar Indian Reservation. The investigation took nearly two years and was successful only because Anderson was so outraged at the nature of the crime—the young girl's body was found hanging from a tree in a grove along the Missouri River—that he simply would not give up on the case. Two men from Mexico were convicted of the murder after Agent Anderson put the case together against all odds, and during a time of intense public pressure from the Indian peoples and the general public.

There was a jurisdictional question in the Stoutwein case that had to be addressed at some point: Where did the murder occur—on the reservation, in the State of Dakota, in another state, or some other place? Where the crime was committed was important, because the location would perhaps establish what law enforcement agency was to be the lead investigative agency, and which jurisdiction would have the responsibility to prosecute the case when the "perpetrator" was apprehended, and if apprehended in a different jurisdiction, what extradition statutes applied.

Law enforcement from all jurisdictions that could be affected was called together to discuss who would be the lead agency. It was finally agreed the FBI was to take the lead, even though the FBI did not generally supervise or take over the lead in an investigation of this nature, for murder is not a federal offense unless committed on a reservation, but rather, a state crime. Due to the fact the location of the crime was unknown and there was the possibility that an Indian was involved, the FBI took the lead in the case. The combined resources of all law enforcement agencies potentially involved were pooled for this particular investigation. The harder question would be which jurisdiction would be responsible for prosecuting the crime. They had a body for sure, but who committed the crime and where?

Agent Anderson was well aware that the laws in "Indian Country," a term sometimes applied to areas of the US where Indian reservations are located, were complicated. Indian tribes are sovereign entities. Tribal governments generally had their own law enforcement and courts. On some major crimes, jurisdiction of tribal courts was concurrent with state jurisdiction and with federal jurisdiction, but there were exceptions and it depended in each case as to who the victim was (Indian or non-Indian) and who the perpetrator was (Indian or non-Indian) and where the crime occurred.

Since Stoutwein was a non-Indian, even if the criminal were an Indian, neither the federal government nor tribal government would prosecute the case. As with a white- on-white murder, the state where the murder was committed would have jurisdiction to prosecute the person charged.

The Federal Bureau of Investigation, with all the resources it could bring to bear on the case, immediately began leading the investigation into the Stoutwein homicide by identifying possible suspects, interviewing family and friends, and checking University of the West records.

The landfill employee, Robert Whitney, who found the body, was immediately contacted by Agent Anderson and interviewed. Before being interviewed, his background was checked for any criminal convictions, and he was clean. Whitney was cooperative with the local authorities and with Anderson.

"I work on a frontend loader and move the garbage that's dumped here into piles, usually every four days, so there is considerable amount of stuff that has been dumped since the last time. I came to work yesterday at my usual time, which is 6:00 a.m. I saw there was a lot of junk. I always get off and walk around to see what's been brought in. You see, Western Gatherers is the garbage company that picks up the stuff at residences and businesses and brings it here and unloads. They run about ten trucks and pretty much cover the city, although one of the routes, I believe, is north of the city in a rural area. I think it extends over the state line to get the stuff of those living next to Three Creeks. But also, construction companies bring in things; sometimes ranchers bring in dead animals. There's all kinds of stuff that people bring in. You would be surprised what some people throw away. Sometimes there are things in good condition that could still be used, or some that could be repaired. That's why I kinda look around before starting to move the junk into piles."

"What happens to the junk piles?"

"Well, the stuff is put into an incinerator and burned. Anyway, I looked around for a while but saw nothing unusual, so I climbed up on my rig and was moving garbage around. I filled the bucket and was moving the load to a pile when I saw what looked like a leg. I thought: what the heck is that? I stared at it for a minute or two. I thought it must be a mannequin or something. You know, what they put clothes on in stores. So, I didn't give it much more thought. As I moved the stuff a bit more toward a pile, I saw some more of what I thought at first was a mannequin. I thought, that looks like it could be a human leg. Whatever it was, it was partially covered by other garbage. I sat there for a while, just staring at it. I was kind of scared, to be honest with you. Finally, I lowered the bucket and climbed down to look closer. I could see it was attached to a human body! Oh my gosh, I thought, what do I do! Well, I uncovered the partially clothed body. I saw it was a guy. He was obviously dead. And get this, the guy had been scalped."

"What do you mean, scalped?"

"Just what I said. Scalped. His hair and the top of his

head had been cut off!"

"Go on."

"I was shaking. I used my cell phone and called 911. I didn't continue my work, just stood there. I knew I shouldn't disturb the body. Then the police came, and I told them what I'm telling you. I didn't work the rest of the day."

"Do you have any idea how the body got into the junk yard?"

"Don't have a clue. I suppose, though, it must have come in on one of the loads Western Gatherers brought in. If it was, it could have been brought in from about anywhere in the area. They pick up the dumpsters at businesses also, not just residential, so I suppose someone could have put the body in a dumpster."

"What days and what hours is the landfill open to the public?"

"8:00 a.m. to 4:00 p.m., Tuesday through Saturday. I work the same days, but 6:00 in the morning to 5:00 in the afternoon."

"Did you ever see anyone near the body, or scavenging in the yard, or whatever, about the time you discovered the body?"

"No, I sure didn't."

He saw no one bring the body to the landfill or anyone near the body at any time. When asked if he had seen anyone hanging around the yard or surrounding streets earlier or any vehicles in the area that day or before, he recalled none. Nothing of that nature was suspicious at all.

"I forgot to mention. I did find the chain and padlock of the landfill fence cut off when I came to work that morning. The chain was still on the gate, as if still securing the gate. I found the padlock to the side of the gate in the grass. My dad was a policeman in Rapid City and so I knew I should preserve the scene and keep the chain and lock, which I did—in a bag in my truck."

He turned the bag over to FBI agent Anderson.

The FBI publicized a telephone number that people with leads could contact and set up a Twitter account and a web site. Law enforcement soon began receiving many contacts that would need to be followed up on, requiring many additional law enforcement and other resources.

"I saw an Indian beating up on a guy at the Horseshoe Bar near Four Mile Town."

"I saw several men and a woman dragging a body to a car on the reservation."

"Is there a reward? I may know who the killer is."

"I saw Red Tail at the dam near Yankton just yesterday."

Students, administrators, and faculty who knew "the Indian Charlie Red Tail" began calling law enforcement as soon as the campus newspaper hit the stands, although many knew little about him and had no information that was helpful, except for Professor Norma Pickenpaugh, who related in exaggerated detail what had occurred in her class regarding Red Tail with respect to the dams on the river. When the interviewing agent passed Pickenpaugh's information on to

Agent Anderson, Anderson was struck by the hostility toward whites that Pickenpaugh had told about with considerable emphasis. He also took note of the underlying angst that Red Tail apparently had toward the dam projects on the Missouri River. Anderson decided he would personally follow up on that bit of information, for it could lead to a motive on the part of Red Tail, since the Stoutwein family no doubt supported the dam project. He would not ignore, however, the possible tie-in of the rape conviction with the murder.

There was no shortage of information being provided by the public, but little was helpful. Finding out what information was in fact helpful to the investigation proved to be a trying, labor-intensive endeavor, but the law enforcement officials endeavored to follow up on any information that might be a lead that could break the case.

CHAPTER 24

THE NEED TO TALK

Johanna Johnson stared in disbelief at the front-page headline of the student newspaper, *The Sly Coyote*: "INDIAN STUDENT AT UW MAY HAVE KILLED FRAT PRES!" The front-page story below the headline was brief: "The body of James Stoutwein, a senior at University of the West and president of the Ranch House Fraternity, was found dead in the city landfill yesterday morning by the custodian of the facility. His throat had been slashed and his body was partially hidden under some of the junk at the landfill. An autopsy will be performed. A member of the Ranch House Fraternity who had contacted *The Sly Coyote* told the paper that he had also called the FBI and told them a possible suspect should be a fellow student at UW, Charlie Red Tail, who several years ago had been convicted of raping Jim Stoutwein's sister at a local dance. No further information is available at this time."

Johanna froze! She stared at the paper for a long time. Then, she began to shake, and burst out sobbing. She cried until exhausted and sobbed, "There is no way Charlie did this. I know Charlie, he wouldn't do this, and he wouldn't rape a girl! I love Charlie! The paper has this all wrong. I must find Charlie and talk to him, I know him. He wouldn't do something like this! It's April Fool's Day!"

As she was gaining some composure, her cell phone rang. "This is Carlos. Have you read today's *Coyote*? Can you believe it! That Charlie Red Tail was the Indian that you were with in the park and that came to an EPS meeting. I can't believe it! Johanna, you must not see this creep again, and you need to watch out for him contacting you. He is dangerous! Do you want me to come over to your apartment?"

Johanna had to restrain herself, as she couldn't think of anything worse than seeing Carlos Madrid, but was able to reply, "No, I am fine. And I am certain Charlie did not commit this murder, or the rape the paper talks about. He is a good guy, and he is being framed!"

"Well, you had better be careful and look out for him. I am here for you if you feel you need someone to be with, to talk to. To protect you if necessary. OK?"

"Carlos. I need to run." She hung up.

The administration at University of the West met in special session the next afternoon. National news organizations were already running with the story. News reporters and TV stations flooded the campus. The board was not sure how to handle the flood of inquiries it was already getting from parents, law enforcement and the news media. Parents were, of course, worried about a fugitive running loose in the area and their children being there at the school. The requests from news media were obviously uninformed as to what privacy rules applied regarding students, but that did not stop them from badgering admission officials and other departments. School authorities did, of course, fully cooperate with law enforcement. The university's legal counsel immediately met with the administrators and advised them as to what information they could release and to whom. An FBI agent also informed them of who needed to be in charge at the university, what could be said, and that until the FBI had more information itself, the school authorities should not say anything nor provide any information. The FBI also advised the school that since the murderer was unknown, and no one knew whether it was a student or a university employee or not, additional security should be put in place to guard against anything happening to another person at the "U." The university should be put in lockdown, they advised.

Meanwhile, Johanna made up her mind to find Charlie and talk to him; first, however, she was going to see her attorney, John Wilson.

John Wilson long ago decided that to be a good attorney, he needed to not only earn respect, but he also needed to feel the pain and the joy of his clients. He has great empathy for his clients. In the field of criminal law, he had been a successful federal prosecutor and later a successful defense attorney; applying the knowledge and skill from his many years in the courtroom, John Wilson learned to not judge others by ethnicity, alleged criminal actions, or appearance. He represented his guilty clients as vigorously as he did the innocent ones. He believed in the American criminal justice system…for the most part!

John Wilson was outspoken about the "wrongs" of the justice system in the United States, and now in his later years, he was filled with total commitment to speak out when injustice was done or being committed. He had made enough money. He had helped a lot of people who needed competent legal advice. He had developed investigative and advocacy skills that imbued him with great confidence, underlaid with great humility. John Wilson was a lawyer's lawyer.

When he received a distress call from Johanna Johnson pleading to see him immediately, he had no thoughts of "Oh no, it's her again." What John Wilson heard on the other end of the telephone was a hysterical person who needed to talk to him. He made time for her. She went to see him right away. And Mr. Wilson knew what the call was no doubt about, for he had read the newspapers and had heard the newscasts.

Johanna was obviously distraught. Wilson quickly determined why she was there to see him. She was awash in tears and she was incoherent, short on facts, and could do little more than talk about the *The Sly Coyote* and the story that all but said Charlie Red Tail had murdered Jim Stoutwein. Attorney Wilson knew that Johanna Johnson cared a great deal about Charlie Red Tail and that she undoubtedly believed in him. When she said she wanted to hire him to represent Charlie if he was charged, Mr. Wilson assured her he would. Johanna said she had little money but could raise some from her family. Wilson said they would worry about that later. As the interview progressed, Wilson asked her if she knew anything about Charlie's conviction for rape. "I absolutely do not!" as she fought back tears and tried to control her shaking. She was obviously distressed by the fact he had been convicted of such a terrible crime; however, she knew in her heart of hearts that Charlie would not have done such a thing. She had spent many hours in tears and sorrow wrestling with the reporting and only knowing the facts reported in the media but not otherwise, except her love for Charlie.

It could be a motive for the murder, Mr. Wilson thought, but did not say.

CHAPTER 25

JOHANNA QUESTIONED

As she left the office of her attorney, the local police confronted her: "Are you Johanna Johnson?" Officer Nick Spencer gruffly asked her.

"Yes, I am, why do you ask?"

"Because we have information that you know Charlie Red Tail and we want to talk with you about the murder of James A. Stoutwein. You need to come with me to the police station."

"What? Are you kidding me?" She quickly thought of running back into Wilson's office.

"No, young lady, I am not. Now please cooperate with us and come downtown where we can talk with you."

John Wilson happened to gaze out the front window of his office. He saw Officer Nick Spencer, with whom he was acquainted, talking to Johanna. He went outside.

"Hi, Nick—what's happening here? This young lady is a client of mine."

"Oh, John, you no doubt read today's papers about the murder of college student James A. Stoutwein. We got a report that this girl knows Red Tail, has dated him, and we want to talk with her about what she may know. She's not a suspect but is a person of interest and could have some information that is important about Red Tail, who is the prime suspect at this time. A fraternity brother of the deceased told us she knows the Indian and that she knew the deceased."

"Well, I do represent her, Nick. Let me talk with her a little bit, and since she is not under arrest, after I have talked with her we will come down to the station and you can talk with her then, OK?"

"Sure, John. I probably shouldn't delay, but go ahead. Make it quick, as a really big manhunt is on for the Indian. I will wait in my squad car."

After the two of them talked for perhaps an hour while Officer Spencer became increasingly uneasy that he was allowing the attorney to talk with her at this point in time, John Wilson accompanied Johanna Johnson to the downtown police station. It was located downtown in the Municipal Building, a short drive from Wilson's office. They were seated in the interrogation room with a one-way window so others could hear and watch as a person was interrogated. Johanna was not to be "interrogated," as such, but rather, "interviewed." Officer Spencer conducted the "interview:"

"Miss Johnson, it is important you tell us the truth even though you are not under oath, for it is a crime to obstruct an investigation or lie to us even though you are not under oath. Do you understand that?"

"Yes, I do."

"You are not under arrest. We have been told you may have information regarding one Charlie Red Tail, an American Indian, who was enrolled at University of the West. We have information that you may know him. Miss Johnson, do you know Charlie Red Tail?"

"Yes, I do."

"How do you know him?"

"I was in a history class with him here at UWest, and we had a few coffees together and went out to dinner on one occasion."

"How many times and where?"

"Heck's. Dinner at Owl Inn."

"Have you seen him on other occasions?"

"Sure, I have seen him around campus."

"Did you know the deceased, James A. Stoutwein?"

"Yes, I did know him."

"How did you know him?"

"He asked me out for a date a couple of times. He lived at the Ranch House Fraternity on Mulberry Street. I live on Mulberry Street and walked by the fraternity going back and forth to school."

"To your knowledge, did Red Tail know Stoutwein?"

"No, I don't think so; however, I do recall one time after I had coffee with Charlie and we were leaving Heck's Coffee House, Stoutwein was with some of his buddies in one of the booths near the door and he started making crude remarks to me as we left. Nothing happened after that."

"OK, do you know of any reason Red Tail may have wanted to murder Stoutwein?

"Absolutely not! And I don't believe he did."

"Did you know Red Tail had been convicted of raping Stoutwein's sister several years ago?"

Johanna almost fainted as she was asked this again. She paused and looked at her attorney, who nodded a go ahead.

"I certainly don't know about any such rape. Charlie and I are not that close. He hasn't confided in me any such things."

"Do you know one Carlos Madrid?"

"Yes, I do."

"How do you know him?"

"From school."

"Do you know whether Madrid knows Red Tail?"

"Yes, I believe he does. I introduced him to Charlie one night in a park here in town."

"Do you know if they knew each other more than that?"

"No, I do not."

Johanna was shaken a bit by the questions about Madrid. She wondered how he came into the picture.

"Did Carlos Madrid tell you that Charlie and I are friends? How do you know Madrid?"

Officer Spencer told her, "I am not at liberty to tell you anything about that."

"Do you know where Charlie Red Tail is?"

"No, I do not."

"If you know anything else about either Red Tail or Mr.

Stoutwein than what you have told me, you should tell me."

Johanna did not reply. John Wilson and Johanna left the police station.

Johanna had felt she could not tell the officer about Charlie being at the EPS meeting, for it would expose her undercover assignment and also could jeopardize Charlie. She did not know of her own knowledge whether Charlie actually knew Madrid, other than when she introduced them at the park. She told the truth. The officers viewing the interrogation through the one-way window were not so sure.

As Johanna left the station, her thoughts quickly turned to the "rape." Could Charlie have done such a thing? She asked John Wilson if he could find out by reviewing the court records and prove Charlie innocent of the charge.

When she left Mr. Wilson, she told herself she must find Charlie before the authorities did.

John Wilson returned to his office for other work he needed to do, but he soon became aware he couldn't concentrate on anything but the Stoutwein murder and Charlie Red Tail. He intuitively thought to himself that the rape conviction would be important somehow, for perhaps Red Tail sought revenge in some way against Stoutwein.

Wilson began looking at newspapers of towns in the South Dakota area near the Horse Creek Reservation. He found an article in a Freedom Leader newspaper that detailed the trial of Red Tail. After reading the newspaper, Wilson knew he had a lot of work to do, as he had agreed to represent Red Tail if he were charged, and it certainly was beginning to look like it would happen.

He decided to go to Tihay to review the court file and transcripts from Charlie Red Tail's rape trial.

Despite the publicity about him, Charlie did not know of the murder or of the manhunt underway to find him. He was reaching to the stars in the Black Hills when he made some decisions about the vision, and about Johanna. He eventually left the forest and headed to the home of Ted Tomahawk to talk with Oscar Big Bull. He headed there with a brave heart, but with a childish anxiety. He had often talked with the great elder he respected and loved, because of the old man's wisdom, and he knew he would be welcomed. His beloved uncle was still recovering from his gunshot wound. The elder was dressed in white-man clothes, drinking coffee and eating a cookie. Charlie had fantasized he would find Oscar Red Bull dressed in beaded deerskin and with a head-dress of eagle feathers. Charlie knew that the era he was pic-turing in his mind had long ago left the Indian culture, but he longed for the peace and tranquility he once knew years before, when they lived on the island in the river and still had the Sun Dance to pray for all of the world and the universe. Charlie had been taught many things by the storytellers and wondered if he would now be taught anything new to help him handle the pressure he was feeling because of the vision of his grandmother and the uncertainties in his heart.

Charlie told the old man of the vision he now felt he was expected to carry out to completion, but the feeling he also had that it would be wrong in his mind to do so and accomplish little to make things right for those who had lost their lands to the government. The old man, because of his wisdom, already knew of Grandmother Yellow Bird's vision and the passing of the vision to Charlie Red Tail. He understood how the vision would be difficult for this young boy of peace. They talked for a considerable amount of time while passing back and forth the tobacco-filled pipe, and then the old man spoke.

"My son, only the Great Spirit can guide you on what to do and how now to act."

The wise elder told Charlie a story:

"Long ago, a warrior of our tribe received a vision that made him feel as though he should be angry, although he did not feel angry; to have hatred in his heart although he loved all of the people, including the white man; that he should fight with all his strength against the white men who had broken the treaties with the Indian people; to count many coup. But the warrior thought that would be foolish and wrong. After the warrior listened to an elder of the tribe, he did as he said and went to the sweat lodge to make his body clean; then he went naked except for his moccasins and breech-cloth to the highest hill he could find, Spirit Mound, there to face the sun for five days. He ate no food, had no water, and was bare to the elements of heat, cold and wind; he stayed erect and in his position while he sought the guidance of the Great Spirit and prayed that he could see clearly what he was to do. An eagle suddenly appeared overhead.

The eyes of the Great Spirit. The warrior had a mysterious feeling that came within him. He felt that the weight of the boulder had been put off him. He felt the highest happiness. When he returned from the summit, the brave entered the sweat lodge without speaking. Then cleansed, he followed his life's road, now in a different direction, and was at peace."

The next day, Charlie went to the sweat lodge to cleanse his body, and then to Spirit Mound for five days and nights. As he survived the struggle of the elements and of the hunger and thirst, Charlie Red tail stood in awe and humility. The sky opened to him. He saw overhead a bald eagle—the eyes of the Great Spirit—and he listened. He returned to the sweat lodge.

He was at peace. Not totally. He knew he needed to explain to Grandmother Yellow Bird why he had made the decision to not pursue retaliation for the construction of the dam. So, he went back to the dam. He knelt in the black dirt and took back the obsidian stone he had buried there. He stood erect. Hands to the sky. A tear in his eye. He talked to his grandmother and explained. Charlie Red Tail heard a voice: "I understand. Go forth."

He did so, and never looked back. He was excited for life and what might lie ahead for him. "I have a real chance for love and service." Johanna entered his mind in a mysterious way. Somehow, he felt different in his heart.

CHAPTER 26

A DESPERATE ROAD TRIP

Johanna decided to drive to the Horse Creek Reservation after having seen John Wilson and being questioned by the police. She had no idea what she was doing, only that she wanted to find Charlie before the authorities did. At the same time, she was conflicted as to why she wanted to see Charlie, for she couldn't resolve in her mind why she felt so warmly toward him after all that had gone on with him, including the EPS surprise meeting and the disappointment she had from it; however, she acknowledged that before she learned of his conviction for rape, she felt she truly loved him. She did not know what she would say or do when she found him, only that she had an irresistible urge to see him before what was going to probably happen—his being arrested—actually happened. She knew she could not help him escape or anything like that, or she would be breaking the law. So, she decided if she found Charlie, she would not tell him of the publicity surrounding the murder of Stoutwein, but rather, would talk to him about EPS and the "rape." And about him and her. What would ultimately come of it, of course she did not know, but she was hopeful that Charlie could explain away some of the disturbing information she had learned from the news article and from the EPS meeting Charlie attended.

She had never been to this part of the country before, the reservation area, and immediately took notice of the rolling hills seductive beauty, the tall grasses and the oak trees, wild turkeys slowly moving away from bushes guarding the road, deer grazing on hillsides. She immediately felt welcome in the scenery and all she was seeing. She felt at home and not afraid. She was not agitated, but not at peace, either—just driven by her feelings about Charlie that forced her forward to whatever was ahead.

She gazed at the stars and listened to the sounds of the prairie as she slept in her car that night, alone with her thoughts and the sky above. A lone coyote's howl comforted her.

When she arrived at the tribal headquarters early the next morning, she was not aware the law enforcement authorities were to start a few hours later from the courthouse in Indian Mound County and drive to the reservation, to also find Charlie.

The staff told her they did not know where Charlie might be, other than perhaps at Ted Tomahawk's and Oscar Big Bull's. The elder had recently gotten home from the hospital and was living with Charlie's other uncle. The administrators at the headquarters were somewhat suspicious about why this white girl was looking for their fellow tribesman; however, they gave Johanna directions to find the house, located many miles from tribal headquarters, on Old Woman Creek, near where Oscar Big Bull's cabin was located, where he was shot by the white man.

Johanna quickly became aware that the road to Old Woman Creek was more a trail than a road, rough and not maintained, over undulating hills and then through open plains. Rocky. Rutted. She was glad she was driving a Jeep. She found the place, though, a run-down cabin at the location that had been described to her. She saw a pickup parked there that had a University of the West parking sticker on the back bumper. Her pulse ran fast. She shut off her car, grasped the steering wheel, and prayed. She knocked on the door. Charlie was there! With a look of amazement, Charlie exclaimed, "Johanna, what are you doing here?" He reached out his hand to her, and she took it as he brought her into the place of his uncles and introduced both uncles to her.

Oscar Big Bull broke into a wide, warm smile and said, "This is the girl you have told me about? She is very pretty. Come sit down, and I will fix some coffee for us."

"That is very kind of you," Johanna said, "but I need to talk with Charlie in private and I am short on time. I need to get back to Three Creeks very soon. Please forgive me. Charlie, could we go outside and talk?"

The two young people from such different backgrounds

sat on a big rock that was on the bank of Old Woman Creek, decorated with lichen of pink, orange, and green. The creek was trickling and the sound of the water over pebbles and rocks joined the birds in the oak trees to serenade them.

"Why did you come here, Johanna?" Charlie asked tenderly while looking into her searching eyes. He knew he had left her the last time they were together with questions unanswered.

She hesitated. He said nothing more.

"Because I care about you, and I have been afraid something bad had happened to you. You abruptly left me, dropped out of school, and have been gone a long time. I had thought we were getting on pretty good, and then you left without another word."

Johanna stood up in front of Charlie and impulsively hugged him. Charlie hugged her also as Johanna began to whimper. "Let's go for a walk," Charlie finally said, and they slowly walked along the creek to the draw up the way, where they were truly alone.

They sat quietly for some time.

"Charlie, do you care for me? I care for you," Johanna said softly. "I need to know how you feel toward me so I can put some thoughts about us together and get some answers to some questions that I have. If you want for me to bug out of your life, just say so. If caring feelings are not mutual, so be it. But if you really like me and want to spend time with me, you need to say so."

There was a long silence again, at the end of which

Johanna stood up to leave. "Johanna, I do like you a lot. I haven't been able to show it more than I have, because there are some things about me that I am afraid would drive you away from me--" he paused "--forever." Charlie hesitated, wanting to find the right words. "I don't have a lot to offer you for hope of a relationship with me, because of a few things in my life that you may not understand. And for the last few years, I have lived in two worlds—the white man's and my people's. I don't know that you could understand what has happened to me, the challenges in my life, and the challenges for you if you join me in a relationship."

His words hung in the air like fluttering birds for a short time, and then settled in with Johanna.

"I hear what you are saying, and"- Charlie interrupted and began to tell Johanna with considerable detail about his grandmother's vision and the obligation to fulfill her wishes that he had just recently refused to honor; about the false accusation of rape and his imprisonment; of the loneliness of prison; about the hoodlums in prison and their demands on him regarding drug distribution on the reservation, and the beating he suffered for refusing to agree to help them victimize his people.

Charlie told Johanna of his fear for his people if Big Bill's or someone else's plan for distribution of drugs on the reservation came about. He told her his dream of becoming a law enforcement officer and returning to the reservation to help his people, about his need to be close to nature and the outdoors, and his religious beliefs in the natural world; about his mother and father and their early deaths, and his being educated in Indian Schools to not be Indian, but to live by the white man's ways. He also told her why he had attended meetings of the EPS. And he told her how he feared from the first day he met her that none of this would be anything she would want in her life and would understand if it was revealed to her, or she somehow found out about his past. Charlie told her all of this over a couple of hours while she listened, quietly and with love, shadowing her deep empathy.

The story he was telling was difficult for him to relate to her and, remarkably, throughout his stunted dialogue, she sat quietly and listened intently without interruption, desperately wanting to understand. This was not easy for Johanna, either.

He then looked deep into her eyes, took her hands in his, and at that moment she knew he cared deeply about her. Her heart began filling with joy, his with warm feelings, but also with some apprehension and uncertainty, as it may have been love and not just warm feelings.

Charlie questioned whether he should have told her all these things, as he was unsure how she would react when she had time to think about what she was being told. He felt reasonably confident he could trust her and that it was OK to have shared so much of his life with her. He also realized he didn't know much about her and her life.

"I need to know you better, Johanna. Will you share with me about your life?"

Johanna sat in deep thought for a while. Then she said:

"Charlie, I have been a loved child by my parents, who are both still alive, although my father is not in good health. My mother is well educated and has worked for years as a bank vice president. My father was, and still is, involved at a high level in the coal industry. I have had many wonderful opportunities in life, not all of which I have appreciated. I received a first-class high-school education in the East. I have raised hell regarding the desecration of the environment and how we treat it, because I believe Mother Earth is sacred and it was given to us to take care of by the God in whom I believe, and society has not treated it in that way. I am earning my degree in elementary education and hope to teach in a school where the young kids have been neglected and are without many advantages in life. I am honest and want to be trusting of those around me and give back to my country what I can for the many opportunities I have had in life. I too love the outdoors and all its creatures and want to do my part to protect it. I draw much strength from the natural world."

Johanna paused a few moments before continuing; then she looked Charlie directly in the eye. Charlie did not look away. "And I feel deeply about you, because since we first knew each other in Pickenpaugh's history class, I felt your passion about the way your people have been treated—I could feel your soul, and I admired it and felt—this is a person who is not only really good looking, but a guy with principles and beliefs that are courageous and with which I want to identify. When we went to coffee and to dinner and I was with you I felt like a million bucks, proud to be with you, for you were not only interesting, but also a listener, and kind. I think I have been in love with you ever since then, but I know we must get to know each other a lot better and share with each other for a longer period of time."

They were comfortable in each other's arms. There on the plains of Dakota, along Old Woman Creek, they continued to share their lives, disappointments, goals, and aspirations. At that moment, each hoped to share the future together.

They walked back to the cabin and to Johanna's car. She kissed Charlie goodbye, then promptly got in her car and drove away. She looked longingly in the mirror at Charlie standing outside the cabin and wondered what was going to happen to him—and to them. She had not been able to bring herself to tell Charlie about the Stoutwein murder and the manhunt.

She was sure Charlie had told her the truth about the past.

As Johanna drove back down the rough road and reached the highway that went to Three Creeks, she saw coming toward her at a high rate of speed several vehicles with red lights flashing. As she passed them, she could see they were not emergency vehicles but were sheriff's cars. She cried, "Oh no!" and instead of driving to Three Creeks, she headed to her parents' home for refuge and understanding.

CHAPTER 27

PLANS DISRUPTED

Charlie's past and his future were finally being reconciled—prison was behind him, he was now enrolled in college, he was in love, and most importantly, he was at peace with his decision regarding his grandmother's vision. The future was looking much brighter! As he had often done in his life, he decided to celebrate his happy state of mind by communing with nature. He decided he would go to Coyote Hill to spend a few days camping there and then to go to his cave in the Black Hills for a few more days before heading back to Three Creeks to find work until the next semester began at UWest. But before going back to the university, Charlie decided he would visit his best friend, Tom Big Horse, whom he had not seen for several months. He wanted to share with his friend the decision he had made about the vision of his grandmother. With excitement and anticipation in his heart, Charlie also wanted to tell his best friend Tom about Johanna and him. He and his uncles said goodbye.

As Charlie went outside his uncle's cabin, he noticed dust in the distance and vehicles driving toward the cabin on Old Woman Creek. Then he noticed the red lights flashing atop one of the vehicles. "Uncle, come here! Hurry!" When his uncle joined him outside the cabin, the vehicles were just pulling into the driveway. Doors slammed, and several men jumped out of the vehicles with guns at the ready. The guns were pointed at Charlie and his uncle. One of the men called out, "Charlie Red Tail, get on your knees with your hands up! Oscar Big Bull, stand away!" The men scattered, to surround Charlie and his uncle. Uncle Ted Tomahawk was not at the cabin.

Oscar Big Bull moved away and Charlie went to his knees with his hands in the air, his pulse pounding as he thought, Oh no, not again!

"Charlie Red Tail, you are under arrest for the murder of James A. Stoutwein," one of the officers screamed.

Charlie yelled back, "What are you talking about? I haven't murdered anybody. You can't do this to me! You must be mistaken. I have not murdered anybody!"

The armed officers closed in. Charlie and his uncle did not move. When two of the officers reached Charlie, they screamed at him, "Put your hands behind your back, you damn Indian! You are under arrest. You have the right to remain silent, et cetera." Charlie was thus partially told his constitutional rights.

Uncle Oscar Big Bull said, "Charlie not a killer. He's not

killed anybody. You doing wrong a second time against this man."

"Oh yeah, old man? Then he can prove his innocence," replied Indian Mound County Sheriff Tex Brutkowsky.

Charlie was placed in a squad car and the posse of law enforcement returned to Tihay. There, in the same cell where he had previously been unjustly held, Charlie would be held again, until his initial appearance before a magistrate, and no doubt for a long time, as he would no doubt have a large bail set and he would not be able to raise it to secure his temporary freedom. He feared he would not receive justice—just like the last time.

The local Freedom Leader was waiting at the jail. The news of the arrest with added color as to where the arrest occurred and the Indian reservation involved was soon on the wire services and used in news programs on television and radio throughout the region.

Charlie Red Tail felt like Chief Sitting Bull at his time in history, a similar time when justice was still a long way off and beyond reach for an Indian. And he felt ashamed of the grief he would now cause Johanna.

CHAPTER 28

LOVE AT HOME

Theodore and Anna Johnson lived in a lovely home in Moose Lake, Wyoming. Ted Johnson had been a very good provider to his family, and he had reached the top of prestige and profit in the coal industry, thereby experiencing respect and stature in the coal town of Moose Lake and in the industry that supplied much of the needs of the country for electricity and power. Neither he nor his wife were arrogant in their success or elitist in their dealings with others, or with minorities and the less fortunate. The Johnsons passed those qualities to their only child, Johanna, who long ago also added to her character the qualities of loyalty and gratitude. She was about to add the quality of being a fighter against injustice. Her parents watched the evening news during the evening Johanna arrived, but did not see her at that time. She arrived very late at night and went straight to bed and did not see her parents that night. Her parents saw the news report on the arrest of Charlie Red Tail. They were a bit shocked, for they were hearing of another crime involving a white and an Indian, and they agreed it was such a sad commentary on an otherwise wonderful state like South Dakota. The Johnsons had for many years contributed to Indian charities and schools, had worked on reservations with Habitat for Humanity, and they were always saddened when a young Indian was involved with some crime. They viewed such incidents as tragic, for they had much sympathy for the plight of the Native Americans. In their minds, the reservations were ill suited for fostering acceptance by the whites of the Native Americans. In their minds, the Indian people did not receive a fair shake from white society. And though they felt that life for reservation residents has improved in recent years, poverty and other life challenges remained a big problem for many of them.

Johanna had not previously told her parents about Charlie and her feelings for him, for she had been waiting until an appropriate time. Now she needed to do so. At breakfast the following morning, she did so with no compunction or regret. She had always enjoyed an open, honest relationship with her folks, except during the time she was estranged from her dad over environmental differences, so though not being entirely comfortable, she believed her folks would understand where she was coming from and the deep feelings she has for Charlie Red Tail.

"Mom and Dad, I have something really important to talk with you about."

"Great, honey—what is it?" replied her dad.

"Yes, dear, is it something to do with school? Do you have a new boyfriend?" asked her mother, who was always interested in her daughter's social life.

For Johanna, her mother's question was a perfect segue into her increasingly complicated relationship with Charlie.

"Well, as a matter of fact, it does pertain to a new boyfriend. His name is Charlie Red Tail."

There was a long pause. Her mother looked at Johanna's dad. Johanna's dad looked at Johanna's mother, each with startled eyes. They both looked at Johanna with a blank stare. Both parents immediately recalled the name of the young Indian arrested for murder, the young boy they had seen on television last night. Johanna's folks did not know what to say as the uncomfortable silence continued.

Finally, Johanna began to tell her parents the whole story about Charlie and her. Johanna's sadness eventually became her parents'. When she finished telling them about what was going on with her and Charlie, and about Charlie being arrested for murder, her parents, of course, expressed many concerns. There were many questions, much agony, and a lot of probing by her folks, but Johanna answered them straight away, expounding on her feelings for Charlie, their meeting on the reservation just yesterday, and her involvement in retaining John Wilson to represent Charlie if he were caught and charged.

Finally, Johanna's mother said, "Charlie sounds like a fine young man. I can understand why you feel so strongly about him, but the circumstances he faces are very threatening and, I am sure, quite scary for you. I, of course, am concerned about you and how this may affect you."

After several hours of tense attention by each of them to the others, Johanna asked her folks to help finance Charlie's legal defense. Her dad said to her, "Johanna, I hear your feelings toward this man. I can tell from your description of him and of your relationship with him that he is someone special in your eyes. Of course, because we love you more than anything in this world, we want to help you in any way that is possible and reasonable. You are old enough and mature enough to know if your feelings are true and not some kind of infatuation. I cannot second-guess you. Although I have only hope that your feelings are justified, I in no way will doubt they are real to you and that you must act on Charlie's behalf. From what you tell us, there is no way this fellow raped and murdered. In other words, your mom and I must trust you and what you have told us. Give your mother and me some time to think about whether we can help. OK?"

After a sustained period of time, to Johanna--an eternity, her parents had an answer for her: "Johanna, we have the money to pay the attorney and we are happy to do so; however, we think it important that all of us go to meet with him to show the support you have in hiring him for this heavy matter." Johanna's mother nodded "yes" in agreement with what her husband said. "Is that OK with you, my dear?"

Johanna broke down in tears and felt deeply the hugs of her dad and her mom.

CHAPTER 29

LAWYER WILSON, AGAIN

Following Johanna's call to John Wilson the next day, the Johnsons left Moose Lake and drove to Three Creeks to see Wilson.

Wilson was pleased to greet them, and he began to talk with them about what he had been doing since Johanna asked him to represent Charlie. He was careful to not mention his representation of Johanna on her undercover assignment.

"When we met last time, Johanna, you asked me to represent Charlie. The police were outside my office and wanted to question you regarding Charlie. A fraternity brother of Mr. Stoutwein had told the police about you and Charlie. I assume you have told your parents all of this and about your feelings toward Charlie, or they wouldn't be here. Let me explain to you and to them what I have been up to and where I see this matter going forward."

"You are correct, Mr. Wilson, that Johanna has told us

about her and Charlie," Johanna's dad interrupted. "Her mother and I want to help with this terrible situation, and we are willing to pay you for your assistance. Johanna has told us how she feels, and what Charlie has told her. We believe our daughter and want to help in any way possible."

"I am pleased to represent Charlie, as Johanna has asked. I must explain a few ethical matters to you before we begin in any substance discussing Charlie. I can represent Charlie only if he requests that I do so. I need to talk with him, and I would expect to go right away to Tihay, where he is being held. Assuming he will allow me to represent him, I will do so on a pro bono basis. This young man is entitled to representation as best we can give him. I will not charge him or you for my services. If you are in agreement, however, I would appreciate your taking care of my expenses that will be incurred. Is that agreeable with you?

"Of course, it is," Mr. Johnson replied, "but we are agreeable to paying your fees in addition to your expenses, just so you understand. Your willingness to represent Charlie without charge is not necessary, but I understand what you are saying and certainly admire you for it."

"Well, it is the responsibility of lawyers to help those who cannot pay for services, and I am happy to do so in this case. I am sure Mr. Red Tail cannot pay any fees. Also, I think a lot of your daughter and want to help her as well; however, I need to tell you that I cannot discuss with you what Charlie tells me without his authorization to do so, as he is the client, and he has attorney-client privilege regarding his entire case.

You all need to know that, because when you ask certain questions of me, I will answer only when that is appropriate. I can keep Johanna aware of the status of the case and where we are from time to time with any charges, but I cannot share any client confidences without his permission.

"I should also add that I have already begun looking into the alleged rape conviction of Charlie and I am reasonably sure he did not rape Betsy Stoutwein. When the time is right, I will seek to overturn that conviction or seek a pardon for him. But for now, I will need to begin investigating the murder charge against him, which I am sure is forthcoming—in fact, I learned this morning that it will be filed soon. In my mind, any charges will no doubt be based entirely on his alleged rape conviction and its supposedly furnishing a motive for the killing and thus his arrest. I am quite sure every white person in Indian Mound County believes he is guilty of both crimes.

"It could be that when Charlie has his initial appearance in court, bail may be set at a level where he can pay it, but I really don't hold out any hope that will be the case. If it is reasonable in amount, perhaps you, Mr. Johnson, could help with it. Any questions?"

Thus, Charlie Red Tail would be represented by a very competent lawyer and have the support of a very significant person in his life, and of her family. If justice could be done, Charlie had a chance despite the prejudice and public outcry against him.

The Johnsons left his office, and John Wilson left for

Tihay soon thereafter. He knew the first thing he needed to do was to interview his client and give him some hope that the legal system this time would have to treat him fairly. Wilson was stressed over the injustice of the other case involving Charlie and the possibility that this effort was going to be a trying case for him to handle, due to the obvious prejudice that had been present in the first case and would no doubt be present in this one. At the same time, Wilson was a very good lawyer. His professional experience and success not only permitted him to accept the challenge with eagerness, but to also expect that justice would ultimately prevail. He was determined to put himself totally into the case and give Charlie Red Tail the very best defense he could receive.

The difficulty of the case immediately presented itself upon Wilson's arrival in Tihay and his picking up the latest edition of the local paper, the *Freedom Leader*.

Blazoned across the front page in large letters: "INDIAN RAPIST STRIKES AGAIN, SAY AUTHORITIES." The article quoted Tex Brutkowsky, the Indian Mound County Sheriff, as saying, "Charlie Red Tail was arrested on the Horse Creek Reservation, after a terrible fight, for the murder of Jim Stoutwein," and that "the Indian had previously been convicted here in Indian Mound County for raping the victim's sister." The story went into detail concerning the rape trial, the prominence of the victim's family, and the sentence meted out to the Indian. The paper also reported that Charlie Red Tail had been released from prison after serving "a lenient sentence." Sheriff Brutkowsky told the *Freedom Leader*, "the motive for the murder is probably that the Indian did not like Jim Stoutwein telling the jury here in the county the truth about the Indian harming his sister."

Jim Wilson knew not what might await him in Tihay, for he had never been there before, nor was he aware of the area's history. Nevertheless, he immediately headed to the county jail to see Charlie, but first to confront the sheriff about his prejudicial comments to the newspaper. The attorney knew he was headed into a fight of some sort and had the hope he could handle it. He had resolve, but also more than a few butterflies in his stomach accompanying the professional challenge Wilson knew lay ahead.

Before going inside, the attorney took several photos of the jail, the gallows starkly portrayed to the side, the statue in front, and the surrounding buildings. Wilson intuitively knew that the jail and its symbolic gallows was a centerpiece of this historical Western town, maintained with pride for the tourists, for sure, but really for the assurance of the people that this was still a "law and order" town.

Wilson entered the jail and was greeted by the sheriff himself, who had been watching him from behind his desk and taking note of his actions. Wilson quickly saw that Brutkowsky was a mustached, tall, heavyset man with a cowboy hat on his head, a badge on his shirt, and his boots on the desk—a man who could have been a US Marshal back in time; at least his appearance gave that impression.

"Sheriff, I am John Wilson, an attorney. I am here to see

Charlie Red Tail, who I understand is being held in your jail."

"Oh boy, you look like a big-city type. You are sure here in a hurry, aren't you?" A pause. "The redskin sure as hell is here in my jail, and he is going to stay here until the feds tell me otherwise." Pause. "Sure, I suppose you want to talk with the brave. You are going to try and get this guilty buck off of this murder, ain't you? Well—if I could, I would tell you to get the hell out of here, but since I can't, I will let you see him. I am going to search you first. Do you have any identification? And you better not be long, as I need to go to lunch. Got it?"

"Sheriff, with all due respect, the stuff you told to the local newspaper was very prejudicial to my client. That kind of pre-trial prejudice may come back and bite you in the ass. You are forewarned. If you persist in trying my client from your office and in the press, I will put you in front of the court and seek a reprimand. Got it?"

"Listen, you slimeball, you best watch your back. You will not be popular in this neck of the woods. You big-city, pious frauds are known for what you are in these parts. Your sway doesn't amount to much in my county, and if you threaten me again, you will be the one behind those bars."

"So be it. Now open up his cell and let me see my client."

Charlie was alone in the smelly, cramped cell at the rear of the jail building. His cell had no windows and only a small steel cot to sleep on, with one ratty blanket that looked as if it hadn't been washed for some time. The only other fixture was a smelly metal latrine. He had seen it before. Charlie looked really tired and drawn. To Wilson, he looked like a man unable to move very well—gaunt, and without expression. He wondered whether Charlie had been beaten up by the authorities but saw no marks on him that could be seen without closer examination. Charlie did not look Wilson in the eye, of course. He said nothing. He received Wilson with no emotion, until he was told who Wilson was and that he had been asked by Johanna Johnson to represent him. When Charlie was told of that good news, a noticeable glimmer of a smile came across the young man's face, but he did not speak.

John Wilson advised Charlie to not talk loudly, but to whisper to him if it was OK for the attorney to represent him, which Charlie immediately did. The attorney explained that Charlie would be taken before a court at about 3:00 that afternoon to have bail set and that it would be very high, and then he would be brought back to the cell. Wilson took notes as he asked Charlie many, many questions about his background, education, possible alibi defenses and accounting for his whereabouts for the last many days. He told him to talk with no one about anything having to do with the charges and not to talk with law enforcement at all without Wilson present. He asked Charlie if there were any relatives or friends that Wilson should notify about what was happening. He explained to Charlie in detail his constitutional rights. He assured him that at all proceedings, Wilson would be present; that he should answer "not guilty" when asked for his plea by the magistrate; that Johanna was doing fine and would be coming to see him soon; that he would be kept advised of what was happening with his case and that if he was ever mistreated, to remember to tell him when they were together the next time.

At 3:00 that afternoon, Charlie was taken in prison garb, leg irons and handcuffs to the court by the sheriff, this being witnessed by throngs of screaming residents, where he pleaded "not guilty" and bond was set at $500,000 cash. The preliminary hearing was set for a month later.

When the court session was over, Wilson turned to Charlie and whispered, "I know you did not rape the Stoutwein girl. I believe you did not murder her brother."

Charlie said to Wilson, "Please tell Johanna and Oscar Red Bull I am doing OK. Tell my uncle I didn't feed his dog before they came and arrested me."

CHAPTER 30

FIGHT FOR JUSTICE BEGINS

Attorney John Wilson had dug deep into the law enforcement and court files on Charlie. For now, he felt
he knew enough about the arrest, trial, and the sentence
on the rape trial. He had formed some preliminary opinions. He vowed he would come back to it at a later time.
Right now, he had a more immediate issue to attack—
the wrongful arrest of Charlie for the Stoutwein murder.
Charlie was remaining in jail on a trumped-up charge,
as far as Wilson was concerned. There was no evidence
implicating Red Tail in the murder—none whatsoever, in
Wilson's mind. Charlie had been arrested without probable cause existing for his arrest. Hell, there wasn't even an
arrest warrant issued. No, Wilson knew in his own mind
that Red Tail had been arrested and charged based on his
rape conviction and the prejudice of the whites in Indian
Mound County, including the person who took a shot at

him and Anderson. Wilson looked again at the indentation on the lock of his suitcase that had stopped a bullet in the racist town of Tihay. "That crazy stunt is another that must be investigated," Wilson said to himself, and he resolved to somehow find out who fired the shot that almost killed him or Anderson.

Since it had not been determined yet what court had jurisdiction for the murder, Wilson decided he needed to try and get Charlie out of jail in Indian Mound County.

Wilson filed three motions in Judge Remington's court. One motion was to recuse Judge Thomas Remington, which would have the effect of automatically disqualifying Remington from sitting on the case, including the motion. Wilson was concerned about what other judge might be assigned to hear the motion, but felt the step had to be taken, for it was clear from Wilson's reading of transcripts of the rape trial that Remington was biased, pro-prosecution, and anti-Indian. The second motion was one seeking to have the murder charge dismissed, based on Charlie's unlawful arrest in violation of the Fourth Amendment to the United States Constitution and the Constitution of the State of South Dakota. The third motion was one of habeas corpus, seeking to have Charlie immediately released for being wrongfully held by the authorities.

The defense attorney asked for an expedited hearing and subpoenaed the arresting officers and Charlie's uncle, Oscar Red Bull. Wilson hoped Remington would be recused and the hearing would be before an impartial judge who would give Charlie a fair ruling on the motions and a fair trial if the motions were denied; however, Wilson would argue that if a trial were to happen, it must be held in a different location, in federal court before a federal judge.

CHAPTER 31

INVESTIGATIONS MARCH ON

Agent Anderson had been chosen to be in charge of the investigation. Obviously, he was not "in control" of the investigative forces, as he knew nothing of the arrest of Charlie Red Tail until he read about it in the newspaper. He immediately called the Indian Mound County sheriff, Tex Brutkowsky. The FBI agent pointed out to the sheriff that the FBI was in charge and the appropriate venue for a trial might not be his county. After being briefed by Brutkowsky, Anderson thought, *I did not hear any facts constituting probable cause for Red Tail's arrest. On what grounds did they arrest him? All he heard from the sheriff in response to his question was that a big-city lawyer had already been at the jail, that the smart-ass was pushing his luck in Indian Mound County just by being there and appearing in court so early in the case.* He was told the lawyer was John Wilson.

The FBI had moved quickly to preserve the scene where the body of Stoutwein was found; however, there was no clothing or jewelry on the body—only his cowboy boots. Anderson found no evidence on the body that could help lead him to the killer, other than what a forensics expert might be able to tell him about the instrument that was used to stab the back, cut the victim's throat, and scalp the poor soul.

No, Anderson really had nothing—no good evidence to go on. He decided he needed to get up to Tihay to interrogate Red Tail. He called his old friend and former federal prosecutor, John Wilson, who, he understood from Sheriff Brutkowsky, was representing Red Tail. Anderson wanted to see if he could question Red Tail. Wilson consented, even though allowing his client to talk with an officer at this stage of the proceedings was not something he would generally permit. He agreed this time because he knew what Charlie had to say and that nothing in what Charlie or Johanna had told him implicated Charlie in the murder; however, Wilson told Anderson he would need to be present during the interrogation and that it had to be conducted somewhere else than in the jail where Charlie was incarcerated. Anderson agreed to abide by Wilson's terms. They agreed to meet at the Cattlemen's Hotel in Tihay in three days.

Rex Anderson and John Wilson respected each other and each totally trusted the other to not resort to BS or misleading information. On the other hand, there was no doubt on the part of either man that each would professionally do his respective job without cutting slack for the other, nor giving an inch on what was needed or expected from the other. They had often worked on the same side of justice while Wilson was an Assistant United States Attorney with the United States Department of Justice. That fact meant nothing more than each would do his best in this case to achieve justice.

When Anderson and Wilson met at the Cattlemen's Hotel, they greeted each other with affection, but spent little time reminiscing. They quickly went to the jail to move Charlie to a room in the hotel for questioning. The jail had no place to talk without others overhearing, and in fact, there really was no place for anyone to sit. The hotel room was secured by the FBI. It was on the second floor of the hotel and had a good view of the town square below. Luxurious it was not, but it did have three wooden chairs. Wallpaper from another time adorned the walls.

Wilson privately explained to Charlie what was happening and that he could answer all questions put to him that he, Wilson, did not verbally object to. He was to pause before answering a question, and then he was to only answer the question he was asked. "For example, if you are asked 'what time is it' don't tell him what kind of watch it is, when you received it, etc. Just answer the question asked. If you do not understand the question, tell him and he will rephrase it. Keep your answers brief."

Charlie's answers were not under oath, but Anderson

quickly perceived Charlie to be telling him the truth. He spoke clearly, directly, and answered the questions without hesitation or equivocation.

The facts Anderson got from Charlie were the same as the ones he had given to Wilson, although Anderson did not know that. Nothing Anderson was told incriminated Charlie in the murder, at least based on what Anderson was hearing and what he knew to date about the crime.

Agent Anderson knew, of course, that Johanna Johnson was working with him on the EPS investigation. He had just been told by Charlie of his relationship with Johanna, and he had a transcript of the interrogation of Johanna by Officer Spencer that covered their relationship. He decided to follow up with other questions of "who," "what," "where," and "when." The skilled agent grilled Charlie, forward and backwards, expecting to find out all he could about Charlie, the rape conviction, and his relationship with Jim Stoutwein. Anderson was aware of the clean record Charlie had while in prison and knew from the warden at the penitentiary, who was not a "bleeding heart," that Charlie was smart, well educated, and was a caring person who often was there for others who needed friendship. The young man was harassed at times for being an Indian; he handled those insults without loss of control, but at the same time standing up for himself.

Agent Anderson wanted to know more about Charlie's relationship with Johanna Johnson. Charlie told him, without equivocation or exaggeration. It quickly became apparent to both Anderson and Wilson that there was an excitement and a respect in Charlie's mind that could arise only from one having and expressing sincere, caring thoughts, uncomplicated by the events of the day.

Anderson also zeroed in on Johanna's friend at the Environmental Protection Society, Carlos Madrid. But he made no mention of the EPS or from where he got the name.

"Do you know one Carlos Madrid?"

"Yes."

"How do you know him?"

"I was introduced to him by Johanna when we were in a park in town while I was going to UWest." Charlie forgot Wilson's advice and said more than the question required in the way of an answer. "He seemed to be a bit jealous of me being with Johanna."

Wilson interrupted. "Rex, I don't know where you are headed with these questions, but I don't see that they have anything to do with this murder case." He was fishing to find out why both Spencer and Anderson were interested in Madrid.

"Well, I don't know that it does, but I need to cover all the bases. His answer may lead someplace for me."

"How could you tell that?" Anderson continued, as Wilson made a mental note to learn more about Madrid from Johanna.

"He seemed angry. He looked at me in a funny way, like he didn't like seeing me there with Johanna. That's all."

"Do you know how Johanna knows Madrid?"

"She said she had dated him a few times."

"OK. I think that is all the questions I have of you at this time."

Back at the jail, Wilson said to Anderson, "Rex, you see the condition of the cell that Charlie is in. It is deplorable. And it is not even clear that he should be incarcerated here, for we don't know where the crime was committed. Can you arrange to have him transferred to the federal holding center in Three Creeks? The victim was found in that location, and at least for now, it may be that a US Attorney's office will prosecute the case against Red Tail, or the prosecutor there in our county. Quite frankly, there is so much prejudice in this area against the Indians, he would be safer someplace else. In Three Creeks, I would also have better access to him for sure. What do you say?"

"Yeah, that all makes sense to me too. He wouldn't be jailed here had the locals not jumped the gun and rushed to the reservation. And I am aware of the racial problems in this area. Let's see what I can do."

As Rex Anderson and John Wilson left the jail, the crack of a rifle shot rang out! Both men hit the ground. "Are you hit, John?" Anderson whispered.

"No, I don't think so," replied Wilson.

The two men crawled on hands and knees back to the jail, where the sheriff had ducked behind his desk with his revolver at the ready. "I think it came from the second story across the street, at the J.C. Penney store. It has apartments on the second story and windows that look out on the square," the excited sheriff exclaimed. "I did not see who shot, but I'll bet it was one of those ranchers that have been clamoring that the Indian be hung. I'll call for some backup." The FBI agents who had accompanied Anderson to Tihay hurried back to the hotel.

After a few minutes, the two law enforcement men snuck around to the back of the store across the street, climbed the outside stairs, and cautiously stalked the second-floor rooms, one by one, but found nothing, not even a shell casing. There was one open window facing the door to the jail. Anderson alerted the Bureau. The sheriff returned to his office.

John Wilson's briefcase buckle had deflected the bullet apparently meant for him, the defender of Charlie Red Tail. The leather case contained Charlie's file; the indentation on the lock would be a reminder going forward of how dangerous this criminal defense would be.

Arrangements were immediately made by Anderson to have Red Tail transferred to the federal holding facility in Three Creeks. Brutkowsky objected but had no superior authority in the matter, and he later made that fact clear to the willing ear of the newspaper reporter who inquired. After all, Brutkowsky needed to make sure his electors knew it wasn't by his doing that the "redskin" was removed from his jail due to concerns for the guy's safety and the inadequate facility in which to hold him.

Undeterred by the sniper attack at Tihay, Rex Anderson moved vigorously forward to further investigate the murder of the body at the dump. While awaiting the autopsy report and the results on the padlock and chain submitted to the FBI lab in Quantico, Virginia, Anderson decided he needed to interrogate Johanna Johnson, the person who apparently knew both Red Tail and Stoutwein. Anderson, of course, was still working with Johanna in connection with the eco-terrorism task force investigation of the Environment Protection Society cell. He respected Johanna for the forthright honesty she expressed when refusing to turn over to the cell the information they were demanding of her, which she in fact possessed because her father had given it to her, but she would not betray him. She readily agreed to proceed with the sting operation once she knew her father was very much in the know about her involvement with the task force. She was doing all that the FBI expected of her. But would she be forthcoming about what she knew of Charlie Red Tail? Anderson decided to find out; however, he knew that Johanna was also represented by John Wilson, for she had told the task force that at the beginning of her undercover assignment. He put two and two together. "Johanna knows Charlie Red Tail quite well and probably is involved with Wilson representing Red Tail," Anderson concluded. Was she capable of lying to protect Red Tail even though she was working with the FBI on the undercover operation?

The agent knew he had to be careful with how he approached this part of his investigation. Johanna Johnson was not just another potential person to interview—no, she was not only someone who no doubt had important information about a possible murderer, but she also was someone already working with the FBI—thus making both involvements more challenging for both Anderson and Johnson.

The FBI agent decided he needed to find out whether Red Tail knew Stoutwein was at the university, for Anderson intended to explore the possibility that Red Tail had a motive of retaliation against the Stoutwein family arising out of Red Tail's conviction for rape of the Stoutwein girl.He felt the better odds were that Stoutwein had been murdered near the university and not at some other location other than the dump. Johnson might have some knowledge pointing to that possibility. The Indian could have known Jim Stoutwein for a lot of different reasons, of course, but certainly from the rape trial, and if he was having a close relationship with Johnson, he may have shared with her that he knew the guy and wanted revenge of some kind. Anderson felt he could move closer to knowing whether Red Tail was the guy they wanted if he could put Stoutwein and the suspect together at the University of the West, where the inference could be drawn that the relationship was such that Red Tail had to know who Stoutwein was and remember him from the past.

"I trust Johanna, though," Anderson wrote in his notes, "and I believe she will be truthful with me on Red Tail." He had reviewed the Three Creeks Police Department's tape of the questioning Nick Spencer had conducted of Johanna, so he had some background on the relationship between her and Red Tail. He felt that part of the interrogation was not very thorough, however.

Anderson contacted John Wilson to set up a meeting with him and Johnson and told him the earlier the better. Wilson said he needed to meet with Johanna first but would advise her to meet with Anderson.

Wilson met with his client and went over what was to happen and how she was to act and answer questions. Very importantly, Wilson told Johanna that Charlie had been transferred to the same facility where she would be questioned. Johanna's anxiety level immediately screamed higher. They talked further. Wilson told Johanna he would ask Anderson to let her see Charlie, that she should know the visit with Charlie would be videoed and recorded by the facility's security cameras, and that she should not ask Charlie anything about the murder charge or the rape.

They were to meet at the federal holding facility on Tuesday, the eighth day of the month of September.

CHAPTER 32

ANOTHER INTERROGATION

The day before Anderson was to meet with Johanna and her attorney at the federal holding facility, he was preparing how to question Johanna when he received a bewildering, anonymous telephone call that changed his thinking about Charlie Red Tail. It also made him question the connection between Johanna Johnson and Red Tail. How involved was she, really, with the Indian? Were they not only sharing coffee and dinner, but also secrets that were important to this homicide, as well as the eco-terrorism planning?

"I intend to find out," Anderson murmured grimly.

The greetings to each other at the federal holding facility were brief. They met in a rather austere room, typically governmental, and with prison-quality decor: steel desk, lightly padded steel chairs, four in number; the room was poorly lighted and windowless. It perhaps contained security cameras and recording devices. The room was devoid of any color and had no wall hangings or other fixtures to add a feeling of humanity to the place of inquiry. The doors made a locking sound when slammed behind them after all had entered.

After a few pleasantries expressed to instill confidence in Johanna that she would be treated fairly and with respect, the Special Agent got down to the business at hand. "Johanna, I appreciate your meeting with me. You and I are involved in another legal matter, one that is also known to your attorney, Mr. Wilson. I have greatly appreciated your cooperation with the eco-terrorism task force and feel we are gaining very helpful information from your involvement with the EPS. The EPS case and this homicide are two distinct cases, unless there develops any overlap of persons, places, or things.

"You should know that I have talked with Charlie Red Tail and I know of your friendship with him, although I am not sure of the extent to which you are involved with him. And I have reviewed the recording of your questioning by Officer Nick Spencer of the Three Creeks Police Department. There is much I would like to cover with you this morning regarding the murder of James A. Stoutwein. Some of my questions may duplicate some of Officer Spencer's; that will not be because I am trying to trick you or cause you to give different answers, but because I may not recall all he asked about, or I may wish to clarify some points. You are not under oath, but I need to point out that not cooperating with the FBI or lying to the FBI are serious federal crimes. So, John, Johanna, should we proceed?"

Both answered "yes," Johanna a bit more reservedly than Mr. Wilson.

Anderson covered many of the same topics Officer Spencer had covered, clarified some of them, and for now, delayed prying deeper into the relationship between Charlie and Johanna. He did ask when they had last gotten together.

"You say you and Charlie got together last week, after the news broke of the Stoutwein murder and the previous rape conviction, is that correct?" Mr. Anderson hoped she had not interfered with a criminal case by aiding in some manner a suspect who may have committed the crime.

"Yes, it sure is," replied Johanna.

"Did you tell Mr. Red Tail about the murder? Ask him about the rape conviction?"

"No, I did not."

"Why not?"

"I did not want to act unlawfully, for starters. And because we found out something we knew about each other but had never said."

"What was that?"

"That we are in love."

"If you are in love, wouldn't that make you want to tell him of the danger he might be in because of his prior involvement with the Stoutweins?"

Johanna studied Agent Anderson very carefully. She thought before answering. "Last week, Charlie told me about what happened years ago—the alleged rape, his conviction, and his prison sentence. Charlie did not rape the

Stoutwein girl or anyone else! He is not capable of such a despicable thing! And as far as the murder goes, I know he is not capable of that either, and after the deep sharing of our love for each other, my heart told me not to tell him of the murder, because deep down I knew he had nothing to do with it! I couldn't believe such would be the case and that the prejudice of the rape arrest and trial would raise its ugly head again and Charlie would be arrested and charged," Johanna exclaimed, choking back tears. "Why are you so out to get him? You don't know how kind and considerate he is! Why don't you arrest Betsy Stoutwein and her dad for perjury?"

"Well, Johanna, I am not out to get him unless he is the one who killed Stoutwein. I have an obligation to investigate this case and to find the killer, and I intend to do so. Wherever the facts lead, I will follow them. Did you ask him how he feels about the Stoutweins, since he said they lied about the rape?"

"He despises them! How would you feel if someone wrongfully accused you of rape?"

"Do you know if Mr. Red Tail knew Mr. Stoutwein was going to the university?"

"Did Charlie know Stoutwein was at the UWest?" Johanna repeated. "As I told Officer Spencer, I don't think he did. There was the one occasion when Charlie and I were leaving the coffee shop and Stoutwein spouted off to me, but I am quite sure Charlie did not recognize Stoutwein—at least, he gave me no indication he did."

"Did Red Tail ever talk to you when you were dating about

the rape conviction and getting even with the Stoutweins for some reason?"

"No, he sure didn't. In fact, I did not know about the rape conviction until he told me about it a few days ago when I went up to find him on the reservation. I told you about that."

"Now, yesterday, I had an anonymous phone call. We traced it. It was from Carlos Madrid. You and I both know who he is and about his involvement with EPS. He doesn't know anything about you working with us, at least to our knowledge. The phone message he left was that he knows Charlie Red Tail, that the Indian had been at an EPS meeting that you were also at, and that Red Tail was seeking help to protest the building of dams on the Missouri River. What do you know about that? Because if he did commit the rape, was willing to blow up a dam, or something like that, he may also have had the capacity and desire to kill Stoutwein. Take your time before you answer that question."

Johanna needed no time and answered without blinking. "Yes, Charlie was at an EPS meeting. I was there. I came late, and Charlie was talking. I did not hear any request of his or indication as to why he was there, other than he was very angry about the dams. I already knew that about him from what he had said at Professor Pickenpaugh's history class and our discussions afterward. Charlie did not know I was there.

"I learned when I last saw him, the time I have already told you about, that he had been at the meeting seeking help in order for him to honor a vision passed on to him by his grandmother to seek revenge for the taking of their tribe's homeland along the Missouri River for a dam project. Charlie explained to me the solemn duty he had felt to carry out the wishes of his grandmother and act on the vision, but that he could not bring himself to do it. You have to understand the spiritual significance of what was being expected of Charlie. He and his people are often guided by the power of the Great Spirit as shown to them in a vision. Because Charlie is a good, kind guy, he could not abide the wrongs he realized would be the effects of his seeking revenge against the white man by blowing up part of a dam."

She then went on to explain again that Charlie had subsequently abandoned any intention of pursuing the vision. She told the agent what Charlie did to free himself of the suffocating obligation he felt under for the honor of himself and his tribe.

"Instead, Charlie wants to obtain a degree in criminal justice and go back to the Horse Creek Reservation and help his people. And I want to go with him!"

"Why do you think Madrid called the FBI and left the message he did? I don't suppose he was just trying to be helpful to law enforcement."

"Madrid has been bugging me ever since we first met. I have told you before how he coaxed me into going to the EPS meetings, and how he has tried to date me ever since. In fact, after the news about the murder and the implication that Charlie might be involved, Carlos called me and offered to protect me. He said Charlie was dangerous and he wanted to help me. I took it as him trying to ingratiate himself with me. His overtures to me in no way capture my affections, nor do they interfere with my work for you; they only reaffirm the slime he truly is."

"Is there anything else you want to tell me that may be important to the investigation?"

"Yes. Charlie was beaten by someone from Denver who wanted him to sell drugs on the reservation. He refused."

"How do you know that? Is that all you know about that matter?"

"Charlie told me. I happened to see Charlie after that, and he looked like he had been beaten, and I know he was hurt. Charlie told me he remembers the guy's name—Horny Al."

"Was that before Red Tail went to an EPS meeting?"

"Yes, a few months before. It was during the first semester. Do you have any other questions of me?"

"I do not."

The session ended. Johanna asked to see Charlie. She saw him and talked to him for thirty minutes; what was said would stay with only the two of them forever.

Special Agent Anderson did not know what to make of what he had been told by Johanna about Charlie. He thought, *I think she is telling me the truth, but how do I independently determine that Red Tail had no motive for killing Stoutwein? Until I can determine that is the case, or I find someone else committed the murder, Charlie Red Tail is the prime suspect. Could it have been Madrid, for example?*

He then turned his attention to information he heard for the first time, this from Johanna during his interrogation. Charlie had been beaten up by someone having something to do with Denver and with drugs. Could the thugs from Denver been involved in the killing of Stoutwein as part of their plan for Red Tail to distribute drugs on the reservation? He felt he needed to check more on Carlos Madrid and better understand the relationship between him and Johanna, as both Red Tail and Johanna said Madrid was jealous of Red Tail seeing her. The task force already had an extensive background check on Madrid and knew of his criminal past and his involvement with eco-terrorism; however, Madrid's buddies would probably know how he felt about Johanna and the Indian. It also could be a pretext for Anderson to try and learn directly from Madrid a little more about EPS.

"Did Madrid know Stoutwein?" Agent Anderson told himself he had better find out.

Since Madrid had telephoned Anderson about Red Tail, the agent had a perfect excuse to locate Madrid and talk further about what Madrid knew and why he called. Was it because he wanted to divert attention away from himself? Anderson wanted to ask him, but he didn't want to tip his hand as to what he knew about EPS; he knew this would be the tricky part of talking to Madrid, because Madrid knew Red Tail had been at an EPS meeting, in addition to having had dates with Johanna. And, in fact, Anderson knew Madrid had talked with Johanna, with Red Tail present, in the park awhile back after an EPS meeting. *It will be interesting to see how Madrid lies about his knowledge of things I have already confirmed with Johanna and Red Tail,* Anderson thought.

CHAPTER 33

FBI HITS THE STREET

The next day, Agent Anderson decided to see if he could locate Carlos Madrid at his house at 510 Mulberry, just three blocks south from the Ranch House Fraternity, two blocks from Johanna's apartment, and one block from Red Tail's apartment. Anderson diagrammed the locations and who lived where; he pondered whether there was any significance to the locations: each was on the path to the university campus; all were on the same side of Mulberry Street. Stoutwein's fraternity residence was north of the others and closest to the university, so it was such as to allow residents at the frat house, like Stoutwein, to see Johanna, Red Tail, and Madrid use the street.

Madrid was not at his house on any of the occasions Anderson had checked before while working the ecotage case, and Anderson did not expect he would be home now if the house were visited again. Madrid did not answer

Anderson's telephone calls to the number Anderson had saved when Madrid had called him and left the anonymous message. The location from which the call had been placed was a landline serving Madrid's residence. Johanna had not indicated to Anderson that another EPS meeting would happen soon, so the agent theorized that if Madrid had killed the Stoutwein kid, he might flee the area. The Agent decided to put out an all-points bulletin to law enforcement to be on the lookout for Madrid's vehicle; he had the description of the vehicle from the county registrations: a Porsche, and the license number. Anderson advised in the bulletin that if the vehicle were spotted, not to approach but report location and direction of travel to the FBI and tail the vehicle within jurisdiction.

Anderson was not totally caught off guard when the Bureau was notified the vehicle had been spotted in Montana and was followed to the US-Canadian border, where the vehicle passed through customs. Anderson's hunch was justified, if not totally so—Madrid could be fleeing the Stoutwein murder, or he could be contacting a terrorism cell in Canada. The agent had the Bureau contact the Canadian Royal Mounted Police to pick up the search and directed the Bureau to provide the Canadian authorities the information then existing between the US task force on eco-terrorism and the Canadian task force. Anderson also told the Bureau to alert the Canadian authorities that Madrid was a suspect in the Stoutwein murder.

After he thought about it for a while, Anderson was pretty

certain Madrid was headed for an eco-terrorism cell known to both countries located along the as-yet publicly undisclosed route of the coal trains headed to the West Coast and from there to Asia. He advised that Madrid be kept under surveillance when found, but not arrested; reports should be forwarded to the US task force, marked for Anderson's attention. The task force had a lot of information on the Canadian cell as a result of earlier cases and knew this would add another layer of difficulty to their attempts to intercept whatever plans the US cell had.

In light of these developments, Anderson felt what Johanna told him about Madrid being jealous of Red Tail made more sense and could have been a motive for Madrid to kill Red Tail, but it didn't make sense as a motive for Madrid to kill Stoutwein. Or did it? What if Madrid wanted to get Red Tail out of the way so he could have Johanna to himself, and he figured one way to do that would be to get Red Tail convicted for a murdering Stoutwein? But why would he pick Stoutwein? *For sure, after the murder and learning of the rape, Madrid could have seen his chance to carry through on that thinking by making sure Red Tail was nailed for the murder. Telephoning me was just another step along the way. But what if Madrid was not the one who murdered Stoutwein? Then who did, if neither Red Tail or Madrid did?*

Anderson hurried to contact the "brothers" of Jim Stoutwein at the Ranch House Fraternity, first in order being Merle Hornsby, the fraternity brother who had contacted the newspaper and named Red Tail as a possible suspect. Anderson quickly learned that Hornsby was Stoutwein's pledge son, a significant relationship in the fraternity; that his pledge father had told him a redskin had been convicted of raping his sister; that the redskin's grandmother had been a thorn in the side his family for a long time because she argued against the building of the Big Bend dam and often spoke out at meetings between her tribe and the whites of Indian Mound County.

Hornsby, like all the members, sure knew Johanna Johnson. "She is one sexy gal," Hornsby told Anderson in response to his question about her. Hornsby also told Anderson he was with Stoutwein when an Indian and Johanna Johnson left Heck's coffee shop and Johnson put Stoutwein in his place for making fun of the Indian. He told Anderson what he recalled being said by Stoutwein to Johnson, but he also remembered Stoutwein said something about getting even with the Indian and wanted to know, "Who was that damn redskin?" He didn't know the guy at that time. Hornsby said he didn't know Red Tail, for he had never met him or been told about him.

Hornsby was anxious to tell all he knew or had heard. Because he was close to Stoutwein, his pledge father often shared things with him he wanted kept confidential. "Jim told me one time not too long ago he had been badly beaten near the entrance to his ranch last year. He told me not to tell anybody. That was before I joined the fraternity. Jim said the guys who beat him up were probably from Colorado, headed to Sturgis for the motorcycle rally, because he saw a license plate on one of the motorcycles and it was a Colorado one. He told me that whoever attacked him seemed to know about the rape trial of an Indian named Charlie Red Tail. They accused him of lying at the trial." Hornsby understood from Stoutwein that Charlie Red Tail had been convicted of the rape of his sister. "But he never really shared any details of that with me," he said. "He seemed a little reluctant to talk about it."

At this point, Anderson made a mental note that the information might be another fact pointing to someone in Colorado, for he recalled that Red Tail had been beaten up and he had told Johanna something about "drugs" and "Denver."

Hornsby also told Anderson a very interesting fact. "When Stoutwein mouthed off to Johanna Johnson in Heck's, after they left, a Mexican, I think Jim said it was—dark-skinned, at least—was leaving behind her and the Indian. The guy, who looked like a dandy, mouthed off to Jim, but nothing came of it. Then, sometime later, as I was thinking about Jim, I remember him telling me he had been sitting in the dark by a door at the Owl Inn one night when the Indian and Johanna were eating dinner, that he had been sort of following them to the place, and that when he snuck out without being seen by them, he ran into this Mexican, and Jim said he felt like the Mexican was the same one he saw at Heck's. He talked with me a bit about why this Mexican seemed to be doing the same thing Jim was doing—spying on the Indian and the girl. He asked me to keep that quiet as well, for he might have 'a come to Jesus moment' with the Mexican as well as the Indian."

"Did Stoutwein say why he was following Johanna and an Indian? Or why he felt the Mexican was also following them?"

"No, I don't think he did. I know Jim was following Johanna because he had this thing about her. He had asked her out a couple of times, to no avail. But as to the other guy, I think it was because the Mexican apparently said something to Jim one day outside our house here, when the Mexican was walking to campus and Jim sort of jumped on him about his following Johanna. The guy told Jim, according to Jim, 'She doesn't want anything to do with you or with the Indian.' They had a shouting match, but I don't know what was said or by who. Jim told me he felt the Mexican had a crush on Johanna or something, and was thinking the Indian was dating her, or why else was he tailing her? And, as I said, I know Jim wanted to go out with her."

Others interviewed at the frat house had nothing important to tell Anderson, other than they all noticed Johanna Johnson when she walked down or up Mulberry Street, and they also saw her a few times on campus with an Indian, but they did not know the Indian's name. When Anderson described Madrid to the others, no one knew him, although one guy said he saw him one time behind the wheel of a Porsche parked in front of their fraternity house.

"We were all out on the lawn. The guy was taking pictures.

Then he sped away. I didn't think any more about it."

"Was Jim Stoutwein out on the lawn with you guys?"

"Yeah, Jim was, now that I think about it."

"We have information that Madrid was taking pictures in front of the Ranch House Fraternity while Stoutwein was on the lawn with others. Perhaps Madrid had also run into Stoutwein when Madrid was going back and forth to the university campus, if he ever walked rather than drove his fancy car," Anderson added to the report he sent to his team. "And, the Mexican that Stoutwein described to Hornsby as stalking Johanna Johnson could in fact have been Madrid. We know Madrid is a Spaniard. Do we have enough to get a search warrant for Madrid's house? I doubt we do at this time, but let's work toward that end. But I don't want to interfere with our task force work on the EPS, so we may not want to get a warrant based on probable cause for the murder unless it is really clear-cut. For sure, we will add Madrid to the name of Red Tail as the prime suspect in the murder of Stoutwein. Let's contact Interpol again to see if we can find out more about Madrid before he came to the US."

Anderson later worked his way south on Mulberry Street to the apartment formerly lived in by Red Tail. As he walked on the wooden walkway to the apartment house, he noticed a series of dark spots on the wood. It looked to him like someone may have been dripping blood. Maybe a wound of some kind. After photographing the spots on the wooden walkway, the experienced FBI agent carefully removed the drops from the wood and put them on an evidence pad for later analysis.

The girl who answered the door of the apartment told Anderson he was the third person who had come inquiring about the prior tenant. She described for him the girl who had come, a description that matched Johnson. The second person was a handsome Spanish-looking guy. "He expressed disgust that the previous tenant was no longer here."

"What do you mean?"

"Well, he asked whether I knew where the previous tenant now lived—he wanted to track him down and make some things right."

"Did he say who the tenant was he was looking for or describe him to you?"

"Only that he said the guy was an Indian."

Anderson continued further south and again scoped the house, which he knew from his ongoing investigation of the EPS and its members to be that of Carlos Madrid. Then, he went back to the alley behind 560 Mulberry. Anderson wanted to determine visibility lines between Madrid's house and where Charlie's apartment was located. He wasn't sure as to why. The agent noted that the south window of Charlie's apartment was directly in line with Madrid's house, unobstructed by trees or other houses. The agent went down the alley again to Madrid's place and looked back to Charlie's apartment from outside a north window of Madrid's. He noticed a spotting scope in Madrid's window pointed at the south window of Charlie's apartment. Anderson wondered why; he wondered if Johanna had ever been in Charlie's apartment. He remembered, of course, Johnson telling him that she had seen Red Tail with injuries, but she did not know from whom or where an incident may have occurred.

CHAPTER 34

TO THE REZ AND BACK

FBI agents were assigned to work the reservation, look-ing for any clues that might be a lead on Red Tail. The agents interviewed tribal law enforcement personnel, health care providers, educators, tribal leaders, merchants, and ordinary citizens. What they were told by the tight-lipped reservation inhabitants was that in no way would Charlie Red Tail have killed anyone; nor would he have raped a girl. Nothing much informative, and certainly nothing deroga-tory, was discovered. Nor could the agents learn anything incriminating about Red Tail from the law enforcement on the reservation or from the elected leaders. Rather, all per-sons they interviewed seemed to be very proud of their fel-low tribal member. All of this was in the FBI's reports. The impression they collectively had and reported in the 302 was that Charlie Red Tail was a born leader: very intelligent, very kind, and very proud of his heritage.

Meanwhile, Agent Anderson stepped up his personal investigation. The dark spots taken from the wooden walkway outside Red Tail's former residence were forwarded to the FBI lab for analysis. He decided he wanted to personally interview the uncle where Red Tail and Johanna had talked recently and where Red Tail was arrested. He wanted to view the lay of the land, and in particular, the area around the cabin. And he wanted to discuss the case with Officer Spencer. Anderson also figured he would go to the state prison and talk to Red Tail's cellmate, Clyde Brown, but he decided he should first go to the reservation.

On the Horse Creek Reservation, Agent Anderson located and then drove to the house of Charlie Red Tail's uncle, Ted Tomahawk. The agent was greeted by a stiff-moving dog supposedly on guard, but obviously a dog who wanted more "lovins" from whomever she found coming to the house.

Charlie's uncle, Ted Tomahawk, greeted him at the door as the agent knocked. He was not invited in, but the uncle came to the outside. The old Indian stood silent, for he long knew there were times more could be learned by being quiet than by talking. The agent introduced himself and told the uncle why he was there. Oscar Big Bull heard the agent and also stepped outside and listened as they were told where Charlie was now being held and that the FBI was investigating the death of James Stoutwein. The old Indians continued to listen but said nothing.

The agent offered the elders a bag of tobacco, with papers, and told them he was not there to do anything to them, just that he was there to learn more as to why Charlie Red Tail might be innocent. There was silence for a while. Then, Uncle Big Bull slowly spoke. "Who do you say was killed? How? Why was my nephew arrested?" He took the pouch of tobacco.

"The victim was Jim Stoutwein, who was part of the Stoutwein family over in Indian Mound County. His throat was cut, and he was scalped. He was found in the dump yard at Three Creeks, South Dakota."

"Oh. That son-of-a-bitch! Good thing he dead. Lied about Charlie raping his sister. Stoutweins are no good. They have always hated us Indians. Even when I was a boy, I knew they were bad. They almost killed one of our tribe they said was trespassing on their ranch. She wasn't. Shot her. I was young then. They tried to stir up trouble with us all the time. I was told to stay away from Tihay by my tribe. I wish the younger kids now would stay away."

"Well, why do you think your nephew did not kill this guy?"

There was a long silence.

"I know Charlie well. He is not of the blood that can kill another. Nor could he rape a woman, Indian or white. His life been good, always. A leader as he is older. Kind. Smart. Was going to go to college. Come back. Help us be safer and kinder. He didn't kill or rape. His grandmother was a leader also. Fought against the government taking our land for the dam."

"Did Charlie live with you when he got out of prison?"

"He lived with me at my house over there," answered Oscar Big Bull, pointing to it. "Until I was shot by the crazy white police. They should be arrested. You leave Charlie alone. That's all I have to say."

When he returned to Three Creeks, Agent Anderson met with Officer Spencer. Anderson had always felt, based on his experience, that the local police on patrol knew more about their town and what was going on than the sheriff's office or that anybody from the outside could find out. Anderson was right when it came to Spencer.

Spencer had been with the campus police for sixteen years, had seen about everything when it came to college students, and was well trained to handle whatever came up. He kept a keen eye on what was going on around campus, and so when Agent Anderson met with Officer Spencer, he had information that was helpful.

"Did you know this kid that was killed, Jim Stoutwein?"

"Yeah. He was somewhat of a troublemaker. I broke up a couple of bar fights in which he was involved. Arrested him one time. Sort of a loudmouth. But nothing other than that."

"Since you live fairly close to the frat house where this Stoutwein kid lived—have you ever noticed anything unusual in the neighborhood that might give us a lead on somebody who might have killed Stoutwein?"

"Nothing that immediately comes to mind."

"Have you ever come across a student by the name of Carlos Madrid here at the University?"

"Oh, you bet. He lives down on Mulberry Street—apparently a rich kid. Drives a fancy car, lives in a nice house, not like most students; has some wild parties. I have been keeping my eye on him for some time. He likes to drive his fancy cars pretty fast."

"Has he been in trouble, do you know?"

"Not that I know of. Well, let me think for a minute. I guess the only thing I might mention—I spotted a motorcycle close to his house one night. Took a look. It had no plates. Serial number scratched off. Called it in and asked that it be taken in and dusted for prints. It belonged to someone out of Denver, I believe. A bad guy with a long record out of Denver—drugs, extortion, and assault—is what I remember. He had a crazy name. Horny Al. His name is Al Gonzales"

"Oh, really! Was there any follow-up?"

"Not really that I know of; however, in that same time frame, as I recall, I saw a red Corvette racing out of town. I thought it was this Madrid kid. I got another call about that time and figured I would get Madrid the next time. Only, several days later, I saw a new car in Madrid's driveway and just figured the rich kid got a new car. Oh yeah, there was another thing I saw the night the red Corvette raced out of town. As I was driving south on Mulberry, at about the four hundred block, I saw ahead a couple of guys out on the lawn, but I did not see anything unusual other than one of them looked pretty scruffy. They had their backs to the street. I didn't see anything other than that, so I didn't stop or anything."

"Would the place you saw the two guys be at about 460 Mulberry?" asked Agent Anderson.

"Yeah, that would be about right," answered Spencer.

"What did the guys look like? You say one of them looked pretty scruffy."

"The one guy had on a motorcycle jacket, as I recall. A cap of some kind. I really couldn't see much. It was pretty dark. I drove slowly by them. I think one of them, not the one in the motorcycle jacket, lives there, because I think I saw the guy there one day, standing out in front by himself."

Agent Anderson then asked, "Do you know anything about another student, an Indian by the name of Charlie Red Tail?"

"Only what I have been reading in the newspaper and hearing over the radio. Our team meetings have certainly discussed the newspaper stories about him, and we have kept an eye out since, in case we see him—but no, I don't know anything about him other than that. But come to think of it, the guy I saw standing in front of the place that I later saw the two guys I was just telling you about; he was an Indian, I think."

CHAPTER 35

TASK FORCE PLAN

Soon after his talk with Officer Spencer, Special Agent Anderson and the eco-terrorism task force participated in a videoconference, called at the behest of Anderson. Anderson explained to the task force that he felt they had enough evidence to arrest the Environmental Protection Society members for the crime of environmental terrorism based on the reports of Johanna Johnson, and more importantly, based on the fact that Madrid had taken an important step in the conspiracy to attack the coal train shipments to be made to the West Coast when he traveled to the terrorism cell in Canada.

Anderson went on to review part of the work that had been done.

"We set a trap for the cell here in Three Creeks with the help of Johanna Johnson and her father. Her undercover work has been invaluable. The cooperation of her father has been so needed and willingly provided. Due to Johanna's providing information to us, we know the terrorists intend to blow up a bridge on a route through Canada. You will recall the qualifying information for Johanna Johnson to provide to the cell membership to be accepted into the cell was her obtaining information from her father as to the route that would be used. Up to the point that Johanna advised them her father told her they would use a Canadian route, the indications were the cell was planning on a northern US route. So when they learned a Canadian route would be used, Madrid apparently knew he would need the help of the cell in Banff, Alberta. The help he needed was no doubt with respect to the explosives to be used. The EPS knew it couldn't get explosives acquired here through customs at the Canadian border. And they needed the other cell's members' expertise in the use of explosives. You all no doubt recall this task force has information on this Canadian cell going back several years, when an oil pipeline was blown up in Alberta, it was thought that this particular cell might have been involved. Also, the cell's location in Banff is somewhat close to the railroad bridge on the route that we led them to believe will be used. Incidentally, the bridge I am referencing spans a large canyon, and it is high above a river—knocking it out, particularly when the train is loaded with coal, would be a huge victory for the terrorists.

"We were fortunate to have learned from a Police officer in Three Creeks a bit about Madrid. He is a rich kid from Spain, a student at the University, and he likes fast cars. He has a record with Interpol that includes suspicion of ecotage in Europe. We obtained from the Police officer a description of the car Madrid is now driving, and we had him tailed as he headed north from Three Creeks.

"Due to great surveillance work by local law enforcement in two different states, we know Madrid traveled to Banff, Alberta. The Canadian authorities picked up the surveillance after he went through customs and followed him to a location known by the Royal Mounted Police to be the location of an eco-terrorism cell which has been on their radar ever since the pipeline was blown up.

"Based on the other information we have gathered over time, I believe we have probable cause to arrest all the members of the cell. We should move quickly at the time of the next cell meeting, which has not yet been set, but when it is, Johanna Johnson will be notified, and she will contact us.

"You should also be aware that in working the investigation on the James Stoutwein murder, I have some leads that point to Madrid as the hit man on that murder. We can't arrest him for that yet, however. Maybe, just maybe, if we can arrest him on the terrorism charge, we can solve the murder case as well."

Anderson was given the authority to proceed. A squad of US Marshals was placed on alert until they would be given the word to obtain arrest warrants, and then proceed accordingly.

Four days later, Johanna contacted Anderson and told him Carlos Madrid had telephoned her to let her know the next meeting of the EPS was to take place in two days, April

15th, at 8:00. She said Madrid sounded psyched and told her he had been to a cell meeting in Banff to meet the guys they had been in contact with and to make arrangements for their help when the time came to get the job done. She had recorded the telephone call. Anderson relayed the new information to Paul Carbine, the Eco-terrorism Task Force chief. The US Marshal's squad was advised of the date, and plans were made to obtain the warrants and make the arrests.

With the critical information coming in from Johanna, and little information of any probative value coming in on the murder, Anderson paused to consider about what to do next. *I must make sure Johanna is safe—that is crucial, so I should have the marshals synchronize their assault to the break-up of the meeting and the moment Johanna leaves the basement and exits outside. She should be instructed to be the first person from the cell to get out of the basement, and if for some reason she is not, she must be told to be sure to place herself in a position that would permit her to run away to the Bachman building where a US Marshal would to be stationed. The other cell members must be led to believe she had escaped and was on the loose.*

The US Marshals' raid on the Environmental Protection Society's April 15th meeting was carried out with precision and without complication. There were no fireworks or stand-offs; the marshals' training and expertise being fully applied assured success was quickly achieved. Five men, including Carlos Madrid, and two women were arrested and transported to the federal holding facility in Three Creeks for prosecution on charges of domestic terror. One woman escaped.

CHAPTER 36

LAB REPORTS

April 15th was a day of madness for Anderson, the agent being practically overwhelmed with all he was doing and what had yet to be done. The raid on EPS had been successfully conducted, but he'd had little sleep in the last few days as the plans were made and the effort carried out.

The autopsy performed on Jim Stoutwein had told Anderson little more than the victim died from having his throat cut and bleeding to death. Anderson needed good news from the FBI lab in Quantico to really have anything to go on. The report received called out that a spot of blood on the right cowboy boot of the victim did not match the victim's blood; however, the blood was not matched with another person or animal. The sample was identified as AB-negative. It was a lead for sure.

Blood type AB-negative is found in less than 1% of the population, according to Stanford University and stated in the lab report.

DNA analysis was to be done; however, it would take a considerable amount of time to do the DNA test because of the backlog at the appropriate lab.

Anderson recalled Police officer Spencer had fingerprints from a motorcycle parked in front of Madrid's house. It took a little time to run Gonzalez through the FBI database and know the criminal record of Albert James Gonzales, aka Horny Al Gonzalez: petty theft, attempted rape, extortion, attempted murder, and aggravated battery. He beat some of the "raps," but not aggravated battery, for which he served a light sentence. He was known to be in the Denver area and perhaps involved with a convicted felon named William Jesser, aka Big Bill, a gang leader involved in prostitution, drug dealing, explosives. Jesser was known to operate out of Denver.

Agent Anderson now had another lead on who may have murdered Stoutwein- fingerprints from a motorcycle parked near Madrid's house, Stoutwein having been beaten up a year ago by riders of motorcycles with Colorado plates apparently headed to Sturgis for the motorcycle rally. Anderson knew he could get a search warrant to search Gonzalez's house if they could locate it, but he also knew he needed more evidence than what he had now—a fingerprint, some blood, and hearsay of a Ranch House Fraternity member learned from a guy who was now a dead man. He knew he needed to find out if there was a problem involving Stoutwein that existed among Horny Al and Madrid, and or/Stoutwein.

Meanwhile, other agents advised Anderson they had found in Charlie Red Tail's belongings a hunting knife, sharp, and with specks that looked like dried blood. The knife had been sent to the FBI lab for analysis and testing. An expert would be consulted later on whether the knife could have been used to slit Stoutwein's throat or to scalp the victim… or both.

Carlos Madrid had obviously been through the booking, incarceration, and interrogation routine before. He already knew his constitutional rights to remain silent and to be represented by an attorney. Accordingly, he said nothing and did not answer any questions concerning eco-terrorism, bad guys from Denver, or James Stoutwein. He kept his mouth shut, as did the others.

Anderson called his team together to decide what to do next. Awaiting Quantico's report on the Red Tail hunting knife and the blood speck on it could be important, he reasoned, but it was a long shot, he felt, and it would take considerable time. He was unwilling at this point to hold up other efforts to find the killer. He directed one of his men to contact Horse Creek Medical Services at the Horse Creek Reservation and see if he could access any medical records of Charlie Red Tail and determine his blood type. Privacy laws aside, Anderson knew this too would be a long shot, but he decided it was worth a try. If it failed, Anderson felt he could have the prosecutor who charged Red Tail with murder file a motion to seek a court order authorizing the Bureau to obtain a blood sample from Charlie, if he did not voluntarily give one. At the same time, Anderson knew Red Tail's attorney, John Wilson, would fight hard against the court authorizing any such search of his client's body to obtain the blood sample. In other words, Anderson felt every effort along the lines of determining Red Tail's blood type would take a lot of effort and a lot of time if the reservation medical care provider did not turn over any blood records on him. The clock was ticking.

The agent decided he needed to get more information on Horny Al. He was known to run with the infamous gang in Denver headed by Big Bill Jesser.

Anderson met with the United States Attorney in Denver, David Platte, to explore whether Big Bill could have had anything to do with the murder. During their meeting, Platte explained to Anderson that his office was aware of Jesser's gang wanting to move drugs into the Horse Creek Reservation in South Dakota, because a young man had tipped them off to that goal of the gang.

"The informant told me that he had been approached to help Big Bill Jesser get started in the business—in fact, he had been beaten up by a guy he knew only as Horny Al, because he refused to cooperate with the drug enterprise."

'What was the informant's name?"

"Charlie Red Tail."

The Denver office of the FBI located Gonzales' home in a trailer park in East Denver. The United States Attorney quickly had an affidavit and search warrant prepared. Rex Anderson and his team acted quickly, too. The ramshackle trailer was put under surveillance. When Horny Al arrived one evening in his red Corvette, the agents moved in. The search warrant was for any objects pertaining to Stoutwein, the murder, or the location where the body was found. Also, the warrant covered evidence of motorcycles in the possession of or previously possessed by Gonzales.

Gonzales offered no resistance but when told the agents were investigating the murder of James Stoutwein, Gonzales told them, "I have no idea who that is, and I have not murdered anybody."

The agents went through every corner of the trailer. They found a receipt from a repair shop for work done on a motorcycle. The date of the receipt would later be compared with the date when Officer Spencer saw a cycle near Carlos Madrid's house, and also with the date of the Stoutwein murder. The searchers also found a souvenir program from last year's motorcycle rally in Sturgis, South Dakota. Three pistols and ammunition were found in the open on a corner table. No knives were found. But as the agents were leaving, Agent Anderson noticed a big belt buckle from an Indian Mound County Rodeo on a belt hanging on the coatrack with the inscription, "All Around Cowboy."

"Hey, Horny Al, where did you get the belt buckle?"

"From a guy." He said no more.

John Sharp, one of the other FBI agents, noticed a black motorcycle jacket in a closet. It too was seized as evidence.

Anderson immediately arrested Albert Gonzales, aka Horny Al Gonzales, on a parole violation, possession of a firearm by a felon, and for suspicion of murder.

"Why Stoutwein?" Anderson said to one of his team after they carted Horny Al off to the federal jail.

Anderson returned to Three Creeks and went immediately to Red Tail's cell after calling John Wilson and asking him to meet him there.

Wilson asked, "What is this all about, Rex?"

"Drugs on the reservation and Big Bill Jesser, a gang leader out of Denver. And your client's alerting the US Attorney to Jesser's plan."

Anderson filled in Wilson on what he had been told by the US Attorney and what they found in executing the search warrant for Gonzales' trailer, leading to the arrest of Horny Al. The FBI Agent said he felt he needed to talk with Red Tail to confirm the information he had learned in Denver and get more details as to how he became involved with Big Bill Jesser.

"Let me talk with my client first."

Charlie Red Tail told the FBI agent everything: He explained how he came to know about Big Bill Jesser from his cellmate Clyde Brown, about the false accusation of rape, about his trip to see Big Bill for explosives and his later abandoning any such plan, about his learning of Big Bill's plans for selling drugs on Charlie's reservation and his asking Charlie to help, and about the beating by Horny Al—whom he remembered was with Big Bill when they met in Denver.

Of great interest to Anderson was Charlie relating that he told Big Bill about Stoutwein and Stoutwein having lied about Charlie committing a rape of his sister. Charlie told Anderson about Big Bill's saying, "He should pay fur what he did to youse. Tell me where the son-of-a-bitch lives."

CHAPTER 37

TEAM MEETING

Anderson's team of FBI agents and state criminal investigators were called together and met to review in a big picture all investigative reports on the Stoutwein murder. They charted everything their investigation found. They analyzed and argued. They went back and forth on four suspects over a period of three days: Carlos Madrid, James Gonzales, Big Bill Jesser, Charlie Red Tail.

Was it Carlos Madrid, whom they already had incarcerated and charged with conspiracy to commit terror? He could have done both crimes. And they certainly had evidence of his jealousy over Johanna Johnson, raising the possibility he had someone "kill the other guy" pursuing Johanna and had that guy charged so he could have the girl. He stalked Johnson and Red Tail.

Was it Horny Al Gonzales, who seemed to be involved at every turn in the case? It was argued he was the killer because he had the rap sheet that showed he was capable of committing murder; he could be placed at Big Bill's meeting with Red Tail because he was identified by the photo shown to Red Tail, although it was not clear that he recognized him from the meeting, but for sure from the beating he took from him; he could have dropped blood at Red Tail's apartment when he beat up the Indian, and the blood found might match the blood found on Stoutwein's boot, and on the padlock to the landfill; he had Madrid's Corvette, so he was in the neighborhood of Stoutwein's fraternity at a point in time when his blood was found at Red Tail's place; he had a belt buckle at his trailer that could have belonged to Stoutwein; and he was no doubt involved with beating Stoutwein near the Stoutwein ranch, because the bartender at the Wapiti put him there in the bar about the time Stoutwein was beaten. Gonzales' motorcycle jacket, the belt buckle, and some of the blood samples, however, were still at the lab.

Anderson questioned whether Gonzales would have acted on his own.

"Sure, he was probably part of the gang that beat up Stoutwein a year ago, but that's different from murdering him. What could Gonzales have to do with Stoutwein in the first place? Why would motorcyclists beat him up? It probably involves more people than Gonzales, for he would never do something on his own—no, it must have something to do with Big Bill Jesser."

Agent Sharp suggested, "Gonzales and others, perhaps Jesser, were paying a visit to Sturgis, South Dakota for the rally and just ran across Stoutwein on the trip. We now know Jesser was wanting to get started selling drugs on the reservation, so the trip they took to that area could have something to do with that plan."

"But how and from where did they know Stoutwein?" another agent asked.

Anderson said, "Maybe Stoutwein was somehow involved with the plan to sell drugs. But how does Stoutwein connect up with Jesser's outfit? The only tie-in I can see centers on Charlie Red Tail."

Or was it Big Bill Jesser, who implied to Charlie Red Tail that he was going to whack Stoutwein, although perhaps all he caused to happen was to bust up Stoutwein, but not kill him. The group knew of Jesser's long rap sheet, his gang influence, and that Horny Al worked for him, but that was about all they had on him at this time. Besides, one of the team opined, Big Bill would never do something like a murder himself—he would have one of his henchmen do it for him.

The team had to first decide whether the one person in custody, Charlie Red Tail, was still the one to prosecute. They each acknowledged there was no basis on which to hold him or to prosecute the kid. He was in custody for one reason, and one reason only, because of a rape conviction that probably was a miscarriage of justice. And with the information from US Attorney Platte regarding Red Tail's contacting him to tell them of Big Bill Jesser's plans for selling drugs on the reservation, they knew they did not have a good case on him yet. The question was, though, whether they should continue to view him as the number one suspect. To a man, the team decided to suggest to the Indian Mound County Prosecuting Attorney that he dismiss the charge against Red Tail. Unfortunately, the prosecuting attorney who convicted Red Tail of rape was the same prosecutor at this point who might have jurisdiction to prosecute him for murder. The team knew that getting his approval was no doubt a long shot.

The investigative team was continuing to discuss what they had and against whom when they received the report from the FBI lab on the blood spot they had found on the knife belonging to Red Tail. The report indicated the blood on the knife was animal blood and not human.

Following the investigators' meeting that adjourned, not knowing who they had for the murder, Agent Anderson researched the FBI databases looking for the blood type of Horny Al Gonzales. What he found from the records was that Gonzales' blood type was A+.

Anderson did not sleep that night, or the next night. He was totally spent and did not know where to turn next on the Stoutwein murder case. He decided to call John Wilson.

"John, I don't believe Red Tail killed Stoutwein or had anything to do with it. Based on what I know at this point, I will encourage the prosecutor to dismiss the charges, and if he won't do it, I will testify at the hearing on your motion to dismiss and indicate the evidence we don't have—that is, none that leads to Red Tail. But I need to know from your client more about his cellmate, Clyde Brown, because the only person on my list that I haven't talked to is him. I plan on going to the state prison and talking to him. Perhaps I can get some information out of him that would implicate one of his buddies in the Jesser gang. Or maybe I can at least put together a conspiracy theory to use to crack down on the Denver boys. Can I have access to your client to find out about Brown?"

"Well, let me think about this. We are still three weeks away from a hearing on my motion to dismiss, and a replacement for Remington hasn't even been assigned to the case yet. Why don't we do it his way: you first go to the prosecutor and get the charges dismissed, and then you can go talk to Brown after talking with Charlie?"

Anderson replied, "Well, it seems like we have a timing issue. Your man doesn't want to be in custody any longer, I am sure. At the same time, I want to exhaust my investigation at this time to forestall as much negative publicity as possible and I guess I can go see Brown without first talking with your client. That's what I will do."

CHAPTER 38

ESCAPE

Not long after Charlie Red Tail was released from prison, having served his sentence, Clyde Brown became very moody. He was lonesome. He missed his roommate, for they had become good friends. In particular, Clyde missed the talks he and Charlie had about reservation life, the animals, even hunting them, and the closeness of the families, something Clyde longed for. As he plunged deeper into depression and loneliness, Clyde plotted and planned a way to escape and to find the same happiness Charlie told him he had enjoyed before the ranch family put him in prison.

When the break finally happened and he found himself on the outside with a new world before him, Clyde Brown knew where he was headed: to the Horse Creek Reservation. He was somewhat familiar with that part of South Dakota. He once lived near a little town called Badger in Indian Mound County. Those days were remembered with happiness, for they were before the life of crime he later lived with Big Bill Jesser, and well before his parents were forced off their farm by the IRS. Now he sought to relive some of those good times but decided he would first go to the reservation and experience what Charlie had told him about it. Before getting to the reservation, however, he stopped in Three Creeks to stay with and old friend from Badger, Harold Springer, who was a janitor at University of the West.

When Clyde showed up on the doorstep of his friend's house, the two immediately recognized each other. They had worked the fields together, gone to high school together, and suffered the poverty of their families' difficult times in life. Harold had not married and lived alone, so he welcomed Clyde to stay with him, unaware of Clyde's past life of crime and his recent prison escape. The two old friends spent several days together and shared memories of their friendship over meals and beers at various places in Twin Creeks. Harold was able to loan Clyde some money. At the Horseshoe Bar one night, while enjoying conversation and a few drinks, a fight broke out.

Harold told Clyde, "The big dude there, that's Jim Stoutwein. You may remember the Stoutweins were big ranchers in our county. This guy's sister was raped by an Indian from the Horse Creek Reservation. He was convicted and put away. That was several years ago."

Clyde did not remember the Stoutwein family, but he sure did remember the Stoutwein name, for Charlie had told him about the clan and fact the brother was the main witness who put him in prison. "I sure do remember the name," Clyde said to Harold.

"Well, look at that. The bouncer is throwing Stoutwein out of the bar!"

Early the next morning, Clyde Brown said goodbye to his friend Harold and took off for the Horse Creek Reservation. But first, he stopped at the post office, pulled a mailing box from the shelf, and went to the Jeep to retrieve a couple of things; he put them in the box and sent the box to another friend of his, Horny Al Gonzales in Denver. He then drove through the countryside toward the reservation, detouring for a bit to drive into and out of Badger to see the town in which he had lived, just for the fun of it. His memories of adult years were not good ones. Too much deprivation of respect, and no sense of belonging; too much family struggle; too little happiness, but much pain of the soul. He drove on.

At the Horse Creek Reservation, Clyde stopped at the casino and figured he would build on the money his friend had "loaned" him. While at the casino, he asked one of the cashiers where Oscar Big Bull lived. The cashier didn't know but motioned the security guard to come over and told him what Clyde was asking. The guard looked Clyde over pretty good. Clyde started to get nervous.

"What do you want with Oscar Big Bull?"

"Well, a friend of mine told me Oscar Big Bull is his uncle and said if I am ever in the area of the reservation to go see him, because the old guy is very wise and to tell him hello from my friend."

"Who's your friend?"

"Charlie Red Tail."

The cashier and the guard looked at each other. The guard nodded. The cashier told Clyde that Oscar Big Bull lived with Ted Tomahawk and gave Clyde directions, before both she and the guard went back to work.

The same day Clyde Brown arrived at the reservation, Agent Rex Anderson of the Federal Bureau of Investigation contacted the warden of the state penitentiary in Indian Falls, South Dakota, Warden Wallace Winston.

"Warden Winston," agent Anderson said, "I am investigating a murder and I would like permission to talk with an inmate in your prison, one Clyde Brown. Can you make arrangements for me to talk with Brown?"

"Oh my gosh, Agent Anderson," Warden Winston replied, "I would have thought the FBI would know! Inmate Brown escaped from my prison about a month ago and is still on the loose. He is no doubt armed and dangerous. We have dragnets out searching for him. The last good information we had was that he was in the Three Creeks area out west. He had been seen in a coffee house there, but we were too late to get him at that location. We haven't found him yet."

"What was he in for?"

"Murder. He was serving a life sentence without parole. I don't understand why he would make a break for it. We had been seeing quite a change in Clyde in recent years. He was a lot more agreeable than when he first came in. Not as belligerent. He was trying to educate himself by making use of the library and materials there. Just was a much better prisoner. No trouble anymore. He was bunked with an Indian named Charlie Red Tail, who I think had a very positive influence on old Clyde. I had heard he was somewhat depressed as of late, however."

The warden reviewed the file and then told Agent Anderson, "The first report we had, five days after the escape, was that an older man with a big scar on his face was hanging around a Three Creeks coffee shop. The coffee shop is a UWest hangout, the report says. Police officer Spencer of the Three Creeks Police had quickly responded after the call came in, but the reporting party said the man had left a day before. Why the guy had waited a day to call the police, heaven only knows. He was unknown to the reporting party. No good description of the guy seen was given to the officer. This was at a place called Heck's.

"The following week it was reported by local authorities over in Indian Mound County that a stranger had been seen around Badger. The stranger was described as a guy and he reportedly was driving a Jeep. We later learned the Jeep was stolen near here about the time Brown escaped. With the description of the guy, we were able to check FBI database and the description given matched Clyde Brown. We flooded the area with state and local authorities. No luck in finding him.

"Colorado DCI advised they are keeping a close eye on

Brown's former hangouts in the Denver area. They are also on the lookout for him if he were to join up again with a gang he used to run with—I think the gang was led by a Big Bill Jesser—but to this point in time, at least, Brown evidently has not caught up with Big Bill or any of his old gang there in Denver."

"After Brown was seen over in Badger, did the search for him in that general area include the Horse Creek Indian Reservation?

"The file doesn't indicate that it did. Let me check with Sheriff Brutkowsky in Tihay. He should know."

Agent Anderson rolled his eyes but said nothing. After the warden had talked with Brutkowsky, he turned to Anderson and said, "No, the sheriff told me that he hadn't sent men there because he was short of officers to cover that area and he knew that if the guy was on the rez, as he called it, he wouldn't get any cooperation in finding him anyway."

There was a long pause, and then Agent Anderson asked the warden to pull the inmate's file.

"I have it," said the warden.

"What is the inmate's blood type? Does the file show it?"

"Yes, it does. Clyde Brown's blood type is AB-negative."

CHAPTER 39

CONFESSION

Escapee Clyde followed the directions given him to the home of Ted Tomahawk. Before going up the driveway, Brown stepped out of the Jeep and gazed at the beauty of the surrounding area. It was just as Charlie had described! He immediately noticed the creek, saw the resident fox Charlie said was always snooping around, and in the distance he heard the red-tailed hawk. For the first time in a long while, Clyde Brown felt serene and safe, at least for that moment.

After several minutes, Clyde drove down the long driveway, parked in front of the cabin, and started for the door. Ted Tomahawk met him with a rifle in his hands. Clyde, by experience and practice, flinched and leaped behind the Jeep. "Don't shoot! I'm a friend of Charlie Red Tail's. I want to talk with Oscar Big Bull. Is that you?"

"How you know Charlie?"

"I was in prison with him."

"OK, come out. Hands in air. I make sure you not armed. Not someone else than you say."

As Clyde came out from behind the Jeep and moved toward the cabin, Oscar Big Bull came out of the cabin and hobbled over to Ted Tomahawk.

"I heard somebody say Charlie's name. What's going on?"

"This white man sez he knows Charlie. Sez he was in prison with him."

"What's yur name?" Big Bull asked.

"I'm Clyde Brown."

"Oh, yeah. Charlie told me when I went to the prison he was in the same cell with you. Come in."

These three men so close to Charlie Red Tail sat down and talked about a person they all cared for, about a boy they all felt was a victim of the white man's injustice and hatred. When Clyde asked, "Where is Charlie now?" the two uncles looked at each other and Big Bull said, "The evil white men arrested him again. Took him away. Said he murdered a guy. Don't know where he is now. FBI took him. We think he is in Three Creeks."

When the cellmate of Charlie Red Tail left the uncles' cabin, he knew exactly what he was going to do. He drove without thinking anything but good thoughts about his friend Charlie. He had some regrets about his escape from prison, but the freedom he was experiencing was a blessing to him, and worth it all. He decided he would drive straight to Three Creeks and get even with those who had taken Charlie away from his freedom and future, wrongfully, and for a second time. Clyde Brown had no thoughts of his own freedom lasting, no illusions that he could now turn a corner and be someone other than what he was, a killer. He headed straight for the FBI offices in Three Creeks. He had been there before. There was no hesitancy in his step or in his mission. He knocked on the locked door. Agent Anderson asked who was there.

"Clyde Brown. I murdered Stoutwein. I am here to surrender. You need to free Charlie Red Tail."

CHAPTER 40

ANOTHER TRIP TO PRISON

Charlie Red Tail and Johanna Johnson were allowed to visit Clyde at the prison. They entered the prison with hearts pounding. The hell-hole still stunk, was stark to the degree of total dejection and hopelessness there residing, still belching sounds of cold, harsh confinement and of the bracelets and leggings snapping shut that brought there the criminally accused, and sometimes guilty.

Johanna grasped Charlie's arm even more tightly. Charlie led forward, flushed with fear, awash with memory of the cruel confinement he had endured as the result of a broken criminal justice system that had turned its back on the concepts of innocence and fairness. His fear paled as he entered the prison, knowing this time it was a free visit that was bringing him here. He was here with gratitude for the act of an unredeemable soul, no doubt committed with a degree of love or respect for this Indian, this Indian of focused purpose in life—not a result of the racist confinement he endured, but rather enabled by an unsolicited act of his former cell-mate, Clyde, whom he now came to see.

"Murder is murder," Charlie said to Johanna. "However, sometimes, perhaps, it is simply a matter of nothing to lose when committed without hope but with an altruistic motive. Clyde killing James Stoutwein was an act of selflessness on his part and done with a belief he was acting for my good. How can I argue with that?"

EPILOGUE

The notoriety of Charlie Red Tail had intensified in Indian Mound County following the overturning of the rape conviction and the freedom of Charlie from the wrongful charge of murder. Prejudice and bigotry of many shook the very foundation of God-fearing citizens in the county and beyond when the Supreme Court of the United States brought into greater public view the wrongs of white society and its law enforcement in Indian Mound County where the Horse Creek Reservation was located. The Supreme Court's decision to set aside the wrongful conviction of Red Tail for the alleged rape of a rancher's daughter, and the Court's critically reprimanding the law enforcement and judicial system in Indian Mound County, raised the bigotry level in the county and its extended area like a huge earthquake's reading on a Richter scale. The high court cited several acts of prejudice against the defendant, violation of his constitutional rights, and harassment by local citizens of federal law enforcement investigating the alleged crime. It also detailed the prejudice and the resulting actions of the white population against the Indian defendant and his white legal counsel. The Supreme Court suggested in the opinion that state government authorize action to remove the officials whose egregious conduct resulted in the wrongful conviction.

The criticism and the reversal did not sit well with many officials in Indian Mound County. "Who in the hell are they to tell us how to run this county," hollered Mac Stoutwein, Chairman of the County Commissioners. "And it just proves the lefties on the Supreme Court are willing to overlook the guilt of an Indian and the suffering of his victim and override the will of the good, hardworking people who have to live next to the uncivilized Indians. We will not kow-tow to their dictates."

With the recent Supreme Court opinion having been issued, Charlie and Johanna now saw their way clear to marry and start a new life together.

Johanna and Charlie were to be married during ceremonies at the Presbyterian Church in Moose Lake, Wyoming, Johanna's childhood home. A second ceremony was to be on the Horse Creek Reservation, Charlie's home. The spiritual belief of the Lakota that marriage is forever, even after death, and the ceremonies to be performed by the tribe, were very important to Charlie, and, therefore, to Johanna.

Johanna's parents were greatly concerned the wedding

notice announcing there would be a marriage ceremony on the Horse Creek Reservation and in Moose Lake would lure the insatiable press to attend as unwelcome guests. Donna Johnson, Johanna's mother, was rightly concerned Charlie's past and a forthcoming ceremony on an Indian Reservation would be something the uncaring, sensational, headline seeking press would decide to cover. The wedding ceremony at the Presbyterian Church in Moose Lake did not seem to Johanna's folks to be a potential problem; however, the ceremony to be had at the reservation Mrs. Johnson feared would draw much unsolicited publicity. The rape trial and the murder charges had generated sensational headlines, radio coverage, and must-watch TV throughout the region. The marriage of the involved Indian to a white girl during a ceremony on the reservation, with all the native customs being performed, would probably be too much for the voracious press to ignore.

The wedding announcement was timely sent to friends and relatives, including to Charlie's friends, wherever they were located. John Wilson, Rex Anderson and a number of FBI Agents were also invited. John Wilson, the attorney who represented Charlie pro bono, and had personally obtained the reversal of the rape conviction in the United States Supreme Court, and Rex Anderson, the FBI agent who had helped to free Charlie of the subsequent murder charge, were especially important invitees for the engaged couple. The couple owed their very lives to those men. Wilson, the Federal law enforcement invitees, tribal officials, and tribal law enforcement were well aware of the possibility of another wrong being inflicted on Charlie Red Tail, Johanna, or the attorney, John Wilson. All peace-loving peoples of the greater Horse Creek Reservation area knew the potential for violence of some of the haters in the area and the violence of which they were capable. There was justifiable concern in the right places that "uninvited attendees" might show up at the wedding ceremony that was to be held on the reservation.

The wedding party, in particular, had four months, until October 7th, to worry as to whether the wedding would happen without incident.

The Horse Creek reservation was to be the permanent home of Johanna and Charlie. The young couple was living their dreams together, and both of them wanted to advance the dreams of the somewhat forgotten people of the reservation.

Armed with a college degree, marrying a wonderful woman who was willing to reside on the reservation, Charlie planned to obtain law enforcement training from the Department of Indian Affairs and become an investigator, then serve his people in a vital role.

Johanna Johnson had aspirations similar to Charlie's—for some time, she had planned to teach young kids on a reservation for no other reason but that she loved children and she wanted to help fight the educational shortcomings of the reservation educational system. She had the college degrees and the teacher training that made her well equipped to make a difference. However, since those dreams, and aware of other needs on the reservation, she had pursued a nursing degree and was but a few credits from that egalitarian goal. She would soon have completed all requirements to allow her to serve in the Bureau of Indian Affairs Health Service, or as a school nurse. Just as importantly, Johanna now had her love for Charlie Red Tail and their upcoming marriage to inspire her in her quest for meaning in her life and for giving back the love she had developed for small Indian children, in particular. Johanna had spent considerable time on the Horse Creek Reservation while she and Charlie had been dating; she had also visited the schools and the medical clinics on the reservation. This talented young woman was excited beyond measure for her future with Charlie and their life to come. During their time together at UWest, Johanna learned a great deal about the Horse Creek reservation and the many challenges she, as a white woman, would face living there. She knew she had to be compassionate and kind, tough, resolved in her work, and viewed as trustworthy by those of the tribe who needed to see all of those qualities and more before accepting her, even though she was marrying a member of the tribe.

Charlie looked forward to returning to the reservation where he grew to manhood and where his people still labored each day under the difficulties created by the reservation system imposed on them, or caused by the Congress of the United States in 1851 when the reservation system was created and the forced relocation of Indian tribes began. Low education standards and achievement, substance abuse, crimes against women, and other serious crime challenges had persisted since. He was well respected by his people and other Indian tribes. He had become a hero of all Indians who followed his victimization by the white man, as he always kept his cultural and personal dignity.

Charlie often thought to himself: *I escaped the scourge of the reservation's lawlessness, but most young people today do not escape. With the increasing presence of illegal drugs on the reservation, peddled from the big cities, mostly Denver, social ills are increasing and existing law enforcement has been wholly inadequate to combat the onslaught of modern-day ills being added to the historical challenges forced on the tribe by the difficulty of survival on the reservation on which they live. Their lives were particularly difficult after the bottom lands of the reservation that were flooded by the reservoirs created by the dams on the Missouri River. The Horse Creek tribe's livelihoods in no small part in the past depended on the now taken lands for the nourishing ecology on the now-flooded fertile bottom lands. Many long-time neighbors are now separated, as they had to relocate to land above the river bottom, seek a different livelihood and in many cases, new friends and neighbors. The prospects for the future for many are uncertain at best. Unemployment is the norm for many tribal members living away from the river bottom, with no real possibilities of jobs to come in the future.*

The flooding of the island where Charlie lived with his grandmother was just one of the terrible losses suffered by the tribe over the course of history.

"How do you explain four years in prison as a character qualification for becoming a law enforcement investigator on a reservation?" the administrator pointedly asked. "I may be able to get your application through the process, but it will take a big effort on your part, with a lot of help from a lot of people. If you are granted the right to enter the investigator program and train with others, the training itself will be terribly difficult. Your strength of character and physical abilities have to prove to be what is desired for such a position and be recognized as a virtue that will overcome your past. Are you sure you want to go through with this, Charlie?"

What the official at the US Indian Police Academy - Bureau of Indian Affairs - Office of Justice Services did not know was that Charlie was a de facto leader of the Horse Creek tribe, although not an elected official. Since high school, Charlie had been seen by the elders of the tribe and by the young people, as someone to be looked up to, an enrolled member to be respected and admired.

Certainly, though, Charlie had detractors, and some enemies, in this shared place challenged to provide a stable environment for relative prosperity through work and self-reliance; one for raising educated children prepared for college admissions; one for having capable law-enforcement providing some assurance of safety from those within and without the reservation who are always poised to exploit Indian people, particularly the young and the women. Charlie knew he was up to the test.

Attorney John Wilson had walked Mulberry Street in Three Creeks, South Dakota, many times as he returned to his home at the corner of Mulberry Street and Oak Street after working late into the evening at his downtown law office, as he had done for nearly forty years. He had handled many civil and criminal cases covering many different subject matters and crimes. John Wilson was a "lawyer's lawyer," with all the respect of the legal system that is given to someone of such high esteem. Over the last year he had been working on a case of "justice versus injustice," the facts based on the latter and the cause he was pursuing being the former. His walk home this summer evening was different than normal due to the fact he had just won an appeal in the United States Supreme Court that was of considerable notoriety—he had successfully overturned a sham accusation, trial, and imprisonment that took four years out of the life of a young Lakota Indian named Charlie Red Tail.

This time, however, his state of mind was different from the normal satisfaction of winning he had experienced in many a legal case, for tonight the success was dampened by an eerie feeling something was not right in his life, a feeling of loss and pain. He walked on toward home, to his beloved wife of fifty-one years, to the black Lab who would be the first at the door for the homecoming, to his many friends and neighbors. As he walked and reflected on the day just past, he gave thanks for all he had in his life, highlighted by a good reputation, a union that had been blessed with two beautiful daughters, and the good health he enjoyed as he and Patricia contemplated retirement.

The explosion was lurid, freighting and telling! The star-studded sky was soiled by a smoky, reddish color. The air was foul, like dead, rotting animals perhaps- or burnt human flesh. As the lawyer drew in the stinking air, the ability to identify the location of the blast vanished under the trauma of fear and the potential reach of the deadly force within sight and sound. Finding the location, the epicenter, was temporarily impossible—unless one backtracked the smoke, protecting one's eyes while being oblivious to the possibility of another blast. The blood-colored fire that engulfed Mulberry Street diminished the possibility of there being survivors.

No one who later would come to the site of the explosion would be able to bring back the love, the happiness, the caring and the Godly beliefs that once resided there. The address at which the explosion occurred was the address of John and Pat Wilson. Pat Wilson, deceased, was seventy-three years old.

Johanna Johnson, a white girl, and Charlie Red Tail, a Lakota Indian, had lived the last five years as the principals in a human tragedy that now was ongoing. When they received the news of the bombing of their lawyer's home and murder of his wife, Johanna and Charlie were devastated, for John Wilson had saved them from injustice and given them a chance at life together. They didn't know what to do for their hero, other than be there for him as they each grieved over

Pat Wilson's death. They cried, prayed, and mourned with many who knew this wonderful wife of a wonderful man, but knew all they could really do was share their love for the grieving husband—their friend and warrior.

Pat Wilson had been murdered, but, beyond doubt, John Wilson was the true target of the hatred of certain whites who despised him even before the Supreme Court's decision. "Johanna, the hatred will continue. Mr. Wilson will still be at risk of losing his life to the hatred. As will we!" said Charlie. "What has happened to us and what has happened to Mr. Wilson is **not water over the dam**. We will remember every evil part of the last four years, and our white and Indian brothers and sisters will carry this bad thing in their hearts forever. We must be strong."

THE END

CPSIA information can be obtained
at www.ICGtesting.com
Printed in the USA
JSHW050314050622
26644JS00001B/6